Kyle liked the tinge on Ava's cheeks.

He preferred that over his own lingering insecurities. The ones that taunted him about his looming deadline. "What's the game?"

Ben rubbed his hands together. "It's called: You Know What We Need."

Kyle knew what he needed. He needed another million-dollar invention. And he needed it yesterday. Yet he wanted to share the teen's enthusiasm, feel that same innocent excitement for something. He'd felt it once. "How do you play?"

"Someone says: you know what we need and then tells everyone their idea. We discuss the idea then vote if we like it or not. You get points if everyone likes it." Ben's eyes widened, and horror lowered his voice to secret-telling level. "But if we vote it down, you lose double the points."

"Or there's no discussion at all because your idea gets voted down instantly. Then you drop to last place. *Last place.*" Ava's disgruntled voice muted Kyle's panic.

The words *vote* and *last place* circled through Kyle. Something hummed inside him. Something he hadn't felt in far too long. That first stirring of an idea.

Dear Reader,

At seventy-five, my dad has built quite a legacy. I had the benefit of working at my father's office during the summer before my freshman year in college. I saw firsthand his work ethic (he arrived first and left last) and his dedication (he never asked anyone to do anything he wouldn't do himself). Yet one moment has stuck with me. It was the end of the day—everyone had long since clocked out and gone home. Everyone except my dad and me (he was my ride home). I remember moaning that we'd been there so long, and couldn't we just leave already (did I mention I was a teenager?). My dad gathered his things, but we never made it to the main door. The janitor had arrived. My dad didn't offer a simple greeting. He shook the man's hand, greeted him by his first name, and asked about the gentleman's wife and kids—my dad knew their names, too. I recall sitting at the receptionist desk and realizing that kindness mattered. That giving five minutes, ten minutes or an hour of your time and yourself can change someone's day.

My father is generous with his time, his talents and his money. However, my dad is proof that sometimes it's that extra moment you take and the part of yourself that you give to someone else that can leave an even more lasting impression. My hero, Kyle Quinn, has the money, but he hasn't quite learned that money isn't always the answer. Thankfully, like I had my dad, Kyle has Ava to teach him a few lessons about the power of love and family.

Cari Lynn Webb

HEARTWARMING

Ava's Prize

———

USA TODAY Bestselling Author

Cari Lynn Webb

HARLEQUIN® HEARTWARMING™

Recycling programs
for this product may
not exist in your area.

ISBN-13: 978-1-335-63386-6

Ava's Prize

Copyright © 2018 by Cari Lynn Webb

This edition published by arrangement with Harlequin Books S.A.

For questions and comments about the quality of this book, please contact us at CustomerService@Harlequin.com.

Printed in U.S.A.

Cari Lynn Webb lives in South Carolina with her husband, daughters and assorted four-legged family members. She's been blessed to see the power of true love in her grandparents' seventy-year marriage and her parents' marriage of over fifty years. She knows love isn't always sweet and perfect—it can be challenging, complicated and risky. But she believes happily-ever-afters are worth fighting for.

Books by Cari Lynn Webb

Harlequin Heartwarming

A Heartwarming Thanksgiving
"Wedding of His Dreams"

Make Me a Match
"The Matchmaker Wore Skates"

The Charm Offensive
The Doctor's Recovery

Visit the Author Profile page
at Harlequin.com for more titles.

To Mom and Dad: For showing me the strength of love, family and faith. I'm grateful for your support, encouragement and guidance. I love you!

Special thanks to my husband and daughters for the endless laughter and willingness to eat leftovers while I'm on deadline.

CHAPTER ONE

THREE. DISASTERS ALWAYS came in threes. Kyle Quinn had two.

First: he was about to lose his fortune.

Second: a woman had just collapsed on the twenty-foot-high scaffolding above him. And could be dead. Only the multiple calls to 9-1-1 disrupted the stunned silence from the photography crew and models looking on from the ground floor at the charity calendar photoshoot.

Kyle ran toward the scaffolding.

A redheaded model sprinted past him wearing trendy jeans and heeled boots.

No, the third disaster wasn't the event.

Kyle had been warned redheads were trouble by his own ginger-haired grandmother. He grabbed the redhead's wrist to keep her from being injured. One model down was more than enough. "The photographer's assistant called 9-1-1. We don't need another casualty for the paramedics when they get here."

She scowled, deep and intense, as if he'd insulted her, not protected her. Her mascara heavy, her eyes narrowed on him like twin rifle scopes. "Then you should stay down here."

With that, she yanked free of Kyle's hold and scaled the scaffolding he'd intended to climb.

"Trouble," Kyle muttered. His grandmother had been right after all. He followed the headstrong model up the ladder, albeit much less gracefully. The redhead scaled the steel structure like a seasoned acrobat from a Cirque du Soleil show.

Francesca Lang, the older model who'd collapsed, had been one of San Francisco's favorite models for decades. Her face had adorned city billboards and commercials alike. She was to be the face of January for the charity calendar. She'd been poised on the platform to look like she'd scaled a high-rise and conquered life. Now she was powerless and barely breathing.

Seeing her, Kyle forgot about his problems and tried to remember the basics of CPR. Compressions and breath ratios.

He needn't have worried.

The redhead confidently checked the older model's airways and felt for a pulse, making him wonder if her parents had encouraged her to have a backup plan to modeling. "Help me get her harness off."

"That's on her for safety." What if Francesca

went into convulsions? She might drop to her death.

"She needs to be able to breathe easier and deeper." The redhead unzipped the older woman's jumpsuit. "Help me, please."

"Tell me what to do."

And she did. For the first time in a long time, Kyle felt vital. There was progress, too. Francesca seemed to breathe easier without the suit, although she still hadn't regained consciousness.

The redhead greeted the arriving paramedics by their first names, calling out a pulse rate and other medical jargon as if she was the trained professional and Kyle was window dressing.

Too many tense minutes later, Francesca finally opened her eyes and was lowered off the scaffolding to the gurney waiting below.

The redhead had never flinched. Never panicked. Never paled like the other scared onlookers nearby. She wasn't just beautiful. She was a hero.

The sirens from the ambulance faded as the EMTs drove off. Beside him, the red-haired model-turned-hero kicked a slate-gray earbud device across the platform with the toe of her high-heeled boot and mumbled what sounded like a bitter curse. "I should have guessed she was wearing one of these."

Kyle eyed the all-too-familiar device with gut-sinking shame. He'd invented the medical ear bud. It was responsible for his instant celebrity. And for his flush bank accounts. It was also the one thing that could bring about his ruin in less than two months.

"Have something against medical earbuds?" He tried to press disinterest into his voice.

"Only if it's a Medi-Spy." She nudged the device farther away from her. "Those earbuds should be remarketed as a toy, not a medical alert device."

He winced. "Really."

She crossed her arms over her chest, looking less like a wannabe supermodel and more like a judge handing out a life sentence. "It gives faulty readings that send people to the ER unnecessarily, and it fails to recognize true emergencies in time." Her frown deepened. "Then there's also the totally unnecessary music feature and its sporadic connection with its own app and the dropped call rate."

"It hasn't exactly evolved in line with its original purpose," Kyle allowed.

He knew the issues with his product, but he'd sold control of Medi-Spy to Tech Realized, Inc. without realizing he'd sold his soul, as well. With every royalty check he cashed, he watched the earbud become more commercialized to increase the profits. Bluetooth? Music options? He wasn't sure he even remembered the heart of the design anymore.

"Anything else wrong with the device?" The harsh bite in his tone was self-directed. He expected her to identify him as a failure next. His reputation and Medi-Spy's were closely linked.

"That's only the highlights of the Medi-Spy's faults." She eased by him toward the ladder. "If you really want to see how often that particular earbud fails, ride along during one of my shifts. I'm a paramedic."

"But you're here," he blurted out. "Don't you mean past tense?" She was gorgeous. The green in her eyes matched the green in her sweater.

"You think I'm a professional model?" Her cheeks bloomed an attractive pink. Doubt, not confidence softened her voice. "I'm part of the local piece of the calendar."

Before he could respond, she'd moved down the ladder, disappearing from his view. Kyle made his way off the scaffolding. Turning, he discovered his model hadn't made it very far. A linebacker-size man and a copper-haired young boy blocked her path.

"I knew I should've waited to use the bathroom." The boy shoved his bangs off his forehead. "What did we miss, Aunty Ava? Did someone fall off the platform and crack their head open?"

Excitement rushed the boy's speech. The linebacker scanned the floor and frowned.

"Nothing that dramatic, I'm afraid." Ava stepped sideways and bumped into Kyle.

He grinned at her and remained in her space. Perhaps not the most polite reaction, but he didn't feel like moving away from her. They were almost on a first-name basis. At least now he knew her name.

The boy's gaze widened, revealing eyes shades deeper than Ava's pale green gaze. The boy's eyes were the color of an avocado skin, Ava's the color of the inside. Kyle rubbed his forehead. He'd scaled a scaffolding and returned to his bumbling adolescence. Comparing eye color to fruit was definitely his cue to leave. And eat. Clearly, he was hungry, or he wouldn't have compared Ava's eyes to an avocado. *An avocado.* He kept his lips firmly sealed.

The boy tugged on the linebacker's arm with one hand and pointed at Kyle with the other. "Dad. That's Kyle Quinn. He's the inventor guy."

Ava reached over and pushed Ben's arm down. "Ben, it's not polite to point."

"But he invented the Medi-Spy." Awe clouded Ben's face and voice, lengthening the word *spy* into several syllables.

Ava looked at Kyle, her gaze assessing. "He doesn't look famous."

Kyle resisted the urge to smooth his hands over his button-down shirt as if to prove he concealed nothing. He never liked to be scrutinized at any depth beyond the surface, and Ava analyzed. Kyle shrugged instead of asking Ava for the results of her analysis. "He's right. I'm the Medi-Spy inventor."

"I hate to tell you this, but…I stand behind my earlier comments." She straightened and locked her gaze with his. "Your device has too many features. It's confused about what it is, like some teenager trying to figure out who they want to be when they grow up."

No apology. No pleasure to meet you. No retreat. Kyle discovered his first real smile that morning. He liked his paramedic-turned-model even more. He reached over, shook hands with the linebacker and learned Dan was Ava's partner in the ambulance, the boy his ten-year-old son, Ben. And according to Ben, Ava had earned the title Aunt, not because they shared blood. Rather, Ava was family from the heart.

Ben extended his arm toward Kyle, mimicking his father. Kyle noticed the paracord band wrapped around the boy's thin wrist. Its silver medical-alert plate all too familiar. Kyle felt the shift of the titanium links of his own medical-alert band across his own wrist. He'd worn some form of a medical-alert bracelet since he'd started walking. He wondered how long Ben had his and gripped the boy's hand in a firm handshake.

Ben's grin spread toward his ears. "Wait until the kids at school find out I met a real famous person."

Soon, Kyle might be famous for being a hack. For losing everything because he had no new ideas. Without a second idea, he'd fail to fulfill his contract. The penalties were stiff and unforgiving. That definitely wasn't the type of notoriety he wanted. He shouldn't still be here. He needed to get back to his office and create something. A new invention to rival the Medi-Spy earbud. The execs at Tech Realized, Inc. would accept nothing less.

"Hey, I was chosen to be a part of this celebrity calendar, too." Ava's arm brushed against Kyle as she reached to tug on Ben's hair. "You already know me."

Kyle wanted to know more about Ava. She had a bold confidence that he admired. But getting to know a woman better couldn't be his focus right now. He needed to stop distracting himself. His mother would tell him to quit procrastinating. If only it was that easy. If only he wasn't stuck as if he stood on a high dive, too afraid to jump. Too afraid to trust in his swimming skills. Fearful he'd sink, because Medi-Spy was exactly what Ava painted it—a failure.

"But Mr. Quinn is in the papers and magazines at least once a week," Ben argued. "And you aren't."

The photo ops were a side effect. Definitely not Kyle's choice. But that was the unwritten part of signing a seven-figure contract and launching a best-selling product. His celebrity had been instantaneous. It had been handed to him and he'd been trying to hand it back ever since. Standing out never suited him.

He'd stood out in school for several reasons, from his scrawny stature to more serious offenses, like his preference for the science lab over the football field. But he'd grown into his height, filled out and tipped well now. Still that awkward kid with the deadly nut allergy—the one that had forced him to sit at the peanut-free table every school lunch—lingered inside him and cringed with every camera flash. "Your dad and aunt save lives. That's the real-life hero stuff that means more than any picture in any gossip page."

"Still, you get to meet other famous people. I've seen the pictures on the internet." Ben edged closer to Kyle. His gaze shifted back and forth between his dad and Kyle. "If I invent something, can I meet Chase Jacobs and the starting offensive line for the Pioneers?"

His dad held up his hands and retreated. "Don't look at me. I sit in the upper section at the football stadium, not the box seats, when the Pioneers play at home."

"I can get you tickets on the fifty-yard line," Kyle offered. "Let me know if there's a home game coming up that you want to see."

Dan shook Kyle's hand again, a grateful, hearty pump. Ben nodded as if his suspicions had been confirmed. Celebrity was good. Confidence tipped the boy's chin up and strengthened his voice. "My aunt and I are inventors, too."

"That's nothing." Ava waved her hands between them as if trying to wipe Ben's words from the air. "That's just a game we play."

Kyle liked the tinge on Ava's cheeks. "What's the game?"

Ben rubbed his hands together. "It's called You Know What We Need?"

Kyle knew what he needed. He needed another million-dollar idea. And he needed it yesterday. Still, he wanted to share Ben's enthusiasm, feel that same innocent excitement for something. He'd felt it once with the Medi-Spy. "How do you play?"

"Someone says, 'You know what we need?' and then tells everyone their idea. We discuss the idea, then vote if we like it or not. You get points if everyone likes it." Ben's eyes widened, and horror lowered his voice to secret-telling level. "But if we vote it down, you lose double the points."

If Kyle played, he'd only lose points. In real life, it was more than bragging rights or his reputation at stake. If he didn't come up with a second invention soon, his parents and sisters would suffer. The women's shelter he funded would be forced to shut its doors. He could handle the fallout himself, but failing his family would be unforgivable. He'd created the Medi-Spy to honor his grandfather, an iron worker who'd suffered a stroke in the heat. He'd always meant for the money to bring his family closer. That wouldn't happen if he defaulted on the terms of Medi-Spy's sale.

"Or…" Ava's disgruntled voice muted Kyle's thoughts. "There's no discussion at all because your idea gets voted down instantly. Then you drop to last place. *Last place.*"

The words *vote* and *last place* circled through Kyle's mind. Something hummed inside him. Something he hadn't felt in far too long. The first stirrings of an idea.

Ben set his hands on his hips. "Aunty, you know your idea for hair dye that changes color with a person's mood wasn't good."

Kyle placed his hand over his mouth and chin to cover his smile. Even *he* doubted there was a market for mood-changing hair dye and *he*, the one without an idea, had no right casting judgment.

Dan laughed. "There really wasn't anything to discuss."

"It could be hugely popular." Ava set her hands on her hips and stared them down. "But we'll never know because you crushed it before I could debate its merits."

"What merit is there in having hair that changes to green when you're jealous? No one really wants green hair." Dan nudged Ava in the shoulder, knocking her out of her standoff mode. "You really need to come to the table stronger in the next round."

Kyle laughed.

Ava pointed at him. "You can't side with them unless you've agreed to the rules."

Rules? That hum shifted to a buzz. Kyle's idea solidified into more than a throwaway thought. Their game could be a contest. First place. Last place. Rules to follow. Perhaps a contest for an original invention. An idea that would keep his parents retired in comfort, Penny's Place open and his sister's college tuition funded through her graduation. Then Kyle would finally bring his family back together like they'd been before his grandfather's death. "You have rules?"

"Every good game has rules." Ben looked at him as if Kyle shouldn't ask such ridiculous questions. "It needs to be fair."

Kyle nodded. His contest would be fair, too. But could it work? Could one simple contest keep him from financial ruin? "What are the rules?"

"Everyone gets a turn. You can tell your idea anytime. Any place, except church and anytime Dad tells you to be quiet. Otherwise you can't interrupt." Ben held up his fingers and counted. "This is the most important one—you can't make fun of an idea."

"Unless they're mine," Ava added.

"We couldn't not comment on the hair dye, Ava." Dan jabbed his elbow in Ava's side. "Even my dad nixed that idea and he likes every single one you have."

Ava shoved Dan back. "Your dad is a good man."

"What does the winner get?" Kyle asked. A family game was all fine and good. But his contest needed a winner. In a viable contest, there needed to be a prize.

"Bragging rights." Dan's voice was matter-of-fact, as if nothing else mattered.

Again, that worked for a family game played

in the car or a restaurant or at home. But Kyle needed more than bragging rights to entice entries.

The *more* that he needed was money. Money motivated people. There'd be no entry fee required. He'd offer a twenty-five-thousand-dollar grand prize for an original idea, provided the winner agreed to sign away their rights to the idea. If his team—the one he'd need to pull together—could develop the idea into a prototype, he'd give the winner an additional twenty-five-thousand-dollar bonus. Then he'd submit the winning idea to Tech Realized, Inc. to meet his deadline and fulfill his contract. Everyone would win.

Kyle searched for a downside, but couldn't see one and wanted to hug Ben.

A hug was hardly enough to thank the boy who'd possibly saved Kyle from bankruptcy. Instead, he touched his medical-alert bracelet. He didn't know why Ben wore the bracelet, but he knew that bracelet made the boy different. Set him apart from his peers. Kyle remembered all too well having his mom bring special food to baseball practice and classmates' birthday parties until he'd stopped RSVPing with a yes. He remembered all too well how it felt to be different, when all he'd wanted was to be the same.

Different might help an adult, but it would hinder a child. "Ben, how would you like to tour my idea tank? Your dad and aunt could come, too, if they wanted."

Ben tugged on his dad's arm. "Can we?"

"We have to check our schedules," Dan said. Before Ben could argue, Dan lifted his hand, palm out. "But I don't see why not."

Ben pumped his fists against his sides. "Can I take pictures?"

Kyle nodded. The kids at school would require proof of Ben's claims about spending the day with a so-called celebrity. Kyle would ensure Ben had whatever he needed to be the envy of his classmates. "As many selfies as you want."

"Cool." Ben stepped to Ava's side. "Aunty, you have to go, too."

"I'm not sure," Ava hedged.

"But you might come up with better ideas if you see how good ideas are made," Ben countered.

Ava crossed her arms over her chest. "I already have good ideas."

Ben rolled his eyes. "Please come with us."

Kyle held his breath, waiting for Ava's response. Totally ridiculous since he didn't care if she joined them or not.

Finally, Ava hugged the boy. "Fine. I'll be there."

Kyle released his breath. One quick tour. One more afternoon with Ava. That wouldn't be too much of a distraction. Nothing Kyle couldn't handle.

CHAPTER TWO

AVA BUSIED HERSELF with the sun-kissed-yellow teapot whistling on the stove and tried not to track her mother's every step from the kitchen into the family room. Today was a good day. With every step Ava's mother took, her auburn curls bounced rather than wilted against her forehead. She'd opted for her cane over her walker—another improvement.

Lately, her mom's bad days seemed to outnumber the good days by almost two to one. Ava should be celebrating these moments with her mom. Not leaving her alone. "I'll call Dan and cancel."

Her mom settled both hands on the cane. Her voice lowered into parental override mode—the one that demanded, not requested. "You'll do no such thing."

"It's no big deal." Ava set the tea mug on the end table beside the couch, along with the bamboo tea chest, filled with her mom's favorite tea blends. She avoided looking at her mom, worried her too-perceptive mother would notice the hint of disappointment in her gaze and call her out for lying now. "I wasn't really interested in touring Kyle Quinn's think tank anyway."

"Ben expects you to be there." Her mom lowered herself onto the couch and settled the cane within easy reach. "You can't disappoint that precious boy."

She also couldn't leave her mom alone. That made Ava feel like a disappointment as a caretaker. Ben was young; he'd recover. Her mom's good days weren't guaranteed. Her stomach clenched around her love for her mom. How many stars had she wished on over the years to end her mom's pain? How many prayers had she recited since middle school? She ignored that knot twisting through her chest and concentrated on gratitude. She was grateful for this day. "Ben will understand if I don't make it."

"Well, I'm ordering you to go." Her mom dropped a ginger tea bag into the mug; her tone dropped into the criticism category. "You need to do something other than work and look after me."

"I like my work." Perhaps not as much as she wanted to, but her work fatigue was temporary. Sleep and a night off would improve her outlook. Ava tugged the teal throw from the back of the couch and tucked the fleece blanket around her mom's lap. "Even more, I like to spend time with you."

"I'm supposed to be doing the looking after." Her mom touched Ava's cheek. Regret stretched into the lines fanning from her mom's pale blue eyes and slipped into her voice. "I'm the mother—it's my job."

"You did that while I was growing up." Ava took her mom's hand and held on, giving and absorbing her mother's strength. Pleased she could be here for such an amazing woman. "Now it's my turn."

Her mother tugged her hand free and smashed the tea bag against the side of the mug as if that would squeeze the bitterness from her voice, too. "You should be making your own life and not have to…"

Ava stopped her. "Don't say it."

"It doesn't make it less true if I keep silent," her mom said.

"Taking care of you has never been a burden," Ava said. That's what family did for each other.

Ava and her older brother had promised each other they'd protect their mom like their father never did. They'd vowed their mother would never be alone. Brett had cared for their mom while Ava had served her country. Now it was Ava's turn to help her family.

"At least your brother dated and finally married." Her mom's words chased Ava into the bathroom.

She grabbed her mom's afternoon meds and walked back to the family room.

Her brother would return from his internship in Washington, DC, before Thanksgiving. Then her mom could switch her attention to the possibility of a grandbaby and away from Ava's lack of a dating life.

Ava was more than happy to leave dating to the unsuspecting singles in the city. The ones foolish enough to believe in love, who easily surrendered their hearts to a man. Ava wasn't about to give her heart to any man. She couldn't trust he'd stick around, and that'd only lead to heartbreak. She prided herself on being smart enough not to invite heartache into her life.

Her older brother would stick with his new wife, Meghan, through the good and bad, sickness and health, like he'd vowed on his wedding day last year. But Brett was the exception.

Men stuck until a true test came along. It was then they revealed their true heart. An argument or disagreement or relocation wasn't life changing or a true test. However, a diagnosis of MS at the age of twenty-six with two children in diapers—that was life altering. That was a *real* test. One Ava's dad had failed when he'd bailed out on his family. Life had gotten hard and suddenly more was expected from her father than he'd ever planned to take on. He'd run away: far and fast.

Ava refused to follow in her father's fleeing footsteps. "I have a very full life. No dating or marriage required."

"Working all the time is not a well-balanced life." The spoon rattled against the plate under her mom's tea mug, along with her mother's disapproval.

Ava's two jobs kept them in their three-bedroom apartment. Her jobs paid for the in-home nurse and therapists that helped care for her mom each week. Her jobs granted her brother and his new wife the opportunity to concentrate on starting their own family without worrying about their mother.

Except Ava had lost her second part-time job as a CPR instructor yesterday. The company had hired an intern full-time and no longer needed Ava. The extra paycheck had covered the costs of her mother's medications and the utility bills. Ava hadn't told her mom, refusing to give her mother any more worries. She'd figure out the finances.

Ava was determined to do what her father had failed to do: stick beside her mom every step of the way. If that meant she had to work more than an average forty-hour week, she'd do that and more for her family. "Well, this is the life I choose."

"Roland tells me that balance is the key to happiness and contentment, which in turn leads to longevity in life." Her mom's voice was thoughtful and smooth like the honey she added to her tea.

"Roland also likes to say that stretching is the gateway to the soul." Ava swiped a chocolate from the happy-face candy dish on the end table and aimed the tip of the chocolate kiss at her mom. "We both know that being able to curve your spine into a full backbend until your feet touch your head is painful and awkward. Hardly soul cleansing."

Her mother's laughter melted through Ava, satisfying her more than chocolate ever could.

"I admit there are a few things Roland says during our yoga sessions that don't seem to apply to real life." Her mom tossed another candy at her.

Ava caught the chocolate in her free hand.

Her mother dipped her chin and eyed the candies in each of Ava's hands. "But he's not wrong about the rewards of always seeking balance."

"I'll seek balance soon." After she balanced her checkbook. Ava popped a chocolate into her mouth.

Maybe she wanted more or something different on those nights when reality and memories blurred into the same nightmare. But bullets ripped open flesh, no matter if the victim came from a battlefield or the city streets. People suffered whether from a lost limb after encountering an IED on a desert road or a miscarriage on the bathroom floor of a homeless shelter. Ava could help the wounded. Just like she helped her mom. She'd worry about herself later.

Her mother looked at Ava over her glasses and shook her head. "You've always been a terrible liar, but a good daughter."

This was Ava's world. Letting a guy in would upset the balance. Relationships required time that she didn't have. She was already committed to her family and her work.

Her mom tugged on the drawer of the end table, but her fingers slipped, unable to keep her grip around the handle. Ava opened the drawer. Her mom had lost more strength, but not her spirit. Ava had to hold on to the positive like her mom always did. Ava was sure she'd find another job soon. "I won't be gone long."

"Take your time. Rick will be here within the hour. We're playing Rummy." Her mom took a deck of cards out of the drawer. One corner of her mouth kicked up with the cheer in her tone. "When you play cards with us, you ruin the fun by calling us out for cheating."

Ava straightened, set her hands on her hips and frowned. Knowing Dan's dad would be with her mom calmed her unease. Still, she'd take the tour of Kyle's place and head back home. "When I win, I like to know that I earned it fair-and-square. Makes every win that much more rewarding and worthwhile."

"Perhaps." Her mom sorted the cards across the coffee table. "But Rick and I both cheat. Trying to outwit the other one makes the game more entertaining."

The light moments offset the painful ones for both of them. Maybe Ava just had to discover more light moments. "Fine. Next time, I'll cheat, too."

The burst of surprised laughter from her mom bounced through the room, pulling Ava's smile free.

"You have too much integrity to stoop so low." Her mom nodded, her own smile lingering. "It's one of your best qualities. Just don't judge the rest of us too harshly."

Ava shoved her phone and keys into her sling bag on the kitchen counter. "I don't judge people."

Her mother covered her cough of disagreement with a sip of tea.

"There's nothing wrong with expecting people to be…better." Ava had worked hard and sacrificed for everything she had. The easy road hadn't been opened to her or her brother. She wouldn't have taken it anyway. She didn't operate that way. She struggled to understand people who seemed to have a lot of what her grandmother had used to call "quit" in them. Her father had too much quit in him.

"Well, today I plan to be a better cheater at Rummy than Rick," her mom said.

Ava smiled. "Call me if you need me."

"I'll be more than fine." Her mom waved her hand toward the door. "Get out and find some fun."

Ava would prefer to find a help wanted sign. She blew her mom a kiss and took the stairs to the lobby. Outside, she paused on the sidewalk and tipped her face up toward the sky. Fall was one of her favorite seasons in the city. The sun warmed the city's locals and the tourists scattered like fallen leaves swept away in the breeze. Ava crossed at the intersection to cut through the park.

A couple strolled along the paved path toward the fountain, their laughter entangled as tightly as their linked arms. A mother pushed a stroller while her young son scrambled after her, a balloon gripped in one hand, an ice cream cone in the other. Shouts echoed from a group of college students embroiled in a rambunctious game of flag football. Others lingered on blankets, books in hand, headphones plugged in, soaking in every ray of the bright Saturday sun. Ava kicked a soccer ball back to a father. His daughter skipped in front of a soccer goal made with orange cones, her ponytails swinging against her bright soccer jersey that matched her blue cleats. The park pulsed with fun, relaxed and easy and welcome. Ava kept walking, her steps rushed as if she feared the trees would join branches and prevent her escape, forcing her to stop. Forcing her to have *fun*.

She slowed her steps, crushing her ridiculous thoughts into the gravel with the heel of her running shoe. She could relax and enjoy a day in the park like everyone else. She simply chose not to.

Later, she'd stop and smell the roses at the floral shop's outdoor stand on her walk to the Pampered Pooch. She wanted to see if her friend Sophie had any senior animals that needed fostering. Ava and her mom hadn't fostered for several months, but they both always enjoyed the extra company of a senior rescue. Surely a four-legged friend in their house would add balance to Ava's world.

Ava blamed her mom and Roland for her errant thoughts. She didn't even attend yoga classes on a regular basis. Yet Roland's affirmations about a fulfilled life followed her around like a shadow. She picked up her pace again, as if she needed to outrun her mom's chiding laughter and Roland's disappointment.

Who cared if she didn't actively search for fun? She usually accepted extra hours at the hospital or filled in to teach a CPR class or worked a music festival to bolster her bank account. Then she slept better.

Surely the fact that she enjoyed teaching CPR and had discovered she liked both country music and indie rock counted for something. Roland would no doubt chide her to seek out more entertainment. If she graduated from a physician's assistant school and transitioned to another career path, then she'd have the opportunity to find fun.

There wasn't enough money to provide for her mom and get her graduate degree.

Even more, there was nothing appealing about putting herself first and being as selfish as her own father. Her family came first. *Always*. If that meant fun waited on the back burner, so be it.

She'd be grateful for what she had and not mourn a life that wasn't meant for her.

That would be enough. She'd make sure of it.

Ava hurried across the street, leaving the park and her private wishes behind, among the trees and birds.

CHAPTER THREE

KYLE CHECKED HIS recent call log and his emails for the tenth time in the past twenty minutes. Not that he could've missed a call. He'd woken up before sunrise, clutching his cell phone, and he hadn't put it down even to eat lunch earlier. Yesterday, he'd called and messaged a dozen former developers and business associates about judging his contest. No one had replied. *No one.*

He couldn't judge the contest he'd created. The contest he planned to use to keep from defaulting on his own contract.

Canceling wasn't an option. The press releases had gone out. Hits on the webpage had multiplied into the thousands overnight. More headlines and sound bites had hit the TV and radio news spots all morning. Kyle couldn't turn back. He needed to keep his reputation intact and run a viable contest, not some hoax that the public would conclude was no more than a publicity stunt. The press liked to speculate about his next PR blitz as if his Medi-Spy creation had only been for attention. Yesterday's newspaper had claimed a reality TV show was his latest pursuit.

He paced through his second-floor suite, ignoring the theater room and the arcade room, instead seeking refuge in the design lab. He shouldn't have invited Ben and his family over. He shouldn't have translated Ben's car game into a contest. He should've left the photo shoot last weekend and returned to his lab. But it was too late for what he should've done.

Right now, he shouldn't be dropping into the industrial office chair and pressing the button to print more contest flyers as if he'd suddenly decided to hone his marketing skills. He should be scanning his brain for an idea. He only needed one.

What was wrong with him?

The groan of the printer spitting out copies matched the groan of panic rolling through him. He shoved his phone into the back pocket of his jeans, closed his eyes and drew in a breath that lifted his entire rib cage and made his stomach bloat. His older sister had taught him how to breathe, claiming he needed to learn to breathe with more mindfulness. More intention.

He counted to five. Nothing quieted those jitters skipping around inside him.

Another five-count and still nothing within

him unwound. Only his to-do list flashed across his eyelids. At the top: create an invention.

His cell phone vibrated in his pocket. Kyle exhaled and lost any intention of quieting his mind.

He clicked the answer button on his notepad propped beside the computer. His little sister's face with her clear lab goggles propped on her head like a new-age headband filled the screen. Kyle dropped the stack of flyers onto the work table in the center of the design lab, set a 3-D printed piggy bank on the stack and walked with the notepad into his so-called inspiration area.

"Still moping around, all alone in your steroid-infused man cave?" Callie adjusted the oversize goggles on her head.

"It's my home." And his offices. He skipped his gaze over the large room filled with both vintage and contemporary arcade games. Darkness and silence leaked from the connecting theater room, yet not the good kind of dark for movie watching or that quiet anticipation before the final fight scene. He'd transformed the entire second floor of the building into the ideal work and living space. He blamed the sandwich he'd eaten for lunch on his sudden indigestion.

Kyle frowned at the computer screen. Although it was wasted on his little sister. Her focus had already returned to her microscope.

He asked, "Did you want something? I have company coming over soon."

That captured her attention. She blinked once at the screen, slow and methodical, like an owl. Only, owls held their silence; his sister had no such filter. "You don't have people over to your place. Except for the rooftop, but that doesn't count since you don't live up there. People are never invited inside your home."

No thanks to Callie. In her clear-cut manner, Callie had asked how he'd know if people came to visit him or his ultimate man cave? Friends might like his man cave more than him. He'd chosen to do what he'd always done: keep to himself. Except today, he'd stepped out of his comfort zone. Hopefully, he hadn't lost his mind at the photo shoot. "I'm turning over a new leaf."

"You can't get distracted now." Callie's eyebrows pinched together, and she shuffled papers around on her desk. "You only have forty-one days before you need to hand in your second idea."

His sister had a memory like a vault. One time, in a passing phone conversation, he'd mentioned the terms of his contract. She hadn't forgotten one detail. "It's under control."

Callie leaned closer to the computer screen as if to study him like a petri dish under one of her microscopes. "You aren't still pining for the past, are you? The days when you were unknown, un-remarkable and an amateur."

That was the life she'd told him no longer existed. The one she'd told him he'd never get back. He dropped into one of the oversize leather chairs and set the notepad on the flat, wide arm of the chair. "I can have friends."

Confusion thinned her gaze and her mouth. Of course, Callie had skipped her senior year in high school to enroll in college and then fast-tracked her way into graduate school to become a medical scientist. She would earn both her MD and PhD titles behind her name in the next year, as long as Kyle kept his contract with Tech Realized, Inc. and paid her tuition.

"How many times do I need to remind you that if you hadn't sold out, you'd still be wasting away in Mom and Dad's basement, a wannabe inventor, living off Dad's meager retirement?" She grimaced as if her test results proved inconclusive.

Now he lived in a man cave on steroids and was poised to lose everything. Was that somehow better? "This isn't about high school reunions and old times."

"That's a relief." Callie sighed. "You and I aren't team players. We can't conquer the world with apologies and regrets."

Kyle wasn't sure he'd ever wanted to conquer

the world. He'd wanted to design something that could keep people from suffering. People like his grandfather. Callie, he knew, had other plans for her life. Plans that depended on his continued funding. And those depended on his next big idea. "I'll make the tuition payment soon."

She looked at him as if she'd never doubted that would happen. As it always happened on the third Thursday of every month. "I wanted to tell you that I've been invited to continue my medical research at Oxford once I receive my doctorate degrees."

"But that's in England." And nowhere near San Francisco or her family.

"It's one of the premiere research facilities in the world." Excitement widened her brown eyes.

How could she be thrilled about living in another country, so far away from her family? How could he not be happy for her opportunity to continue her life's work? "Have you told Mom and Dad?"

"They're ecstatic. At least from what I could tell." Callie tapped a pencil against her bottom lip as if she struggled to work out the exact sequence of a DNA genome strand. "They were walking on the beach. Mom found a giant sea shell with only a small chip. Maybe they were cheering about that." She paused, grabbed a notepad and scribbled across the paper.

Kyle waited. His sister spoke in logical order. But her thoughts always came out in scattered spurts like air in a waterline. He'd always assumed her genius brain never quieted. If she didn't pause to record her thoughts every so often, she might miss the next big medical breakthrough.

Finally, Callie blinked into the screen. "No, I'm sure Mom wished me safe travels and Dad wanted hotel recommendations in the area. Or maybe that was the couple with them. I think they're planning a trip up the Gulf Coast. Doesn't matter. Oxford wants me."

Kyle wanted to wish his sister well. Share her excitement. But only sadness circled through him.

Four years ago, their grandfather had died unexpectedly, and their family had splintered without the glue that had been Papa Quinn. Kyle had inherited his grandpa's vintage 1965 Mustang. Along with the last of his grandfather's wisdom on a handwritten note left inside the Mustang's glove box: "When you take a wrong turn, Kyle, a guiding hand and full heart will lead you home where you belong."

Kyle's family had taken several wrong turns after Papa Quinn's passing, and the distance between his family had only widened further. Then Kyle had signed his contract with Tech Realized, Inc. Honoring his grandfather's memory had filled his bank account. The money he'd always intended to help guide his family back together.

Now he funded dual degrees that would only take his sister farther from home. Worry mixed with the sadness. She was a scientist, not an experienced world traveler. How was he supposed to protect her from a continent away? He should protect her. She'd always been there for him in grade school. More than once, she'd stepped in to deflect the bullies' attention off him and on to her with her oversize books and even thicker bottle-size glasses.

The buzzer from the street entrance hummed through the suite. Kyle tucked his concern away, certain he'd come up with something to entice his little sister home. Something like her own research lab, custom built to her specifications. "That's my company."

Callie had already returned to her notepad and had pulled her microscope into view. "Don't be like Iris and get distracted, Kyle. Send them away and get back to what really matters. You can't lose focus of what's really important."

With that, Callie clicked off. No "I love you." No "talk to you soon." No "I hope you visit me in England." Only an order to work and a caution not to be like their oldest sister, Iris. Kyle's problem was he struggled to focus on what was important: a new idea.

He checked his emails on the way to the entrance. Still no response from his potential judges. Not even a terse thank-you, or any thank-you at all. He'd take his sister's advice. Offer a quick tour and then send the trio waiting outside on their way. They'd understand he had to work. If they didn't, what would it matter? They weren't friends, and this was a onetime offer.

He pressed the button to unlock the main entrance door that led into the lobby and spoke through the intercom, telling them to come up to the second floor.

Kyle opened the door to the suite and welcomed his guests inside. He would've explained his plans to work that afternoon if Ben hadn't disrupted the silence with a drawn-out *whoa*.

Kyle shut the door and turned around to find the young boy bouncing from one foot to the other, his gaze darting around the suite. Ben never moved from his father's side, as if he waited for a referee to blow a start whistle to let the games begin.

"You work here?" Ava stood with her arms crossed and one eyebrow arched. Clearly, she wasn't as impressed by his personal arcade space (aka inspiration area) as Ben.

"I live here, too." Kyle grinned at the disbelief Ava failed to hide. His grin widened at her resistance to smile. Suddenly, all he wanted was to make Ava smile. Suddenly, that became important. That became his focus, even as he told himself to concentrate on something else.

"Cool." Ben failed to hide his awe.

Dan rubbed his chin and nodded. "Can't see anything I'd add."

"How about books or candles? Maybe some colorful throw pillows or picture frames to break up all the gray and black," Ava suggested.

Ava, with her red hair sweeping past her shoulders and green eyes, brought color into the monochrome room. The room was quiet and subdued without the arcade turned on, the screens lit up and the sounds of the *game over* music playing. All the room wanted was someone to press Play. Kyle didn't know what he wanted. But he liked welcoming Ava into his home. "It wasn't designed to be a meditation room."

"Clearly," Ava said. Her gaze jumped around the room, taking everything in. Even better, she never retreated toward the door.

"This should appeal to you, Ava." Dan shoved her shoulder. "You love that pub with the '80s arcade games and pool tables south of the city."

Busted. Ava avoided Kyle's gaze. He longed to laugh. She didn't want to like his place. Too bad he didn't want to like having her there. He'd planned to send them away quickly and without much fanfare. Now he hesitated, and that irritated him.

He'd always have to question whether a woman genuinely liked him—the guy with the deadly nut allergy, who preferred arcade games and comic books and his family. The one who tended to believe if the money went away, so might the woman.

The news reports about him wanting to find love on a reality TV show were completely false. Yet there was something about Ava that tugged at places deep inside him. Places he'd learned to ignore years ago. Places he buried under his flush bank accounts, confident money would fill any void.

He admitted Ava was attractive like he acknowledged a flaw in one of his 3-D designs. He'd fix an error in his design with several keystrokes on the computer. The only way to fix Ava was to ignore his interest in her. Ignore that tightness inside his chest. File her into the same category as every other attractive woman he'd met: unavailable, off-limits and a disruption to his life.

"Aunty, you always want to play Skee-Ball." Ben pointed across the room. "Here we don't have to wait in line."

"Or wipe down the machines before we use

them." Dan looked at Kyle. "I'm not kidding. She carries those antibacterial wipes with her everywhere we go."

Ava threw up her hands. "Just trying to keep everyone from getting sick."

Dan wrapped his arm around her shoulders and squeezed her. "We appreciate it, even if you act more like an overly cautious grandmother sometimes."

Ben giggled and followed Kyle farther into the room, cutting between the pool and foosball tables.

"You have basketball shoot and off-road driving games." Ben touched the Ping-Pong table and stared at the far wall. "And four pinball machines."

Kyle had always wanted a pinball machine in the basement of his parents' house. In the gaps between his invention design sessions, he'd make lists of every game that would've improved the basement dwelling. Every game that might've enticed the kids from school to come over and play with him. Each one of those games waited inside Kyle's inspiration suite now. Kyle had stopped waiting for friends to come over in middle school. Now he'd assumed the more fun and games that had surrounded him, the more ideas he'd have.

For now, inspiration hadn't arrived, no matter how many arcade games he jammed into the room. Not even Skee-Ball, his favorite childhood game, inspired him. "There's a ninety-two-inch flat-screen TV with surround sound and gaming consoles right through that door."

"Like a real theater room." Ben dragged his hand across the air-hockey table and edged closer to the twin Skee-Ball games.

Surprised Ben wasn't racing into the theater room for the video games, Kyle looked at the subdued Skee-Ball lanes. "I never replenished the prize tickets in Skee-Ball, but they work."

The blank chalkboard wall—the one he'd always meant to be like a graffiti wall to write inspirational sayings or draw pictures on—caught his gaze. The box of colored chalk had yet to be opened, and he'd bought it a year ago to celebrate the completion of the remodeling. His sister's earlier claim about him being alone drifted through him. He chose independence and self-reliance. The blank wall mocked him. "The highest score gets full bragging rights and their name listed on the wall of champions."

Ben hopped as if anticipation bounced through every limb, forcing him to move. He tugged on his dad's arm. A plea widened his eyes.

"Ask Kyle if you can play." Dan dipped his chin toward Kyle. "This is his office."

Kyle grinned at Dan's hesitation over the word

office before meeting Ava's gaze. "I refer to it as the inspiration room inside the think tank. There's also a design lab with 3-D printers and more professional equipment. Everything required to make this place look like a real business."

One corner of Ava's mouth twitched as if daring Kyle to try harder. He'd never turned down a dare in his life.

Dan stepped back and raised his hands. "Definitely not judging."

"He's just jealous." Ava wrapped her arm around Dan's waist, easy and comfortable.

Dan hugged Ava. "I won't deny I'm jealous."

Jealous. Kyle watched Ava and Dan's casual interactions. In that moment, he understood jealousy on a very different level. But relationships complicated life. Relationships required effort and focus and time—everything he needed to put into developing an idea. And everything he required for his contest to be a success. He acknowledged that twinge of envy that tinted his eyesight green and filed Ava in the if-only-he-was-a-good-team-player-and-this-was-another-time category.

Both Dan and Ben shared twin looks of excitement.

Ben rubbed his hands together. "So, can we really play?"

"We don't want to take up too much of Kyle's time." Ava touched Ben's shoulder. "I'm sure Kyle has plans for the afternoon."

This was where Kyle agreed with Ava. He should explain that he had to work. This was his cue to hurry through the rest of the tour and make the offer for them to come back another time. Or never. This was where he regained his focus and concentrated on his priorities.

That chalkboard wall trapped Kyle's gaze as if reflecting some void deep inside of himself. But Kyle liked his life. "It's Saturday, you can play as much and as long as you want."

"Seriously?" Ben asked.

Ava kept her hand on the boy's shoulder, as if holding him in place, and eyed Kyle. "One hour."

He should accept her terms. One hour was already overstaying their welcome. He held her green gaze, locked on as if they'd entered some staring contest where the winner received more than simple bragging rights. "As it happens, my afternoon is wide-open."

Ava never flinched. "One hour should be more than enough time."

Challenge accepted. He'd make sure one hour wasn't long enough. Kyle pointed to the wall again and grinned at Ben. "I feel I should warn you that I don't lose easily, and I intend to have my name up there."

Ben shrugged one shoulder as if unconcerned with Kyle's skills. "I like to win, too."

"I can't decide where we should start." Dan's laughter mixed with Ben's as the pair ventured around the room.

The cheerful sound seeped inside Kyle as if trying to fill that void. He'd once shared that same joy with his sisters, playing Ping-Pong in their parents' basement that they'd converted into a teenager's hideaway. Kyle looked at Ava. "We can continue the tour or play a round of pool."

She opted for the tour, but her gaze landed on the Skee-Ball lanes and stuck as they passed.

Kyle guided Ava into the development lab. The state-of-the-art room had multiple desktops, a dry-erase-board wall and tinted glass windows that overlooked the city. More hand-held games and toys littered the entire space. Multicolored puzzle balls and cubes sat among the various plastic building blocks scattered across the empty worktable. Three-dimensional printed items, ranging from a bottle opener to the first pieces of a chess game, stood sentry around the room. Each piece a reminder of his continued unoriginality. Middle school kids printed more complicated designs on their 3-D printers.

"You're running a contest?" Ava pointed at

the contest time line Kyle had written in colored markers on the dry-erase board.

"I put it together this week with my legal team, and we issued a press statement yesterday morning." Kyle eyed the list on the dry-erase board. Acting as tour guide to Ava accomplished nothing productive and only reminded him of that awkward boy he'd long since outgrown. "I need to thank Ben for the idea."

"Ben?" Ava stood beside the sleek metal table and picked up the piggy bank he'd used as a paperweight for the stack of contest flyers.

"I got the idea when Ben talked about that invention game you guys play." Guilt pricked into his skin like a rough tag in his shirt collar. He'd done nothing wrong. He had nothing to confess.

He'd launched a contest. Planned to give the winner money. He'd even written in the rules that the winner's idea became the property of his company once they accepted the cash payout. He'd spent hours with his legal team. Even required the entrants to click an "I accept the terms and conditions agreement" box to enter the contest. That wasn't guilt scratching at him; it was panic. He had to find judges and mentors immediately.

Ava picked up a contest flyer and searched the paper as if searching for understanding. "What's behind the contest?"

His chance at success. Albeit from the mind of someone else. Still, the winner would get money and Kyle would fulfill his contract. Everyone won. That scratch dug deeper into his neck like a razor pressed at the wrong angle. "It's a way to give back. People have great ideas, but no platform to build them."

"You'll supply the platform." Ava smiled, sincere and wide. Surprise drifted through her voice as if she'd doubted his altruistic streak. "That's really impressive."

Somehow her smile only sharpened that razor against his skin. He stepped forward and grabbed the flyer.

Ava held on to the paper. "Afraid I might enter?"

Kyle didn't want to encourage her. After all, playing a game about invention ideas in the car was much different than coming up with a viable idea that could potentially change lives. Ava was certainly a pleasure to be around, but she wasn't an inventor. Nor was she his conscience. "The contest is open to anyone with an idea."

Ava released the paper. "I'll keep that in mind."

Kyle placed the flyer and his guilt back under the piggy bank paperweight.

"Your contest can possibly change someone's life," she said.

Or return his life to how it should be: with his family home, where he needed them. "I'm not sure it's life-changing money."

"Trust me. It is." Ava's earnest tone drew Kyle's focus. "You're going to change someone's world."

He only wanted to bring back his old world, where he'd always belonged—the one he'd relied on before Papa Quinn's death. Before his family had splintered and had fled in different directions. Without a new idea, the contest was his only chance. "The contest has to be a success first."

"It has your name and you're already a success," Ava said. "How could it fail?"

Kyle concentrated on her wide smile, refusing to list all the ways his plan might fail. Or the ways he might fail. If only her smile was enough to lessen the unease building inside him. He grabbed a puzzle cube from the table to keep his hands busy. But no matter how many turns he made on the cube, he couldn't quite organize his guilt back under that pile of flyers. Or rearrange his unease.

He rushed out of the design room. In his haste to retreat, he led Ava into his living quarters. His personal space. Not the place he should've taken her. The apartment area was too small. Too compact. She was too close.

He couldn't avoid her gaze that was too pene-trating, as if she could read his secrets. She was supposed to have stopped at the game room. Been enthralled by the glitz and the glamor of the theater room. Been in awe of the state-of-the-art development lab.

She wasn't supposed to look any deeper at Kyle.

He wasn't supposed to let her.

He feared if she looked too close, she might glimpse the fraud inside him. For some unknown reason, he didn't want her to see him that way.

"There's no separation between work and home." Ava opened his college-dorm-style re-frigerator that had leftover pizza and an assort-ment of Greek-style yogurt inside. She grinned at him over the door, a tease in her voice. "Don't cook much?"

"One of the perks of selling the earbud. I got to add a personal chef to the payroll." He kept his tone easygoing but touched his medical-alert bracelet.

Her gaze tracked to his wrist. "What's the bracelet for?"

He stiffened, but kept his voice mild and in-different. As if his condition was no more life-threatening than a hangnail. In the summer before the sixth grade, he'd wanted nothing more than to fit in with the other boys. He'd boasted about his allergy and embellished his stories about ambulance rides to sound cooler than they ever were. Troy Simmons—one of the boys Kyle had wanted desperately to call a friend—decided to test Kyle's claims and hide a nut in Kyle's lunch. That single nut had sent Kyle on another ambulance ride. His three-day hospital stay had taught him a life lesson in trust. His family became the only ones he'd ever fully trust. He'd returned to school, confident that it was easier to be alone with his secrets than to be betrayed by so-called friends. "Nut allergy."

"How severe is it?" she asked.

"Enough that I need to wear this." And the personal chef had been hired to ensure his employees didn't bring food into the building that would cause a reaction that sent him to the hospital. He wasn't about to confess that weakness to Ava. She was a stranger. A temporary guest in his building.

In middle school, he'd stopped discussing his food allergies with people outside of his family. Now, even though his personal staff had moved on to other jobs, his chef still delivered meals twice a week. He'd grown tired of the five things he knew how to cook that wouldn't make him reach for his EpiPen and dial 9-1-1.

"You don't talk about it much." She shut the

refrigerator door and watched him. "At least from what I read."

"You looked me up?" He wasn't sure if he should be flattered or worried.

"I wasn't bringing Ben into a stranger's house." Her voice was confident and sure. Her stance, with her hands on her hips, was unapologetic.

"I'd be even more cautious after reading anything about me on the internet." The news reporters and gossip columnists were just another reason he kept to himself.

"You don't like to talk about yourself, do you?"

"I like to keep my private life private."

"But you're a local celebrity and the public wants to know." Ava leaned against the counter as if in no rush to continue the tour. "I imagine everyone wants to spill your secrets."

Good thing he didn't have too many. And none that he'd risk sharing with another person. He eyed Ava. No makeup concealed the freckles across her nose. No designer labels peeked out on her yoga pants and oversize sweatshirt. As if she really wore those clothes to work out in. She'd dressed for herself and her own comfort, not to impress. Such a refreshing change, yet everyone had an agenda.

What was Ava's? Was she looking for a fast

track to her fifteen minutes of fame? Looking
for an easy payout with a story to sell? He hoped
she was. That was more than enough for him to
escort her out of his suite and sever his interest
in her. "It's a good thing that I don't have any
secrets, then."

"Well, you've got one," she challenged.

Alarms blared through him. He knew she'd
been too perfect. "What's that?"

"I never read a quote or story about you from
your private chef."

"She's discreet." He paid Haley Waters, his
chef, very well for that discretion.

She nodded, as if content with his answer.
Content not to press for more. "We remodeled
our kitchen, but it might've been wiser to invest
in a personal chef."

Like his chef, Haley? Did Ava have secrets?
Kyle should walk her back to her friends. Not
linger in his kitchen as if he wanted to get to
know her better. As if he wanted to *know* her.
Yet he should discover what she wanted from
him. "You don't like to cook, either?"

"It's not the cooking. It's the shopping." Ava
grimaced. "Although now I get our groceries
delivered."

Our. Kyle scanned her fingers for a ring. Even
without a ring, she could be involved with someone. That thought knocked around inside his gut

like the break of the balls on the pool table. Definitely not his business. Those were only hunger pangs making his stomach clench. Nothing food wouldn't quiet. Before he could shove a spoonful of yogurt into his mouth, he asked, "You cook for more than yourself?"

He had to stop talking or she'd question his angle. As if he had one.

"My mom and I live together." She walked out of the kitchen, toward the game room, as if she'd revealed more than enough.

She wanted to keep her private life private, too. That put them on common ground. And intensified his desire to learn what else they might have in common. Why couldn't she have been like the women he'd met who were only interested in what his money could do for them? Why did *she* have to be interesting? And standoffish, as if she didn't trust him with her secrets.

She pulled out her phone and tapped the screen. "We should get going."

He'd asked one personal question and she wanted to leave. "Play one game of Skee-Ball. It'll be hard to talk while you're trying to beat me."

Her gaze shifted toward the lanes. Temptation was there in her half grin.

"Come on, Ava," Dan urged. "I talked to

my dad. Your mom is good, and they already planned dinner without us."

"One game." Ava stepped up to the first lane.

Kyle pressed Play on the second lane. "Let's see what you've got."

He already knew what he got: a game room that wasn't empty or silent. He'd enjoy the moment. Then get back to work. What harm was there in one round?

One game turned into two. Then three. The moment extended into the evening. Then through dinner. The foursome moved together from one section to another. Challenges issued. Teams made and disbanded. Everyone proved to be poor losers and even worse winners. Between the boasting and bragging, more challenges were tossed out. Laughter threaded through every minute: good-natured and contagious.

Finally, Dan called a halt. Ben had exceeded his yawn limit and bedtime beckoned.

One last debate followed.

Ava grabbed the chalk and walked to the wall. "I claim the top spot."

"For Skee-Ball only," Dan argued. Both Ben and Kyle nodded, drawing out her frown.

"Fine." She filled up the wall with a swirl of blue chalk. "Here are the final standings."

Kyle earned: Expert Ping-Pong Player.

Ben: Highest Score 11 and under.

Dan: Best Off-Road Driver.

Ava: High Score Skee-Ball.

Kyle walked the trio out and returned to the suite. Time to work. His reprieve had ended much like all good times had to. His gaze stuck on the chalkboard wall. Ava had added a smiley face after her name: bold and challenging, like her.

He skipped turning off the lights and instead pressed the start button on the Skee-Ball lane.

One more game wasn't a big deal. It meant nothing. It wasn't as if he wanted to extend the moment. As if he couldn't accept the evening had ended.

As if he wasn't ready for the silence of being alone. He preferred the quiet.

He just wanted to play one more game. Nothing wrong with that.

CHAPTER FOUR

KYLE FINISHED A direct deposit into Penny's Place bank account to cover the shelter's expenses for the month, submitted Callie's tuition payment early and logged out of his banking website. His ringing cell phone disrupted the silence that had blanketed the suite the past week. The heavy quiet draped like sheets over the furniture of an abandoned house.

Or perhaps the real damage had come from Ava, Dan and Ben last weekend. Their laughter no longer lingered and that amplified the still-ness surrounding him. He'd never have noticed if he hadn't opened the door that day. Even more disturbing was that he wanted to invite them back. He needed an idea, though, not friends.

He pressed Answer on the phone screen.

Over the speakerphone, the brusque voice of Terri Stanton, VP of Tech Realized, Inc., dis-rupted the still, sterile air in the development lab. "Kyle, you can help as many amateur in-ventors as you want with your contest, as long as you submit your proposal as outlined in the contract you signed."

"You'll have a proposal by the due date." Kyle double-checked the time line on the dry-erase board. The contest ended two days before his idea was due. Late last night, he'd added the last judge to the panel. The official contest open house happened tomorrow afternoon. Everything was proceeding as planned.

Everything but creating his own original idea. That wasn't proceeding at all.

He'd spent the entire week inside the lab. The result: a 3-D printed chess game board, complete with all the individual chess pieces. And a growing list of ideas he'd thought were original until a quick search on the patent website proved him wrong. It seemed everyone had gotten to his ideas first.

The contest was quickly becoming his plan A.

"Hey, I like an altruistic streak as much as the next person," Terri added. The graciousness in her voice was cut by the bluntness in her tone. "Just not at the expense of your commitments."

"And the bottom line," Kyle said before he could shut his mouth.

There was a pause in the air over the speakerphone. Then Terri cleared her throat as if strengthening the firmness in her voice. "We've all enjoyed the Medi-Spy profits, even you, Kyle.

You can't deny it. That doesn't make us bad people."

No, bad people stole others' ideas and passed them off as their own. Kyle ran his hands through his hair. He wasn't really stealing an idea. Every part of the contest had been vetted and approved by his legal team at Thornton, Davies and Associates. Every contestant had to sign an agreement and a waiver. No one was being duped. No one was being forced to submit an entry.

Besides, he wasn't taking every idea. Only the winner's. The winner received a monetary prize. A quite nice reward. Maybe if he increased the payout, he'd decrease his guilt.

This was for his family, after all. That didn't make him a bad guy. A bad guy wanted to line his own pockets. "These inventions have to be about more than money."

"Do they?" Terri laughed as if his innocence amused her. "Money opens doors."

And was supposed to solve any problem, wasn't it? "It really is all about the money."

"It's about making more money. With your new invention." Terri's voice increased, as if she picked up the phone and spoke directly into the receiver to get her point across. "Then we can do whatever we want. Even sit around and philosophize about the dangers of money if we choose to."

Several clunks echoed down the hallway, followed by the clatter of bells. Kyle was supposed to be alone. Like he wanted. Like he chose to be. "I'll have my proposal to you on time, Terri. I need to get to a meeting."

"Make it a profitable one. I promise you won't regret it." Terri laughed and clicked off.

Kyle stood up, stuffed his phone into the pocket of his jeans and walked into his inspiration area. A curly-haired petite woman in four-inch red heels and a charcoal-gray business suit picked a ball out of the Skee-Ball queue. One underhand toss and the ball flipped up the ramp, landing in the forty-point circle. The points flashed in red lights across the digital screen on the top.

Kyle walked up to the second Skee-Ball lane, pressed the start button and switched his greeting for his older sister into a question. "Shouldn't you be at work?"

Specifically, his older sister should be at the job he'd secured for her last week at the Zenith Law Firm.

"Who's Ava?" Iris threw her second ball, garnered another forty points and never glanced at him.

"Ava is Ben's aunt." Kyle faced his lane and aimed a ball at the white rings. "What about your job?"

"Things weren't going to work out at Zenith." She kicked off her heels and adjusted her stance as if her future was riding on the next toss. "Who is Ben?"

"Ben is Dan's son." Kyle landed a ball in the fifty-point ring. "What happened at Zenith?"

Thanks to a connection through his own legal team, he'd found his sister a position as a receptionist at the Zenith Law Firm. The position was perfect for Iris; between her pleasant voice and animated disposition, she'd been ideal to answer calls and greet clients in the reception area. The position paid well, offered benefits and had no mandatory overtime.

"Besides the requirement of having to be seated at my desk at precisely 8:00 a.m., there were other unrealistic expectations." Her ball failed to make it into the scoring range. "Who is Dan?"

"They're friends." Kyle grabbed another ball and glanced at his older sister. "Tell me why you got fired."

This was Iris's sixteenth job in the past twelve months. That had to be some sort of employment record. His sister was quickly becoming a serial job-hopper.

"You don't have friends." She tossed her last ball from one hand to the other and looked at him. Nothing sparked in her blue eyes, as if she guarded herself from Kyle. "It was a mutual parting, by the way. I told Lacey Thornton you'd see her at the Harrington fund-raiser tonight."

Kyle's ball dropped out of his hand and onto the lane. His voice dropped, too. "Why would you say that?"

"Because Lacey helped get me the job at Zenith." She pointed the ball at him. "You are friends with both Drew Harrington and Lacey, so you should be there at the fund-raiser to support your friend's family."

"I don't have friends." He threw her words back at her.

"You don't have friends who come here to hang out, play arcade games and write their names on the chalkboard wall." She turned to the lane, tossed her ball into the fifty-point ring and smiled. Her voice came out more like an accusation. "But you do have business friends."

"Fortunately, I have those business connections." Kyle ran his hands through his hair as if that would contain his frustration. He didn't mind supporting his sister, especially since her disaster of a marriage and the extreme fallout after her divorce. But she needed something of her own. Certainly, she wanted that for herself, too. All she had to do was stay longer than a week at a job and she'd start to build something. "It's been those business friends who've been willing to offer you employment. But I'm running low on those connections."

"Then you can network tonight at the Harrington event." She frowned at her final score and restarted the game. "If it makes you feel any better, I really intended to be at that job longer than a week."

He'd intended the very same thing. Had even bought her an entire work wardrobe for this particular job, believing this would be the one she stuck with. Her suit jacket bagged around her shoulders—she still hadn't regained the weight she'd lost after her divorce. Her frame had always been frail, but now she looked even more fragile. More vulnerable. He sighed and softened his voice. "Tell me what happened."

She watched the balls roll into the queue. "When am I going to meet your new friends?"

Iris released information according to her own schedule. In her own way. She'd continue returning his question with one of her own for the rest of the morning. Determined to end the game, he said, "I met them at the calendar shoot for juvenile diabetes research several weekends ago. I offered to give Ben, who has juvenile diabetes, a tour of the place. He likes to invent things."

She cradled the ball and turned to face him, but her gaze refused to meet his. "It was a mutual parting of the ways at Zenith. Wade and I agreed I wasn't right for the job. I've already made plans to meet up with Wade and his entire team at Rustic Grille for appetizers and drinks next week."

His sister had remained friends with every one of her prior employers. *Every single one.* She'd crossed the employee-employer boundary, proving they were better buddies than coworkers. He might've envied her ease at making friends if not for the fact that her friends wouldn't pay her rent or her credit-card bills. "What now?"

"I have options." Both her voice and small grin lacked confidence.

More like Kyle would have to find her another employment option. He rolled his last ball up the ramp. "Options that can pay your rent, bills and food."

"Why is it always about money?" Irritation dipped into her normally sweet tone.

He'd just asked Terri of Tech Realized, Inc. the very same thing. He repeated Terri's response. "Once you have enough money, you can do whatever you want. Whatever you're passionate about."

"Are you living your passion now that you have money?" Iris tossed her ball from one hand to the other as if debating whether or not to launch it at him. "Living alone in an arcade. Is this the life you always imagined?"

When had it become about him and his life? Or his passion. Whatever she meant by that. He could count on his hand the number of people he knew that were passionate about their work. Maybe he needed to extend his circle of acquaintances. They weren't discussing his life right now, anyway. "Come with me tonight to the Harrington event. We'll find someone with a job opening that you can be passionate about."

"I have another commitment tonight." She turned back to the game.

"For a potential job?"

"Maybe," she hedged.

Kyle studied his sister. He wanted her to be happy. She deserved to finally be happy after a marriage that had left her isolated and scared to trust anyone, even her own family. His throat closed as if a Skee-Ball lodged there. "Iris…"

"I'll change my plans around." She eyed him. Her chin tipped up in challenge. "As long as you introduce me to your new friends."

Simple. Easy. "Done."

He had no idea when he'd see Dan, Ben or Ava again. That promise wouldn't be difficult to keep. Smiling, he walked toward the back of the suite, grabbed his checkbook from a desk drawer and wrote out a check in his sister's name. He knew by heart how much she'd need to cover her monthly expenses—he'd written the same check every month for the past year. Returning to the inspiration area, he handed her the check. "It's enough to cover rent and food for the month."

"I've got everything covered." She focused on the lane, both her voice and grip on the ball intense.

"You've already lined up another job." He couldn't quite pull the surprised sarcasm from his voice.

She tossed the ball, pumped her fist as it rolled into the highest point ring. "Not yet. But I will."

"Then you're going to need this." Kyle thrust the check at her. "Just take it."

His sister launched her final ball. Landed another high point and jumped up in the air. "Where's the chalk?"

"The what?" he asked.

She waved toward the chalkboard wall. "The chalk. I need to write my name over Ava's."

"What are you talking about?" he asked.

"I'm the new high score." She jumped again and pointed at him. "You can tell Ava I said, challenge accepted."

Why couldn't his sister be this competitive in the workforce? "You need to go home and iron your suit—the one you wore for your job interview at Zenith—and not worry about being the high score."

"No ironing today." She erased Ava's name

and wrote hers with her trademark flourish and flower to dot the second lowercase *I* in her name. "I have an appointment with Roland Daniels to de-stress and unwind."

He needed to de-stress. How could his sister be so unpredictable and stubborn? She'd just lost her job. Again. "Stop at the bank and deposit this check on your way to the yoga studio."

"I already agreed to go with you to the Harrington event. You don't need to pay me like I'm your employee or something."

Kyle cleared his throat to release the truth. The truth she never wanted to hear. "You can't go back to Penny's Place, Iris. Take the check."

Iris crossed her arms over her chest and frowned at him. "Why not? They understand me there."

"It's a shelter for abused and abandoned women." He still cringed at the memories of seeing his sister in the doorway of Penny's Place. Her bruised eye. The stitches circling her wrist and crisscrossing her forehead. A nauseous fury still stormed through him at the reminder. "You aren't either of those things now."

She yanked the check from his grip and stuffed it into her suit pocket. "Because of your handouts."

"It's not like that." If she'd keep a job, she wouldn't need his handouts. He smoothed the frustration from his voice. "I want to help. That's all."

He wanted his sister to have security and protection—everything she never had in her brief marriage.

Iris slipped her heels back on, once again looking the part of a corporate professional ready to conquer the business world, one promotion at a time. "Mom and Dad called to congratulate me on making it a full week. I tried to pretend, but it only disrupted my inner zen. Luckily, they were off to snorkel, and their lecture ended quickly."

Neither Iris nor Kyle had told their parents the full details of her divorce. No one besides Kyle knew where Iris had ended up a week after she'd signed her divorce papers. No one besides Kyle knew about the darkness in her marriage. Kyle intended to help his sister now.

"Did Mom and Dad tell you when they wanted to move back?" Perhaps with his parents back home, they could work together to get Iris into a full-time job. Kyle was beginning to think he needed reinforcements.

Iris tipped her head and gaped at him. "You do realize they retired to the Florida Coast, right?"

"But their family is here." Their home was here. At least once he built the family estate in Sonoma. Then their family could be together again. Close again like they'd been before Papa

Quinn's death. Like his grandfather had always expected them to be.

"Speaking of family, can your family members enter that contest of yours?" Iris pulled a folded piece of paper from her oversize purse. "Wade showed me the flyer this morning before I left."

"No. You're ineligible to win." Besides, he'd already advanced her double that amount over the past year.

"I have a great idea that's worth more than your contest prize." Enthusiasm lifted her voice. "I only need paint brushes and…"

"Painting the ceiling in here to look like the sky isn't a great idea." Kyle crossed his arms over his chest. He'd given Iris free rein to design the bathrooms and hang her own artwork in the elevator. The arcade, he intended to leave alone. The family basement never had a ceiling painted to look like the sky. He didn't need that now.

"With the right lighting in here, it'd look incredible." Iris adjusted her purse on her shoulder and stared up at the ceiling. "You have no imagination."

He used to have one that helped him create endless ideas. He wasn't sure where his imagination had fled to or how to find it. "I don't need an imagination to recognize when something is a waste of time and money."

"Art is never a waste of time." Her voice was confident, her tone defiant. "But I don't expect you to understand."

He understood his sister needed a job with a regular paycheck. "I'll pick you up at seven tonight."

"Any other orders?"

He couldn't resist the urge to bait her. "Get a class calendar from the yoga studio. When you start working full-time again, you won't be able to attend a late-morning yoga session with Roland."

Iris glared at him and yanked open the door. She exited without a goodbye. He shouldn't have baited her. Yet when she was riled, she lost her fragility and vulnerability. Whenever Iris was riled, he saw a glimpse of his older sister—the one with the backbone and spirit that had come to his defense more than once. The one he'd grown up wanting to be like. Was it wrong that he wanted the sister he once knew?

CHAPTER FIVE

AVA RUBBED HER eyes and looked out the passenger window of the ambulance, idling in their usual curbside spot on the street. Three hours ago, the clock had chimed for Cinderellas everywhere to return home before the magic disappeared. Now Dan and Ava were stuck in the middle, between midnight and sunrise, with four hours left on their work shift.

The darkest hour of the night might've already passed, but the city only ever went completely dark in a rare power outage. Tonight was no different with the stoplight lighting the intersection and the surrounding buildings lit in awkward checkerboard patterns.

Tourists knew the city for its landmarks: Golden Gate Bridge, Alcatraz and Lombard Street with its eight hairpin turns. Ava marked the city by patients and victims, especially the ones that had left the deepest mark inside her. Six blocks ahead on the left was the cardiac plaza. Chest pains and shortness of breath were the main reasons for 9-1-1 calls from that particular office building. Four blocks to her right was her first hit-and-run intersection. Every time she passed the corner of Cliff Street and Gate Street, the anguish of a mother's cries over her stillborn baby echoed through her.

Ava stared out the window, searching for a less morbid memory. Only gloom overtook her. That was her own fault for inviting her financial problems inside the ambulance. She should've stuck to the cute puppy and kitten videos she usually watched between emergency calls and not opened the help-wanted website on her phone.

But watching endless videos wasn't going to pay the rent or cover the cost of her mom's prescriptions. Neither was her paramedic's salary. She had to supplement her income.

She scrolled through the job ads on her phone and groaned.

"Nothing promising?" Dan asked between bites of his cheeseburger.

"It's a toss-up between airplane repo man, exotic personal assistant or nude housekeeper." Ava dropped her phone on her lap.

Dan choked on his bite of french fry.

Ava handed Dan his bottle of water. "In all fairness, the nude part ends when the guy's wife returns from her vacation. Then it's just regular housekeeping."

Dan wiped a napkin over his mouth and muted

the laughter in his voice. "How much does the housekeeper get paid?"

"Not nearly enough." The housekeeping would barely cover the expense of her mom's daily medications. That left rent, electric and food.

"For the fast, easy payout, you should enter Kyle's contest. You get to keep your clothes on, unless of course your invention involves being naked." Dan crumpled the empty foil wrapper from his cheeseburger along with the tease from his tone. "Although that doesn't seem like the kind of X-rated idea Kyle wants in his contest."

"How do you know what Kyle wants?" She wanted to see Kyle again. But only in the can-I-play-Skee-Ball kind of way. Nothing more. She had no time for a man in her life.

Even if she did, Kyle wouldn't make the cut. Anyone who could fund a random contest with fifty thousand dollars in less than a week, on a whim no less, played on a different field than she did. One that was no doubt carefree, worry-free and extra green from his money. Her field consisted of financial debt and possible job burn-out—not exactly greener pastures or enticing.

"Ben and I checked out Kyle's website." Dan polished off the last of his french fries. "We're trying to come up with a winning invention."

That money, along with the potential bonus,

would allow Ava to go to school and pay for her mom's care. No naked housekeeping required. Temptation swirled through her. But she had to come up with an idea better than mood-changing hair dye. She'd need a serious, workable idea. One worth twenty-five grand. "Surely you guys have something on your list of wins from our You-Know-What-We-Need game."

"Nothing worthy of fifty grand," Dan said.

"Then it's not such an easy, quick payout." Like everything in life. Life was never that easy or simple. Ever.

"You just need one idea." Dan held up his index finger. "One."

"One really good idea that hasn't been thought of already." Ava stretched her legs out and flexed her toes inside her boots, rolled her ankles. Nothing smoothed out the sudden restlessness inside her. "An invention that can also be made into a prototype."

Dan scrunched up his napkin and threw it at her. "You looked into the contest, too. What is your idea?"

"I talked to Kyle about the contest when we were there." She'd considered the contest in a the-sky-is-always-pink-in-that-world kind of way. Putting her energy into a fantasy made her selfish like her father. She had to do what was right for her family, not only herself. Believing she could win a contest was a risk she couldn't afford. She tapped on her phone screen to search for more job ads. "My only idea is to find a legal, non-nude, part-time job that pays well."

Dan tapped the steering wheel. "You have better odds with the contest or the lottery."

She refused to believe that. She had to be thoughtful and methodical in her job search. Entering a contest and wishing on stars wasn't practical. "I just have to search the right job-ad website."

Dispatch interrupted the conversation. Codes. Location. And more details rattled over the speaker, focusing Ava.

Who was she kidding? She wasn't an inventor or a forward thinker. She was a paramedic who'd served her country and now took care of her mother. She tended to the wounded and sick—that was what she knew how to do. What she excelled at. Ava buckled her seat belt and left her ridiculous thoughts about inventions outside, in the gutter.

"Time to roll." Dan buckled his seat belt. "Told you that you should've eaten while we had the chance."

Stress had stolen her appetite. With each block closer to the victim's location, she crammed the stress deep inside her, where it wouldn't distract her. She couldn't rescue her struggling finances, but she could help save another life.

FORTY-EIGHT HOURS after her late-night job search in the ambulance, the reality of Ava's life crashed over her. Game night at Kyle's place seemed like a distant memory—an imagined one.

Her reality was a domestic fight and a victim with multiple stab wounds. An overdose. One early-morning heart attack. A stroke. Not everyone arrived at the hospital alive. Those were only the life-threatening calls during the night.

Five hours into their shift, Ava had checked the full-moon calendar, looking for something to explain the hectic pace. The full moon was still more than eight days away. Her shift had been another routine night on the job. A routine night that had left her hollowed out and exhausted.

Ava walked into her apartment, her legs wooden, her steps slow. Surely a few hours of sleep would right her world enough to take on the day.

But her home life collided with her professional life, adding a bleakness everywhere she looked.

Joann, a registered nurse and her mother's caregiver, sat at the kitchen table, her fingers wrapped around a wide mug. Worry and exhaustion faded into the older woman's wide brown eyes and thinned her mouth.

The long-time nurse—and second mother to Ava—didn't need to speak for Ava to know her mom had relapsed during the night.

Ava worked her voice around the catch in her throat. "How is she?"

Joann sipped her tea as if requiring the warm liquid to loosen her own words. "We made it through the night."

They'd never called Ava. Not that she would've been able to answer, given their call load. She thanked the powers that be for Joann. She'd be lost without the remarkable woman caring for her mother.

Joann pointed to a dry-erase board on the side of the refrigerator. "Doses and times are on the board. You'll want to repeat."

Ava scanned the med list and her heart rolled into her stomach. This wasn't a mild relapse. Nothing that would resolve in the next few hours. "You need to get some rest."

"I'm thinking the very same thing about you." Joann tipped her mug toward Ava; a familiar motherly scold laced her tone. "Child, you look like you're about to drop out to that tile floor. If you dare to do it, I'm leaving you right where you fall."

"Can you at least cover me up?" Ava asked, a small smile in her voice.

"Fine, but I'm not getting you a pillow." Joann rinsed her mug in the sink and set it in the dishwasher. "Go to bed before you really do faceplant on this floor."

Ava hugged Joann and watched the nurse leave. Exhaustion made her feet drag down the hall. She already knew sleep would be difficult to hold on to with the worry for her mom weaving relentlessly through her. She showered and changed, and then headed out of her bedroom. Her gaze drifted over the contest flyer she'd tossed on her dresser last week.

She tiptoed into her mom's room and curled into the recliner beside her mother's bed. Concern pulsed through her, making her entire body ache.

Her mental health needed a career change and soon. She'd never really paid attention to statistics, never considered herself a number on a survey. Until recently. Statistics listed a paramedic's burnout rate at five years. If Ava listened hard enough, she could hear that clock ticking. She hadn't shared with Dan or her mom that her past and present intersected during any quiet moment. In those moments, memories stole her sleep and haunted her with fear-induced adrenaline rushes.

The more she worked, the more her empathy dwindled away. Last night's first call had been to a car accident involving a seventeen-year-old who'd been texting. The teen had cried his life was too hard with balancing school and girl-friends and expectations. He'd swerved into on-coming traffic, too absorbed by the videos on his phone to watch the road. Ava had wanted to lecture the teen that *hard* was having both legs blown off from an IED and living to talk about it. Hard was leaving your pregnant wife at home while you served for a year overseas and not knowing if you'd return at all. Hard was bury-ing your child. Too soon. Too early. Because of irresponsible drivers like him. Anger warred with her compassion. But teens should be hav-ing fun and being carefree, shouldn't they? They weren't adults yet. And didn't everyone deserve a second chance?

She wanted to believe she could attend physi-cian assistant's school, shift into an office envi-ronment with normal hours and less stress. Then she'd rediscover her empathy and passion for helping people. But attending graduate school would sacrifice her mom's care. She'd never risk losing Joann. If only there were more hours in the day. Then she could have everything.

Kyle's contest was another option. A chance—however small—to change her future if she won.

Maybe all she needed was to just take the risk and enter the contest. Maybe believing she had a chance to win would be enough to quiet the past and give her hope. Hope that would surely bring back her compassion.

Her brain was too exhausted to think logically. She wasn't actually considering entering Kyle's contest, was she?

She had an idea of sorts. Something she'd considered over the last few nights in the lull between calls. Something she'd woken up thinking about yesterday afternoon.

Ava slipped out of her mom's room, grabbed her laptop and returned. She opened the contest website and clicked on the entry button. She'd enter and not tell anyone. If nothing came of it, at the worst, she was out a few hours' time. She'd wasted more time scrolling through TV stations, searching for something to watch.

Filling out the entry form gave her a chance to decompress—something the facilitators of the Critical Incident Stress Debriefing group recommended.

More than an hour later, her mother woke up. Her smile barely twitched across her lips; her voice was no more than a raw scratch. "Glad you're home safe."

Ava set the laptop on the bedside table and

held her mom's pale hand. "Sleep, Mom. I'm here."

"I have two guardian angels," her mom whispered. "What would I do without you both?"

Ava waited for her mom to drift back to sleep. She wasn't qualified to be a guardian angel. Joann had earned that distinction more than once. Ava might not be guardian-angel eligible, but she was there to protect her mom.

She reached toward the computer with her free hand and pressed the submit button on the entry page. She had to try for her mother and herself.

She shut the laptop and curled into the recliner. She fell asleep cradling her mom's hand between her own, wanting to hold on to the dream of a different future. Not the pink skies and fantasy future, but one that might be a real possibility. If only…

CHAPTER SIX

KYLE WALKED AROUND the outdoor garden oasis he'd designed on the rooftop of his building, checking the ice bin, appetizer trays, and avoiding the guests mingling around him. Small talk had never interested him. Too much politeness and too many gracious compliments made him suspicious. He always ended up searching for the flip side—the criticism wrapped inside the sweetness.

At eight, his grandfather had declared Kyle was man enough to learn how to shake a hand and stand behind his word. Papa Quinn had taught him to rely on the strength of a handshake, not empty promises. His grandfather looked people in the eye, always had a firm handshake and listened.

Sam Bentley, one of Kyle's judges and soon-to-be mentors, walked over to the buffet table and shook Kyle's hand. Sam had a handshake Kyle could rely on.

"Quite the crowd," Sam said. "I didn't expect so many people to be here."

Neither had Kyle. The contest open house had been last weekend. The number of contest entries had exceeded his expectations by more than double. "You might want to try the shrimp before they're gone."

"Good idea." Sam piled several bacon-wrapped shrimps onto a napkin. "You doing okay?"

Kyle paused and looked Sam in the eye. His grandfather had always cautioned Kyle not to ask a question if he wasn't fully invested in the response. Sam seemed prepared to listen. Sam's wife, Glenda, bounced between them and air-kissed Kyle. "You've outdone yourself, Kyle. How did you manage this so fast?"

The effervescent woman answered her question with another one. "Did you see Vanessa Ryan, the news anchor from Channel 15, and Brendan Payne from Channel 10? Brendan looks better without all that studio makeup. Do you think they might be an item?" Glenda glanced at Kyle. "Don't you get nervous talking to reporters? Worried you might say the wrong thing."

Sam handed his wife the napkin with the shrimp and grimaced at Kyle. "Honey, try these. They're quite delicious."

"I can't eat now." Glenda adjusted the cashmere scarf around her neck. "Nikki James—also from Channel 10—is headed right this way."

Kyle disliked the press even more than small talk.

Nikki lifted her champagne glass in a toast to the threesome. "Kyle, are you going to show us where the finalists will be working on their inventions?"

"Not tonight." *Or ever.* Kyle motioned to Sam. "Mr. Bentley can answer any questions you have. We designed the lab together the last few days."

Glenda widened her smile and tugged her husband closer to Nikki James. Grateful, Kyle slipped around the buffet table and escaped. He checked his watch. Only twenty minutes until the finalists were announced.

The finalists with the ideas that would save him.

He'd spent another endless round of nights pretending to work inside his lab. Even the five-star meals prepared by Haley Waters, his personal chef, had failed to inspire him. He'd played Skee-Ball more than once in the early morning hours, searching for something with every toss of the ball. All he'd discovered was that the game was better with Ava challenging him and Ben and Dan's laughter surrounding him. The ideas remained stuck inside him.

He'd considered arranging another visit for Ben, Dan and Ava, but nixed that thought. He wasn't that lonesome to have people around.

Even his sister hadn't popped in to disturb the silence. Iris had texted to tell him about several job interviews she'd scheduled for the week. She hadn't texted with news that she'd secured a new job. How was he supposed to judge his sister while he failed at his own job?

Iris circulated through the crowd, bringing her usual cheer to every guest. Not only did his sister excel at small talk, she made every person she met feel special and comfortable. She treated strangers like cherished old friends, claimed she'd never known a stranger. For one breath, he envied her. Wanted to be like her. Wanted to belong with such effortless ease.

Fortunately, his survival instinct forced him to inhale the evening air, driving that senseless wish away and returning him to more secure ground. He might stand apart, but at least he was safe there.

His gaze caught on an all-too-familiar redhead. The same redhead he'd imagined challenging him to a late-night game of Ping-Pong. The same redhead he'd want as a friend if friends were his goal.

He'd stopped looking for friends in the sixth grade. He'd been wary and distant on his return to middle school after Troy Simmons had tested Kyle's allergy claims. In high school, he'd accepted that inviting the guy who might need an

EpiPen jammed into his thigh and an ambulance ride was too much of a party buzzkill. By college, that twinge of missing out had faded. He'd been too busy with his studies and sharing his inventions with his grandfather.

Yet that almost-familiar clench to his insides, as if he'd missed being around Ava, surprised him. He'd moved on from his past and was more than satisfied with his life. After all, he had more important priorities than a misplaced wish to belong.

But Ava was here. Dressed in a bold bottle-green dress and looking like the model she never claimed to be. Kyle wanted to be near her again. That should've made him run in the other direction. Instead, he moved through the crowd, offered a chin dip acknowledgment to different guests, yet never lost sight of Ava.

Finally, he stood within touching distance. And hesitated like he'd stepped back into middle school and watched the party invites flash across cell phones in the hallway. He'd always held his breath, waiting for his phone to vibrate with a new text alert. The invites had never arrived. He'd long since stopped hoping. Stopped holding his breath.

Until now. With Ava. His breath stilled. That deceitful hope flared. *Had she come to see him?*

Ava stepped forward, embraced him without

hesitation. The hug was too quick. Too impersonal. He wanted to reach for her again. Pull her against him and hold on, for longer than appropriate, until all those tense places inside him calmed. Until he tackled that awkward boy from his past and wrestled every old insecurity back into place. Until the hope faded.

Ava motioned to an older auburn-haired woman in a wheelchair with a bright multicolored shawl draped around her thin shoulders. "Kyle, this is my mother, Karen."

Kyle jolted, yet managed to keep his expression contained, his smile in place. Her mother? He hadn't expected family introductions. Friends met families. Boyfriends met parents.

Ava and he weren't…anything. *But could they be?* That urge to take Ava into his arms lowered to a simmer and refused to fade.

He ignored those useless thoughts. His schoolboy days of crushes and old wishes were in the past. Forgotten underneath his master's degree and practical business pursuits. He took Karen's hand, kept his grip steady and gentle. "Pleasure to meet you."

"I haven't been this nervous since Ava deployed for her last time." Karen held on to Kyle's hand. "I hope they make the announcement for the finalists soon."

Ava touched her ear, and then her bracelet.

Her hands fluttered around her, but never stilled. Only her smile settled on Kyle. "Can't deny my own nerves, either. Or that I'm still in shock about getting the call from your contest people."

His people? That hope splintered. He'd known better than to trust it anyway. Ava wasn't here for him, but for the contest. For the money. He pulled out his best host smile—the one that Iris had taught him and leveled the alarm out of his own voice. "Can I get you anything?"

"I'll celebrate when Ava is officially announced as a finalist." Her mother smiled. *A finalist?* Now Kyle knew what it felt like when the world tilted on its axis. Ava was just an acquaintance. Someone he might want as a friend. Someone he might like… No, that was wrong. This was very wrong. Ava wasn't supposed to be a contest entrant. Most definitely not a finalist. He wasn't supposed to know the finalists. He wasn't supposed to *like* the finalists. He wanted one of their ideas. Not any complications, like friends or his conscience. Panic and dread pooled inside him like quicksand.

"We were just asked to attend, Mom." Ava searched his face as if looking for a clue. "It doesn't mean I'm a finalist."

Kyle patted Karen's hand and tapped composure into his tone. "I'm afraid I can't tell you. I don't know the finalists myself."

"But it's your contest." Karen peered at him, pride and love for her daughter reflected in her open gaze.

The last time he'd hugged his own mom, only grief had filled her gaze. That'd been one month after his grandfather's unexpected death. At the airport before his parents' one-way flight to the Florida coast. He'd expected to see joy and pride in his mom's gaze when he'd brought his parents home to the house he'd built for his family.

Kyle held on to his neutral expression. He'd always excelled at masking his emotions—a downfall for his few previous relationships. His exes had always complained about his emotional unavailability as if it was a bad thing. Finally, his skill proved useful. "I've intentionally stayed out of the selection process." Although he was second-guessing that decision right now. "That's why I chose the judges I did."

"Important to remain impartial." Karen squeezed his hand as if giving him her approval and encouragement. "You wouldn't want to appear biased."

"That would ruin the integrity of the contest." Kyle managed that without a flinch. He'd ruin the integrity of his contest later. Right now, he needed to get through the next half hour without demanding a do-over. *How could Ava be a finalist?*

"You aren't going to give us even a hint?" Dan walked up, tapped Kyle on the shoulder with his fist before shaking Kyle's hand.

The rest of Ava's friends swarmed across the rooftop and surrounded Ava like bees around their queen. His family had gathered around Papa Quinn the same way, with the same love and support. But they were family and that had been expected. These were only Ava's friends, yet they acted like protective family members.

There was that pinch in his chest again. As if he'd missed something important. But he had everything he needed with his family. All he needed was his family back with him.

That quicksand surrounded Kyle as doubt made his world roll off its axis into a tailspin. His voice was the only part of him not spinning. "Even if I knew, I wouldn't ruin the moment."

"I'm Rick Sawyer, Dan's dad." The man was as tall and wide as Dan, but with deep red hair. He gripped Kyle's hand, looked him in the eye. "Ava is the daughter I never had. I couldn't miss this."

A blush tinged Ava's cheeks. Her fingers shook before she smoothed her hands over her dress.

At least Kyle wasn't the only one uncomfortable. That slowed the tailspin into a slow slide. Enough for Kyle to regain his balance and his words. "You're Ben's grandfather and the one that supports Ava's ideas in the You-Know-What-We-Need game."

Rick laughed, the sound booming and infectious. He pointed at Ava. "It's always wise to remember the ones who stood beside you before you made it big, my girl."

"Well, let's hope she didn't submit her idea for mood-changing hair dye." Dan's smile stalled. He stared at Ava; alarm stretched his words out. "You didn't submit that idea, right?"

Ava hugged Rick as if she needed an anchor and frowned at Dan. "Rick, you've always been my favorite Sawyer."

Kyle would like to be Ava's anchor. The one she reached for without question. Without reserve. *No.* What was wrong with him? He hadn't even decided if he wanted her as a friend. Kyle shifted his weight from one foot to the other to regain his footing. If Ava truly was a finalist, he couldn't be Ava's anything. Nothing more than an advisor. That thought churned like sour milk inside him.

Dan shrugged as if unconcerned about Ava's allegiance to his dad. "You need someone to keep you grounded. I accepted that role the day you climbed into the passenger seat in my rig."

"I love you, too." Ava blew Dan a kiss and settled her head on Rick's shoulder.

Jealousy bit Kyle hard. Unbidden. Unstoppable. As if he wanted Ava's head on his shoulder, her arms wrapped around his waist, his arms around her. Like they meant something more to each other. As if he wanted that kind of trust.

Kyle clenched the back of his neck to stop that churn of sour need from creeping up into his throat. He had to get it together. He had to breath and collect himself. Focus on something other than Ava. She couldn't be his focus. Definitely not a confidante. Because he could never open himself up to someone else. That wasn't a risk he'd ever take. His family accepted him. That had always been enough.

Kyle excused himself and tracked down his head judge, Barbra Norris. Barbra had been his freshman professor in his computer engineering program at college and later his mentor. He'd consulted her before he'd signed his contract with Tech Realized, Inc., although he hadn't taken Barbra's advice two years ago. She'd cautioned him not to be swayed by the money. Warned him about agreeing to the terms of a second idea, as it'd taken him years to perfect his Medi-Spy. But he'd been full of himself and riding on cloud nine. Yet he hadn't realized that clouds were no more substantial than his own inflated ego. A mistake he was paying for now.

He might've called Barbra a friend, but he

feared that label. He'd never wanted to disappoint her. If she was a friend, there'd be something sharper. Something more lasting about disappointing the woman who was someone he wanted to grow up to be like. Someone with integrity. Principles. Standards.

He guided Barbra behind the outdoor kitchen for more privacy, praying he was wrong about Ava and the contest. "Is Ava Andrews a finalist?"

"Ava was slotted in early this morning. The other finalist used an idea that was patented three years ago." Barbra grimaced, making her opinion on cheaters quite clear. Then she clasped her hands together and her eyes widened with delight. "But it's wonderful that we have two military veterans as finalists. It's a publicity windfall for everyone involved."

"That's terrific." Kyle's smile cracked his lips like sandpaper. More publicity—not exactly what he'd intended. Barbra expected the contest to continue for years and build into something that aided young inventors across the country. Kyle only expected to aid himself. This one year. This one time.

Back to his current problem: How had Ava finaled? "I thought you told me there were well over four hundred entries."

Barbra tapped a finger against her mouth like

a seasoned librarian quieting a noisy kindergarten classroom. That had always been the clue that she was calculating something inside her brilliant mind and interruptions would not be tolerated. Her finger stilled, and her hand lowered. "The exact number was five hundred and thirteen. Seventeen were disqualified immediately for false applications. Of the four hundred and ninety-six, seventy-seven contained copyrighted and patent-pending ideas. That left us four hundred and nineteen solid entries to choose from."

Yet Ava Andrews had finished in the top two. *The top two.* "Do you know what the finalists look like?"

The contest couldn't have been about appearances. Ava had qualified on her own merits. She was a paramedic who saved lives and, it seemed, a legitimate inventor. Kyle only saved himself and was willing to pay for someone else's idea to use as his own. He was everything Ava was not. He couldn't want her. She'd never want someone as damaged as him.

"Not until tonight." Barbra grinned. "The two finalists make quite the pair. The press is going to adore them."

Kyle resisted the urge to run his hands over his head and yank on his hair. Part of the contest rules stated that Kyle would work with each finalist to help refine their ideas. To make sure one of those ideas met Tech Realized, Inc.'s terms. To make sure one of those ideas would save him from financial ruin.

The finalists were supposed to be strangers. It was easier to ignore his conscience with strangers.

Ava was not quite the stranger he needed her to be. Something inside him knotted at the thought of using Ava's idea. What if he convinced her to drop out? It wasn't too late to stop this disaster. They'd slot in a stranger. An unknown.

Barbra checked the time on her watch and grasped his arm. "Time for the announcements. I'm so glad you convinced me to take part in this."

Would Barbra be glad when it all ended? When he was outed as the fraud he pretended not to be? No, he wouldn't let that happen. There was time to figure something out. Still time to find the right thing and actually do it. He had thirty days to turn in his proposal to Tech Realized, Inc. One month to develop an idea that wasn't already on the patented list. Miracles happened in less time. He only had to believe. "Let's find that microphone."

Barbra walked beside him toward the small stage set up in the middle of the rooftop. "The next four weeks are going to be exciting."

Exciting or excruciating, Kyle couldn't decide. But there was no way to stop the ball from rolling down that mountain. He just needed to keep two steps ahead of the ball and jump out of its path before it flattened him. Nothing he couldn't handle.

Ava was a contestant. He'd keep her at an arm's-length distance. He'd been with Ava less than a handful of times. She was more stranger than friend. He rolled his shoulders, knocking that tap of his conscience away.

His gaze landed on Ava in the crowd as if guided there by an invisible hand. That wasn't good. He had to stop looking for her.

His gaze shifted to Ava's mom, smiling and cheerful in her wheelchair. That invisible hand punched him in the gut, stalling his breath. He knew without asking that Ava needed the money from the contest. Ava needed to win for her family, too.

He had to fulfill his contract for his family and the women at Penny's Place, who depended on his support to keep the doors open and the heat on in the building.

Ava must have read the rules and requirements surrounding the contest. She had to click on the "I agree" box to submit her entry. He wasn't responsible for any confusion. She shouldn't have entered if she hadn't understood the expectations. The expectation that her idea belonged to him if she cashed the prize check. She had to win first.

He cleared his throat, tried to swallow around the sudden dryness. If he hadn't known better, he'd have thought he'd choked on his own lies.

Barbra accepted the wireless microphone from Iris and quieted the crowd. She put her glasses on and read from her prepared notes. Kyle scanned the rooftop that had become standing room only. Surely the crowd violated some sort of city code. When had so many people arrived? Were they all related to the finalists? All family and friends of two people who'd selflessly served their countries?

Kyle's head buzzed. He was about to take advantage of a veteran of the United States military. He struggled to remain upright on the stage.

The contestants were supposed to have been starving college kids. Not two adults with families, friends and expectations. Not upstanding citizens and overall good people. Because Kyle wasn't a good person.

His neck strained against his too-tight tie. He wanted to remove his suit jacket, unbutton his collar and inhale a clean breath. He grabbed a glass of ice water from the tray of a passing server.

He'd double the prize money. Triple the bonus. Money always solved any problem, didn't it?

It had to. That buzz shifted into a roar inside his head.

He needed to call a stop to this fiasco. End it here and now.

Be a man.

His sister waved at him from the seating area. She'd linked arms—as was her habit—with another familiar woman. Penny Joyce was the house manager of Penny's Place. Penny had rescued Iris from the streets after her divorce. She'd moved Iris into her house, gave her food, shelter and solace. Penny had saved his sister. He couldn't fail the generous woman or the countless women she protected. The pride on the women's faces lodged in his chest like a blade.

Barbra finished her welcome and thanked everyone for their patience. She held up an envelope and asked who was ready for the finalists to be announced.

Excitement hummed through the air around the crowd.

Kyle clenched the cold glass. A numbness radiated from Kyle's very core.

Barbra read the first finalist: Grant O'Neal.

At least Grant was a stranger. Still, the numbness squeezed into Kyle's throat.

Barbra announced the second finalist: Ava Andrews.

Definitely not a stranger.

That massive ball flattened Kyle as if he was nothing more than an ant.

Cheers filled the night air, bouncing off the high-rises crowded around Kyle's building. Guests jostled each other to offer congratulations to Grant and Ava. Several members of the press demanded Kyle's attention, cornering him near the makeshift stage.

Several glasses of water and too many questions later, Iris linked her arm with Kyle's and leaned into his side. "My feet are about done in these heels. Tell me that we're about done tonight, too."

"I'm ready to call it a night." Kyle switched directions when someone called out his name. He headed toward the group gathered near the empty dessert bar at the far end of the rooftop.

"That's Drew Harrington calling your name." Iris waved to the tallest man in the group who was also one of her former employers. "Finally, I get to talk to your friends and learn more about them than their first names."

He'd promised Iris that he'd introduce her to his new friends. He just hadn't expected that to ever happen.

After Drew released Iris from a bear hug and

shook Kyle's hand, the city's best assistant DA introduced them to Dr. Wyatt Reid and Mia Fiore.

"Do you mind?" Mia aimed a large, intimidating camera at Iris and him. "*The Chronicle* contracted me to take pictures of tonight's event."

"The only recent family photographs I have with my brother are from events like these." Iris edged closer to Kyle and smiled. "Although we managed to avoid the cameras at your mother's fancy charity event last week, Drew."

"I'm jealous that Kyle has such a lovely plus-one for his events," Drew teased.

"Drew, you don't turn on the charm unless you need something." Iris set her hands on her hips and faced the lawyer who towered over her by a good foot. Ironic she confronted Drew yet cowered from her ex-husband, who'd never accepted his lack of height. "What is it?"

Drew's shoulders slumped. Chagrin dampened his voice as if his mother scolded him, not Iris. "My paralegal's birthday is Monday."

Iris stared him down, her foot tapped. Even Kyle shuffled from one foot to the other under his sister's disappointed look.

"I might've forgotten to make lunch reservations," Drew rushed on.

"You forgot, or you have no idea where to take her?" Iris's foot tapped double-time.

"Both," Drew admitted. "But Elena mentioned you guys still take yoga classes together several days a week."

His sister had found a workout partner in Drew's paralegal. Kyle wanted to be surprised. His sister's circle of friends grew in proportion to every failed job. Kyle had tried to expand his circle after he'd signed his lucrative contract. He'd hosted rooftop parties that were featured in the gossip pages weekly. Then one night he'd discovered he was more alone inside that crush of people on his rooftop than he'd ever been. The gatherings became more about social climbing and attention. And Kyle retreated back into his safe zone and the parties became gossip history. He grabbed a glass of champagne from a passing waiter, certain that the scratch in his throat was from the crisp night breeze, not regret at his lack of friends.

"Skip lunch," Iris said. "Elena started a new detox program last week. Get her a gift card from Bits and Bites Pantry. They have the organic juices she likes."

"Iris Quinn, you're the best." Drew picked her up in another hug.

"Tell my brother that." Iris laughed. "He can't hear it enough."

Kyle liked the sound of his sister's joy. He couldn't recall the last time he'd made her laugh.

But finding a job wasn't a game. Kyle wasn't sure he could do enough to make up for the years he hadn't been there for Iris. There wasn't a time he could recall growing up that Iris hadn't been there for him. When his sister had needed him the most, he'd been absent. True she'd shut her family out, but Kyle should've tried harder to get in. He shouldn't have given up on her then. He refused to give up on her now.

Drew pointed at him. "Your sister is terrific, but you've both been holding out."

Kyle drew back and sipped his champagne. Drew's brother was a PI in the city. He'd seen Brad Harrington and his fiancée, Sophie, circulating through the ballroom with Mayor Harrington, Brad and Drew's mother, last Friday night. What had the Harrington siblings discovered about the Quinns? Kyle crossed his arms over his chest. "Not sure I'm following."

Drew glanced at Dan and then grinned at Kyle. "Both Ben and Dan haven't stopped talking about your game room on steroids."

Kyle coughed.

Drew handed Kyle a napkin. "We've all read the newspaper articles about this legendary arcade space that's supposedly part of your offices. But there haven't been any photographs published in the paper to verify the stories."

Mia lowered her camera and turned toward

Kyle. Laughter drifted through her voice. "What they want to know is if they can tag along the next time Ben and Dan get to play at your place."

Kyle blinked at his glass as if searching for an answer in the champagne bubbles. Inviting Ben and his family over had been a onetime offer. The contest preparations had been his focus, and now seeing the contestants to the finale would be his priority. If a repeat of that afternoon with Ava and her friends filled him with anticipation, he'd have to get over it. He hadn't started the contest to expand some unnecessary friendship circle. He'd done it to ensure his family—the only circle he wanted to be a part of—could return home, where they belonged.

"You don't have to tag along." Iris bounced on her heels, appearing to have resolved her earlier foot pain. "We'll head down there as soon as Kyle escorts his other guests out. Shouldn't be much longer."

No. He wasn't heading to his suite with a group of people, as if he intended to throw an after-party at his place. He never held parties at his place. But Drew had lined up three of Iris's past jobs. He owed him. Surely a gift card to Rustic Grille would be more than fine.

"Where's Ava?" Iris asked. "I'm ready to accept her Skee-Ball challenge."

Iris grinned wickedly at Kyle, as if daring him

to rescind her offer. She'd vowed retribution for Kyle making her do interview speed dating at the Harrington event in the crowded ballroom last week. Clearly, she intended to make him pay now.

Those champagne bubbles burst inside him. Why wasn't he putting his foot down, opening his mouth and saying no? Kyle switched out his champagne flute for a glass of water. His sister hadn't pressed the mute button on his voice. Surely Ava wasn't the reason for his hesitation. As if he had a crush on a redheaded paramedic and the mention of her rendered him tongue-tied.

"Ava never mentioned a challenge." Wyatt scratched his chin and glanced at Mia.

What had Ava mentioned? Not that Kyle cared. He crunched on a piece of ice to numb his tongue and keep that question from escaping.

"Ava doesn't really know about the challenge." Iris sipped her wine. "She was the high score on Skee-Ball until last week, when I replaced her."

"She'll want another chance to take back the top spot." Mia laughed. "Ava hates to lose."

"Then it's settled," Iris said.

Nothing was settled. Kyle didn't want a game tournament or friends. He wanted an idea. A proposal for his contract that would keep away his financial doom. Tongue thawed by his worry, he worked his voice free. "It's been a long night. Maybe everyone would rather head home."

The entire group around him grinned like middle school kids invited to the cool kid's house. Kyle had never been the cool kid.

Drew said, "We'd love to keep the party going."

"Should we tell Grant and his friends?" Iris never waited for Kyle's reply; instead, she motioned for Grant to come over.

Not more people. That'd make the evening even more of a thing. A social thing with friends.

Finished extending her invitation to Grant and the contest judges, Iris jumped up in her heels. "This is going to be the perfect end to a rather terrific evening."

Kyle tried to smile and nod in agreement. *Perfect* wasn't quite the word he'd use.

CHAPTER SEVEN

AVA SNUCK INTO Kyle's suite and slipped into the women's bathroom. The empty room was a reprieve from the arcade playland right outside the bathroom door and the crush of people up on the rooftop. The perfect place to pull herself together.

Ava paced the lounge area and avoided looking in the mirror. She was certain she still had that shocked look of a bad driver's license photograph—the kind where the DMV employee failed to offer a warning to smile.

She was a finalist in Kyle Quinn's Next Best Inventor Contest. Her idea could win. *Her idea*. She'd have the money to pay for her mother's care while she completed graduate school. She could build a different future that only yesterday had seemed like nothing more substantial than a wish made upon a star. The tremors in her fingers speared up into her arms. She gripped the marble countertop, stared into the glass sink and reminded herself not to get too carried away. After all, she still had to win.

First, her idea had to become more than a few pages of notes. More than a concept. It had to work.

But that was for tomorrow. Tomorrow, she'd meet with her mentor—one of the judges from the panel—and would learn how to develop her idea into a product. Tomorrow, she'd begin to turn a wish into reality.

Tonight, she wouldn't stack up even more worries. Or brainstorm fallback plans. She'd already answered enough questions from the reporters. Already smiled for the cameras until her cheeks ached. The center of attention was the last place she ever wanted to be. She'd step aside now, avoid all that and try to enjoy herself. Then the nerves and adrenaline could stop misfiring inside her like a fuse box struck by lightning. Her stomach could finally unwind.

The main door swung open. Ava spun, teetered on her heels, expecting to see Iris. Kyle's sister had designed the elegant bathroom, with a vintage fainting couch in the seating area and three private stalls, each with their own chandelier. Surely Iris would prefer this space over the understated coed bathroom offered on the rooftop.

Ava didn't know the attractive woman smiling at her. There'd been a moment of rapid introductions after the finalist announcement. Ava most likely met her upstairs already. That'd explain why the woman seemed familiar to her.

The woman stepped to the sink beside Ava, turned on the water and washed her hands. "Congratulations on being a finalist."

"Thank you. I'm still a bit shocked." Ava thrust her hands under the cool water to wash away that insistent tremor. Adrenaline ping-ponged through her once again, making her want to simultaneously dance and gag. She'd never danced with abandon and only ever cleaned up the stomach contents of a patient. "I've never done anything like this before."

"You've never snuck into a celebrity's private bathroom before?" The woman never wobbled in her five-inch heels that seemed like an extension to her already too-long legs.

Ava blinked. This was Kyle's place, not some celebrity's apartment, and she wasn't some over-zealous fan. Kyle and she were…nothing. She'd entered his contest. Played games one time at his place. Thought about him every day since that Saturday. Only in the most casual way, of course. Like the way a coworker thought about a work peer after hours: fleeting and offhand.

The woman watched Ava. The shimmer in her eyeshadow sharpened the blue in her eyes.

"I've been here before." Ava dried her hands. The woman had to wear colored contacts. No one had eyes that piercing. "No sneaking required."

The woman's eyebrow lifted into a perfect arch, like an arrow nocked in a bow.

Ava waved her hand, but the motion failed to slow the spill of her words. "I meant that I'd never entered a contest like this before. I'm not an inventor. I play an idea game with my best friend's ten-year-old son. But that's only a game we play to pass the time."

"You're a novice inventor." The woman dried her hands with a soft cloth from the stack between the two sinks. "And friends with celebrities."

The woman's voice dipped as if she sipped vinegar. Her gaze probed as if she searched for Ava's other flaws.

"I'm a paramedic." And natural redhead with green eyes. Nothing artificial about her.

The corner of the woman's mouth tipped up, softening her earlier disapproval. "Perhaps with a fifty-thousand-dollar idea."

The reminder of the money distracted Ava. She had to win to change her future. Her hands shook again. "We'll see in four weeks. There's a lot to do between now and then."

"Like spend more time with Kyle Quinn?" The accusation in the woman's voice tempered any sincerity.

Like fill out the applications to physician's assistant graduate schools. Like submit those applications before the deadline. And create a prototype—whatever that meant. Definitely not hang out with Kyle as if they were friends. Friends who wanted to become something more like a couple. "I'm not sure how involved Kyle will be with the development side of our ideas."

The woman tossed the cloth into the basket and refreshed her bold red lipstick. "Kyle told me he'd be a mentor and guiding both finalists through every step of the process."

Kyle would be with her. Every step. Like a partner. That thought lodged inside Ava before she knocked it away.

The woman's gaze connected with Ava's in the mirror.

Ava's cheeks warmed as if she stood under the desert sun. But she wasn't one for blushing. Or getting gushy over a guy. She wouldn't start now. This wasn't a dating game or love-match contest.

She didn't want Kyle like that. She didn't want any distractions. She wanted to win. But right now, Ava really wanted the woman's prying gaze to latch on to something other than her. She blurted, "Hard to believe that Kyle got the idea for the contest from my best friend's son and pulled this together so quickly. We went from playing Skee-Ball to this in a matter of days."

The woman leaned her hip against the counter edge and faced Ava.

Ava pressed her lips together. Her plan misfired. She considered running, but her heels and long dress would only trip her up. She'd missed the high-heel benefit race for cancer awareness this past spring. Now she regretted her decision to accept that extra work shift instead of learning how to run in stilettos. The skill would've come in handy now.

"You get to hang out here with Kyle." The woman's smile was too relaxed and too open like a shark about to attack. "Now I'm really envious."

The woman was beautiful and polished. The kind of woman Ava expected Kyle would want to be with. The very opposite of Ava, who wore boots to work and preferred workout gear to sequins and high heels. The woman watched Ava as if she'd already catalogued Ava's shortcomings.

She'd escaped into the bathroom to unwind, now everything inside her seemed tangled up even tighter. Flustered again, Ava said, "Kyle and I just met at the benefit calendar shoot for juvenile diabetes last month."

"The one where Francesca Lang collapsed?" The woman held open the bathroom door.

Ava followed, refusing to cower in the bathroom. She'd meet the woman heel-to-heel. "Yes, that was the event where we met. I hope Francesca has recovered."

"Francesca is recovering very well. I interviewed Francesca after her ordeal." The woman pressed the up button on the elevator. Her voice was mild, as if she assumed Ava had known who she was. "The piece ran on the evening segment at Channel 10."

Ava's stomach dropped out, as if the elevator became unhinged. She hadn't seen the woman at the hospital or around town or upstairs. She'd seen her on TV every weekend.

Ava knew nothing about dealing with reporters and the press. She hit Rewind on their conversation. Had she said anything that she shouldn't have? Should she warn Kyle? "I'm sorry I missed that segment. I work the night shift."

Once she was in the elevator, Ava willed the vintage carriage to suddenly shift into fast gear. She didn't want to be locked inside the small box with the reporter any longer than necessary. Ava concentrated on the floor numbers—all four them—and avoided the newswoman. The elevator seemed to stop between floors. Why hadn't she taken the stairs?

"Can I offer you some advice?" the woman asked.

No.

But the woman translated the silence to be Ava's consent. "If I was standing in your heels, I'd concentrate more on Kyle Quinn and less on the contest."

Ava jerked her attention to the woman.

"Don't tell me you haven't considered that angle." The woman tossed her head, sending her hair sweeping across her chin in perfect timing. "You'll gain more than the money the contest offers if you win Kyle Quinn instead. Kyle is one of the city's most elusive bachelors and quite sought after."

The top-floor button finally lit up. The elevator took its time pulling to a full stop, as if to taunt Ava.

"Of course, the other finalist, Grant O'Neal, seems like quite a catch, too." The woman brushed her polished nails across Ava's arm and stretched her smile wide. "I believe, Ava Andrews, that this is a contest you can't lose if you play the game right."

"I'm not interested in playing a game. I want to win." Ava wanted to pry the doors apart and escape. At the smallest gap, she pushed through the unopened doors and launched herself onto the rooftop.

"A word of caution." The woman stopped Ava's retreat with a hand on Ava's wrist. "Don't become the heartbreaker contestant. That headline doesn't play well with the public."

Ava didn't want any headline with her name in it to play well. Didn't the woman have real news to report on? The woman might've hooked and netted Ava, but Ava hadn't sunk yet. She walked away, her head high despite the unease churning inside her.

Ava scanned the rooftop for Kyle. She wanted to apologize for anything that might get taken out of context by the reporter in the bathroom. What happened to the bathroom being a safe zone? Women were supposed to bond over smeared mascara and lost lipstick in the ladies' room, not dig out each other's secrets to reveal to the world on the local news at six.

Kyle stood on the far side of the rooftop between two gentlemen that Barbra Norris, the head judge, had introduced as her fellow judges. Ava wove through the crowd and paused to accept congratulations. She stepped away and only then noticed that the bathroom reporter tracked her every move. The woman lifted her glass of champagne in a silent toast, as if giving Ava kudos for making nice with Grant's friends.

Ava changed directions midstep and veered toward the buffet. She strolled along the table, stopping as if considering her options. One glance over her shoulder confirmed her bathroom reporter still watched her. Ava grabbed a plate and piled food on it, in no particular order. Stacking the crackers on top of the cheese, she balanced fruit on top of the crackers. Adding a strawberry for color, she studied the plate. If she added another layer, would it collapse like she worried her own world might? Perhaps being a risk-taker wasn't her thing after all.

Before the crackers toppled sideways off her plate, Kyle stepped into her path and curved his fingers around her elbow, steadying her arm and her world.

"Can I offer you something?" Ava lifted the plate and too late realized her error. She appeared to have filled the plate for Kyle, not herself. Perhaps her bathroom reporter had left the building to report on a real news story.

Kyle plucked a strawberry from the stack, along with a piece of cheese. "Iris invited you, Grant and all your friends to the game room for a tournament."

Ava shifted, and her gaze collided with her bathroom reporter. The woman hadn't left. Worse, she appeared to have locked on to Kyle's hand still on Ava's arm. Unfortunately, Ava struggled to ignore the warmth of Kyle's touch herself. For one insane moment, she considered edging even farther into his side, using his strong shoulders to block her view of the reporter. But her own shoulders were the only ones Ava relied on. She'd never hid behind a man before, and she wouldn't start now. Ava straightened and stepped back, out of Kyle's personal space. Too quickly, she regretted the loss of his touch. Annoyed at her flighty thoughts, she glared at her bathroom reporter.

The irksome newswoman covered her smirk with a sip of champagne.

Ava asked, "Will the press be there?"

Kyle grimaced as if he'd bitten into a moldy strawberry. "No."

Ava nodded, relieved to get away from the woman. Her family and friends would be with her. What could possibly go wrong?

CHAPTER EIGHT

"DAN, YOU READY for this?" Wyatt, Mia's husband-to-be, pressed the down button for the elevator and rubbed his hands together.

Ava wasn't certain she was ready for this. Sure, she'd enjoyed her trip down memory lane in Kyle's arcade room a few weekends ago. Right now, she wanted to kick off her heels, hang her dress in the closet and put on her workout clothes. She never second-guessed herself in the everyday, regular clothes she preferred. Or better, she could put on her uniform—the cargo pants, button-down shirt and boots—to remind herself what she was good at. Where she belonged.

"You could take out your wallet and pay me now, Doc." Dan cracked his knuckles and laughed. "Save us both some time."

"Come with me." Mia pulled Ava into the waiting elevator. "My feet hurt too much in these adorable shoes. The guys can bait each other on the stairs, where we can't hear them."

Wyatt lunged inside the elevator. "There's nothing wrong with a little trash talk."

"It's good for the blood." Dan rolled his shoulders. "Keeps us sharp and focused."

Ava needed to keep her focus off Kyle and stay on guard for more reporters. She'd watched Kyle escort several couples down the stairs. Surely only friends remained.

Mia ran her fingers over the textured paint on the elevator wall. "This is fabulous. We could do something like this in the upstairs bathroom, Wyatt."

"You want the bathroom to look like an elevator," Wyatt said, not bothering to hide his confusion. His gaze tripped around the seven-by-seven-foot square box with mirrored doors and merlot-colored walls.

Mia shook her head. "Look at the design work bordering the painted sections."

Both men peered at the wall. Wyatt looked at Dan and said, "Not getting it. You?"

"Let me see." Ava shoved the guys apart. "Mia, why did you ask them? They're too busy plotting arcade domination."

Mia rolled her eyes at Wyatt and Dan. She curved her fingers along the detailed edge. "This is hand-painted. Exquisite. Intricate."

Had Kyle commissioned someone to design his elevator? Ava glanced at her clearance-rack dress and practical heels. Nothing intricate or exquisite about her. She preferred low maintenance. There was nothing wrong with that. One more thing to blame on her bathroom reporter. If only the newswoman hadn't talked about Ava's winning over Kyle. As if Kyle was the real grand prize.

The cash prize from winning the contest would be there to bail Ava out when times got tough. She couldn't say the same for Kyle Quinn. He'd kept to himself most of the night. Participated when expected. Yet he'd remained politely closed off, answering questions without giving any of his true self away. She wondered how much of himself he'd hold back in a relationship. She'd want an equal partner. If she ever risked her heart, she'd want to know that she hadn't leaped alone.

Not that it mattered. She'd vowed when her father had walked out that no man would let her down like that again. So far, she'd succeeded in keeping her heart intact.

Dan and Wyatt continued making wagers on their way into Kyle's apartment. Ava held the elevator door open and waited for Mia to finish taking pictures of the elevator's interior. Mia swung around and snapped several pictures of Ava before she could duck. "I have first right of refusal on any picture with me in it."

Mia checked her camera screen and followed

Ava into Kyle's apartment. "You don't have to worry. You look terrific."

"You do not lie well." Ava reached for the camera. "Let me see."

Mia held the camera away from Ava and rushed toward the sofas. Dan's dad, Rick, adjusted her mother's wheelchair near the love seat and dropped onto the smaller leather sofa. Mia sat on the end of the larger sofa, tucking her camera between herself and the square arm of the couch. Ava frowned and lowered herself onto the center cushion.

"Kyle, you should hire Mia as your official event photographer." Iris carried a tray of drinks from the kitchen.

Iris's heels added much-needed inches to her height. But that hardly mattered. Iris was a burst of color in her tie-dyed dress and curly hair loose around her shoulders. Her eyes even sparked like some fairy from a children's storybook. Kyle's sister made it impossible not to like her.

Iris added, "That way you can control the images given to the press."

"You don't really need a photographer for the contest, do you?" Ava leaned back into the leather, trying to appear and sound relaxed. "The press can't be that interested."

Iris set the drink tray on an end table and called to Grant's friends at the pinball machines to help themselves. She smiled at Ava. "The press and the public are both interested in anything Kyle does."

"They're fascinated with the money." Kyle leaned against the pool table, not fully a part of the group sitting on the couches or the ones gathered around the games. "I'm not all that interesting."

Ava found Kyle interesting. Too much so. She grabbed a cold bottle of water, wanting to douse her wayward thoughts.

"Your love life is very interesting, little brother." Iris talked fast and moved even faster on her tall heels, handing more drinks out. She reminded Ava of a hummingbird, flittering from person to person, leaving a streak of colorful perfume in her wake.

Iris laughed. "I was asked more than once tonight if my brother was going to be the next one to find love on the TV show *Marriage Material*."

"Are you considering starring on *Marriage Material*?" Karen shook her head as if she couldn't believe Kyle would do such an extreme thing. "Ava and I have watched every season."

Ava ignored her friends' laughter and shrugged. "It's entertaining. Even Dan and Rick watch several episodes with us. Each season, I should add."

Rick stared at her over the rims of his glasses.

His bright red hair and thick bushy eyebrows ruined the stern note in his voice. "I was tricked into watching that show. I've regretted letting you talk me into it ever since I set my TV to record it."

Iris perched on the arm of the couch and studied Ava, her blue eyes wide. "Then you believe you can really find true love on TV?"

"Sure." Ava straightened to add strength and confidence to her voice. "Anything is possible, right?" Except perhaps finding a man who would stick. He might fall in love, but sometimes even love wasn't enough to make a man stay.

Kyle crossed his arms over his chest and eyed Ava. "You're telling me that you'd go on a TV show like *Marriage Material* to meet your soul mate?"

His focus fixed on Ava as if he searched for her soul. One look that both awakened her and struck into her core. Too many emotions stirred inside her. Worse, his full attention released an inner sigh from deep inside her that softened everything within her. An all-too-dangerous sigh.

The kind that she could become addicted to, if she wasn't careful—very careful.

Ava gathered that wisp of a sigh before she released it and made it into something more than a wish. She shook her head. "TV isn't my thing."

Nor was Kyle Quinn.

"Neither are soul mates." Mia nudged Ava with her shoulder. "You can't take offense, Ava. You know it's true."

Ava pushed off the sofa, and Wyatt dropped onto the sofa in her place. Ava had never been the girl who blushed and giggled from a boy's notice. The only problem: Kyle wasn't a boy. And the woman inside Ava—the one she'd tried to ignore—had ideas of her own. "We should be asking Kyle if he believes in soul mates and true love. He's the one going on *Marriage Material*."

Kyle pushed away from the pool table. "Mia, would you be interested in being my event photographer?"

Ava took that as a definitive no. Kyle did not believe in soul mates. She wanted to ask why. Worse, she wanted to change his mind. Ava paced away from the couches.

"Definitely." Mia clasped her hands together and grinned at Wyatt. "Looks like I'm going to need to find an assistant after all."

Ava glared at Kyle. He wasn't supposed to give Ava's best friend work that Mia could really use to build her photography business. He was not supposed to give Ava another reason to sigh over him. Ava pressed her lips together, refusing to sigh. "Mia, I can be your assistant."

Everyone shook their heads at Ava.

"Why not?" Ava set her hands on her hips and glared at her friends.

"You already work way too much." Mia rested her head on Wyatt's shoulder as if she'd just decided on a movie to watch, not turned down her friend. Wyatt's arms curved around Mia's waist, pulling out a sweet smile from Mia.

Something knocked around inside Ava like a pang of envy.

But Ava had no time to cuddle and watch movies. She needed the assistant job Mia had available, not a relationship like Mia's. She skipped her gaze away from Mia and Wyatt.

"You have no social life," her mom added. "It really is work and more work all the time."

Ava slipped off her heels and curled her cramped toes into the carpet. She had to work, not date. Working for Mia would resolve her frustrating job hunt. Maybe she could pull Mia aside and convince her friend to hire her.

"Nothing wrong with working hard." Rick propped his feet on the ottoman and linked his hands behind his head. "But you have to make time for fun, too."

What was it with everyone telling Ava that she needed to have fun? First, her mom. Now, Rick. "I'd have fun working for Mia."

"You don't like photos." Mia frowned at her. "Or standing around. You complained the last time we walked across the Golden Gate Bridge to capture the fog."

"The fog looked the same at the beginning and the end of the bridge." Ava waved aside her friend's argument. "I don't like being in photographs." But she liked getting paid—she preferred that.

"My sister can teach you how to have fun," Kyle offered. "She prefers fun over work."

Iris frowned at him. "It's not unheard of to have fun at work, Kyle."

"Then you've found a fun new job?" Kyle asked. "Painting only counts if you get paid, by the way."

"Not yet." Iris stretched her legs and her smile out. "But like Ava said, anything is possible."

"Iris, did you do the painting in the elevator?" Mia sat up, her voice almost breathless from her contained enthusiasm.

"That was me." Iris grinned at Mia and twisted away from Kyle. "I did the elevator and the bathrooms in the suite before Kyle could object."

"This is totally out of left field. Would you be interested in working with me?" Mia held out her hands, stopping Iris from speaking. "I can't pay much, but I could really use someone with your eye for lighting and color on several upcoming projects."

Ava wanted to stomp her feet and yell, why her? But she knew. She'd seen the detailed artwork in both the elevator and bathroom. Mia and Iris shared that elusive quality that Mia referred to as an artist's vision. Ava's vision was practical.

"You're serious?" Iris jumped up and pointed at her chest. "You want to hire me?"

Mia nodded, but her voice was suddenly hesitant. "Only if you have time and don't mind poor pay."

"I'd love to." Iris pumped her arms over her head, her smile infectious. "I got a job without your help, little brother. I can do one thing right."

Everyone around her grinned, too, including Ava. She would've worked hard for Mia, but that wouldn't have helped her friend. Ava wanted some of Iris's abandon. Her fearlessness to be herself, despite onlookers. Despite judgment.

"Look, Iris," Kyle started. "Maybe we should…"

"Have some fun." Ava cut in. She stretched her arms out in front of her and added, "Get warmed up for our Skee-Ball challenge. I'm ready to reclaim my top spot and earn the spa day that I heard was going to the winner."

"I'm already warmed up." Grinning, Iris extended her arms behind her back. "But take all the time you need. I can wait."

"If a spa day is on the line, I want in." Mia pushed off the couch and called for Sophie. "She'll want in on this, too."

Sophie rushed over and set her hand on Karen's shoulder. "I have another idea we need to talk about for the benefit gala."

Karen smiled. "Text it to me and I'll add it to our agenda."

Ava lowered her arms and looked between her mother and Sophie. "Mom, when did you get an agenda?"

"Your mother has agreed to be our liaison with the local chapter of the Institute for Multiple Sclerosis. She's going to help with the charity gala for A City That Cares coming up next month." Mia walked over to stand beside Sophie.

Ava's friends bracketed her mother as if her mom required backup.

"Karen has agreed to give us advice about the decorations for the event," Sophie offered. "I'm not the best at the silent auction setup, so I'm looking forward to her help."

That sounded like a lot. Too much, really. "Is it a small event?"

"The concept was on a small scale," Sophie hedged.

Mia laughed. "Then somehow it ballooned, with an expected attendance of over one thousand people."

"The guest count keeps climbing," Wyatt added, pride in his voice.

That wasn't an intimate gathering. Events like that needed event planners and full-time staff. At the very least, a large committee of volunteers. Not her mother. Ava said, "You're planning this all yourselves?"

"The hotel staff and events coordinator have been wonderful to work with," Sophie said. "We're also lining up quite the list of volunteers."

"I'm honored to be included," Karen said.

"Not as much as we are to have you on board." Mia glanced at Ava and frowned. "You never mentioned your mom used to be the director of special events for a software company."

Ava nodded. "My mom is quite talented."

But her mom and she never talked much about the past. Never talked about what her mother used to do before MS decided to make routine appearances and alter her mom's entire world. They dealt with the present and tried not to worry about the future. Her mom often told her that if she spent too much time looking back and wishing for a redo, she'd miss out on the moments that were given to her now. Only the decisions she made in these moments would affect her future. Ava prayed her mom's decision to work on such a large event wouldn't have negative side effects.

"Well, we're going to take advantage of those talents." Sophie smiled at Ava, understanding in her quiet gaze. "I hope you don't mind, Ava."

Yes. Ava minded very much. Her mother needed rest and calm. She didn't need stress and pressure.

Before Ava could respond, her mother said, "It's nice to feel useful."

Her mother's voice was soft and all the more breath stealing with her sincerity. Ava straightened as if that would open her own airways again. She wanted her mom to feel useful. Even more, she didn't want her mom to suffer. Her mom's tendency to overdo things while forgetting to pull back and take breaks had forced her into a very early retirement.

Ava knew that inner drive well—she'd inherited it from her mom. But Ava wasn't dealing with the complications of MS like her mom was. The Andrews family's all-in attitude was both wonderful and dangerous. There was useful, and then there was overworked. Last year, her mom had started out as a volunteer for an MS fundraiser; she'd then somehow stepped into the organizer role. After the event had ended, her mom had been bedridden for several weeks.

The payout for being useful wasn't worth the price.

Ava had accepted that she'd need to be the moderator and offer common sense. She intended to put her foot down. Intended to tell her two friends to find someone else. Someone healthy and capable of meeting their demands. She'd find another way for her mom to feel useful.

She opened her mouth, but Kyle set his hand on her shoulder and squeezed.

Ava's eyebrows drew together, and the words backed up against her teeth. What did he know about anything? She'd been taking care of her mother with her brother's help for years. Not him.

Kyle said, "If you want to win that spa day, you should play now while the lanes are free."

The spirit of competition enveloped the women within minutes. A spa date, a lunch delivery at work and a weekend brunch on the line, the women laughed and headed toward Skee-Ball. Sophie pushed her mom's wheelchair and called for Grant's friends to join them. Mia and Iris debated the rules. They settled on only one: win any way you can.

Kyle's hand landed on Ava's lower back, stopping her from following her friends. "Ava and

I will be there in a minute. We're going to get some things from the rooftop."

Speculation bounced across her friends' faces. Ava's gaze skipped from one person to the next. Each one, even Dan, eyed her and struggled to contain their grins, as if they'd all been let in on a really great secret. Iris tilted her head and looked between Kyle and Ava.

Ava turned her back on the entire group and their unabashed interest. Instead, she smiled at Kyle, only to discover the worst of the speculation lingered in his solemn gaze. She forced an upbeat note into her voice. "What did you need?"

Kyle guided her outside, into the hallway. "To tell you that we're even now."

"What does that mean?" Ava tugged the door shut.

"We stopped each other from telling our family members no. That makes us even."

"You didn't know what I was going to say." Ava followed Kyle up the stairs. "Maybe I was going to agree with their plans to let my mom help with the charity event."

"Your posture stiffened like you were ready for battle and your hands flexed." Kyle faced her. "If you'd been gripping your mom's wheelchair, you would've raced out of the building within seconds."

Had she been that obvious? She only wanted

to protect her mom. There was nothing wrong with that. There was everything wrong with Kyle being able to read her so accurately. Ava planted her bare feet and her spine on the top stair. "Mia is one of the best photographers in the city. She's also an award-winning filmmaker and has a résumé that makes most Hollywood filmmakers look like amateurs. You should be grateful she hired your sister."

"I know about Mia's impressive accomplishments." He ran his hands through his hair. "It's why I hired her."

"Yet you were going to refuse to let Iris work for her," Ava countered.

"It's not Mia that concerns me." He stepped away as if only just realizing how far into her space he'd gone. "It's my sister."

His sister? This was about Iris. Ava stepped toward him. "She's lovely."

"She is lovely, delightful and whimsical." Kyle crossed the rooftop, picking up empty wine bottles on his way and tossing them into the recycling bin. The glass clanged together like his words. "Except in the workforce, where she becomes unreliable."

"Maybe she just hasn't found her niche yet," Ava suggested hopefully.

"Her most recent job ended last week, after only five days." Kyle handed Ava a half-full case of water. "That was her sixteenth job in the last twelve months."

"But your sister seemed so excited about working with Mia."

"My sister is excited when the sun rises." Kyle picked up a case of mixed soda and walked toward the elevator. "She gets excited about the design that raindrops make on a window pane and loves to make shapes out of the clouds."

"That's not a bad thing." Ava envied Iris for appreciating the beauty in the ordinary. That was her artist's eye, no doubt. "She has a very positive spirit. That's a rare trait."

"Well, rare traits, like believing in wishes made on falling stars, aren't exactly what prospective employers see as strengths." Kyle pressed the down button for the elevator with his knuckles.

Neither did Kyle, apparently. "She's a talented artist."

"Her art can't protect her," Kyle argued. "She needs a decent job with a decent salary. Money will give her security."

But security couldn't always be bought. There was a certain security in being true to yourself and being loved unconditionally by those closest to you. Ava knew that firsthand. Thanks to her mom and her friends. "My mother never wades into anything. She jumps all in and forgets to use caution."

"Maybe this time will be different," Kyle said. "Maybe this is your mother's niche."

Ava's smile was brief. She recognized the words she'd thrown at Kyle about his sister. This was exactly her mother's niche. That was the problem. "Do you think Iris will work differently for Mia?"

"No." Kyle shook his head. "Unfortunately."

"I feel the same about my mother." Without the crowd, a breeze swept around the rooftop. The chill added a crisp edge to her concern. "It's who they are."

"They could surprise us." Kyle tipped his head toward the sky as if searching for a falling star to wish upon.

"I never liked surprises." Every time her father had promised to surprise her, he'd failed with the follow-through. On those rare occasions her dad had come through, the reality had never lived up to her father's overblown hype. A promised horseback ride at the lake became a carousel ride on a plastic horse at the mall. Not that she hadn't liked the carousel. But at thirteen, she'd wanted more than a toddler's miniature carousel ride run by quarters. Surprises always disappointed. "I prefer to be prepared."

"Then we'll have to watch out for your mother." Kyle stepped into the elevator.

But this was her mother. It was her responsibility to look out for her mom. Besides, Kyle wasn't on the list of the select few she trusted to watch out for her mother. Her response came out in an irritated stretch of one word: *"We?"*

"You're going to be busy developing your idea and working." Kyle held open the suite door with his foot. "I suppose I could get more involved with Sophie's event."

Reluctance, not eagerness, threaded through his tone. She pushed, wanting him to admit they weren't a *we*. Not even close. "What are you going to do? Work on the setup, too?"

He pulled back, his eyes narrowed as if her doubt bothered him. "I have more skills than offering introductions and a donation check."

"But have you worked on an event like this before?" she pressed. *Admit it. You don't want to look after my mom any more than I want you to.*

He shrugged and dropped the sodas on the bar at the back of the theater room. "I've attended more events like theirs than I can count."

"Hardly the same." Ava dumped the case of water on the bar and faced him. "You don't really want to volunteer for Sophie's gala."

He pressed farther into her space. "I will for you and your mom."

But she wasn't asking. "You have a lot on your plate."

"As do you." He touched her chin, tipped her face up to meet his. "I'm going to help, Ava, whether you ask me to or not."

He didn't play fair. One small shift and she could press her lips against his. Quick and brief. Taste his lie. "I think it's best if I tell Sophie that Mom can't do this."

It was best that she walked away from Kyle. Now.

He motioned her toward the game room and joined her in the theater room doorway. He nodded at the group gathered around the Skee-Ball lanes. "Do you really think that's the best thing for your mom?"

They'd included her mom. Wyatt had maneuvered her wheelchair at the perfect angle for her to take a turn. Everyone else lobbied to be beside her mom, while the others took their turns as if each one wanted to protect her. As for her mom, Ava hadn't seen that kind of joy light up her pale cheeks or filter through her laughter for so long.

But how long would that last? Would this one night out force her mom to remain in bed for the rest of the week? Would her mother tell her that the fallout was worth it?

Ava already knew the fallout of a broken heart wasn't worth it.

She adjusted her stance to steady her uncertainty.

This was about her mom, not Ava's heart. She hadn't asked her mother what she wanted or needed in quite some time. She'd made the decisions, assuming she knew best. Had she been making the best decision for her mom or herself? "I'll talk to her when we get home."

"For now, everything stands as it is then." Relief and surprise circled through his voice.

Ava nodded. Although she had the sudden sensation as if nothing would be the same ever again.

Kyle unbuttoned his suit jacket. "It could be fun working behind the scenes of an event."

Or a disaster. Looked like Ava would be getting involved in the fund-raiser, too. She had to watch out for her mom. Now there was one more thing that'd put her in close contact with Kyle. One more reason to spend even more time with him. What she really needed were more reasons to stay away from him.

"Iris was serious about playing a full tournament." The frown in his voice eased into his face.

Ava glanced at him and grinned. He wasn't as accommodating as he pretended to be. "Did you want it to be an early night?"

"That'd been the plan." His frown never softened.

Her plan had not been to be part of a *we*. In any sense. Plans changed. She had to adjust. Now, so could he.

She stretched her arms over her head as if prepping for her gold-medal match. "Well, I'm going to enjoy beating you in Ping-Pong before I leave. You should know that I've been practicing racquetball at the gym."

His head dropped back, shooting his laughter toward the ceiling. He walked toward the Ping-Pong table. "Impressive, but that's not going to help you now."

"Want to bet?" Ava challenged. He deserved this for inserting himself into her life.

Kyle turned the handle of his paddle and eyed her across the table.

Ava blamed him for that pull inside her that she fought to ignore. She'd been tempted to give in tonight. To give in and discover what was going on between them.

This was all Kyle's fault. The man was too nice to her friends. Too kind to her mom. His worst offense: he made her want to sigh. She wanted to beat him at Ping-Pong. Just maybe she'd bang her attraction to Kyle out of her system once and for all.

"What kind of bet do you have in mind?" His

mild tone contrasted to the blast of interest in his blue gaze.

Ava's cheeks warmed. The heat swept down into her chest and stole her voice.

His smile, satisfied and confident, kicked up one corner of his mouth. The blue in his eyes only intensified.

"No side bets," Iris chided. "We're all playing for the same prizes tonight and I intend to win them all."

Kyle's soft laugh curled around Ava.

"Can't deny that my sister can be irresistible sometimes." Kyle's love for his sister braced his one-sided grin.

Ava knew what he meant. Iris's brother could be irresistible, too, if she let her guard down. Fortunately, Ava never let her guard down.

CHAPTER NINE

THIS WASN'T A get-to-you-know meeting. Or the game Twenty Questions.

This was the first official meeting of the contest crew: two finalists and three mentors. The first day that would launch the next four weeks. Yet no one seemed in any hurry to begin developing the very thing Kyle was reimbursing the mentors to do and the very thing the contestants had to do in order to win the prize money.

Kyle stood in the hallway. A lively conversation flowed from his conference room. The group had more than enough time last night over Ping-Pong, pinball and cards to learn everything they needed to know about each other. But it was as if they'd pressed Pause on last night's conversation and this afternoon simply pressed Play to resume right where they'd left off. They'd circled back around to continue their debate over the best places in the city for Grant to live. And discussed potential part-time jobs for Ava. They talked like they'd known each other longer than twenty-four hours.

Was Kyle the only one who understood that the finalists had to remain strangers? Fleecing friends had never been part of his plan. Not that Kyle was conning anyone. Last night, he'd decided to increase the prize money. He expected that more money would've offset any guilt. Kyle was wrong.

He never should've allowed his sister to invite the contest group into his home last evening. He should've ushered everyone from the rooftop garden the same way he'd escorted the reporters and other guests down to the street and into waiting taxicabs. Instead, he'd let Iris step into the hostess role, welcoming everyone into his place and offering more food and drinks. Then he'd joined Ava's Ping-Pong team as if he belonged beside her. He hadn't even minded that he'd lost to her twice at Ping-Pong. Worse, he liked being with her. He'd have to get over that immediately.

Ava wasn't interested in what his money could give her. She'd probably expect him to give her something impossible, like his heart. But opening his heart always ended in pain. Always left him even more empty. He'd locked down his heart and made no exceptions these days. One impromptu game night and one particular redhead would not change anything.

Besides, this group had been assembled for

the contest. One professional to another, working together to fulfill the terms set forth in the contest rules.

Ava's warm voice wrapped around him. Joy brightened her story about the latest odd job postings she'd found that morning: one for a superhero sidekick, another looking for a time-travel companion and one in desperate need of a pretend girlfriend. Questions were launched around the room about wages, best time periods to travel to and the benefits of a pretend relationship. Their laughter swelled. A smile relaxed through Kyle before he censured himself. He'd smiled too much, too freely last night. No thanks to Ava. There was nothing wrong with laughter and smiles. He enjoyed a good joke, even liked to laugh. But he preferred to be in control of his emotions, and this was business. Everyone knew emotions had no place in business transactions. He'd treat everyone, including Ava, like a professional acquaintance. He'd be polite, but single-minded and centered on their purpose for being together: the contest.

Kyle strode into the room; his brisk greeting stifled the laughter. Time to focus. "Ava, the clear choice is superhero sidekick. What's your superpower and superhero outfit?"

Not quite the professionalism he'd been reaching for. No matter. It wasn't as if he was biased toward Ava. That would be bad. He looked at Grant and repeated his question. That proved he was fair, impartial and totally unfocused.

Grant O'Neal, former army counterintelligence officer, looked like a drill sergeant in civilian clothes. Kyle expected Grant to yell, "Drop and give me twenty," at any moment.

Grant's grin faded, his eyebrows pulled together and his face shifted into serious. As if the question had been about national security, not superhero powers. After several quiet moments, Grant said, "I'd have super power tattoos and keep wearing my jeans and sweatshirts."

"I'd be your sidekick, Grant, with my invisibility powers and business suit outfit." Chad, one of the mentors, swiveled his chair and dunked a piece of his donut into his coffee mug.

Chad Green, with his wide baby-blue eyes, round glasses and cropped blond hair, looked like he hadn't reached voting age yet. Chad was in his midthirties and, on second consideration, would make the perfect sidekick for Grant. Kyle rubbed his forehead.

"I'll stay behind and run the command center like Alfred, Batman's butler." Sam picked up a croissant from the plate of pastries in the center of the glass conference table.

Sam Bentley was always the sensible one. One of the reasons Kyle chose him as a mentor. Sam always stopped and considered every angle to every situation before he responded. What had happened to the man who'd hired Kyle as an app designer right out of college? That Sam wouldn't have continued this conversation.

"I'll be The Healer and wear scrubs." Ava grinned and slathered cream cheese over a bagel. "At least we have our Halloween costumes covered."

This wasn't a Saturday afternoon coffee date with friends. Who'd been considerate enough to bring snacks? He glared at the pink box with the silver imprint of Chateau Dough on the cover. Chateau Dough catered to people like Kyle with food allergies and sensitivities. He blamed Barbra for her thoughtfulness.

Grant tapped Ava's phone on the table. "Call that guy from the employment ad. See if he's interested in the Super Squad we just created. Tell him we'll work for a group rate."

Super Squad? Kyle had wanted to be a part of a secret squad in grade school. Not now.

His gaze tracked back and forth between Grant and Ava. The pair made the perfect superhero match—her red hair and strength a complement to Grant's defined features and inner self-assurance. Just like Barbra had mentioned at the contest party. Kyle dialed back the jealousy knob. What had gotten into him? Ava and

Grant looked good together. No big deal. Now he needed to drop and do twenty himself until he regained his focus.

Maybe if he referred to Ava and Grant as Finalist One and Finalist Two, that'd create some much-needed detachment. He'd create even more distance if one or both of his current finalists dropped out of the contest. All he had to do was give the pair the right incentive, and he'd replace his current finalists with strangers. That'd end the talk of Super Squads. And sever any temptation of his to join in.

He walked to the oversize dry-erase board, away from the pastries and the group. "With the part-time jobs settled, let's get serious. I want to talk about the very long evolution of an idea, like the Medi-Spy, from concept to prototype to product."

"So, you didn't get the idea to build the prototype and become a millionaire overnight?" Sam asked, a light tease in his usually sober voice.

"Sam, you know full well that didn't happen." Not even close. Kyle added, "Maybe if you'd designed for me back then, we'd have been that lucky."

Sam could've earned the award for one of the top innovators in the city if not for his poor choice of employer. Sam threw up his hands as if he was guilty. "I admit it. I chose to work with the design team at Corsky over Kyle."

"Corsky, as in the technology company that filed for bankruptcy last month?" Grant asked.

"One and the same." Sam's voice was grim.

"Ouch." Ava rubbed Sam's shoulder as if he was a family member of a victim she transported.

Grant winced.

"But that's the point." Kyle pointed a dry-erase marker at each one of them, stepping into his role as leader of the Harsh Truth Squad. "No one knows what ideas will take off and which ideas will flatline."

Barbra smiled and nodded. "I might make a professor out of you yet, Kyle."

But teachers encouraged. Teachers inspired.

"That's not inspiring." Ava crossed her arms over her waist.

Exactly. Kyle was eager to explain. "That's the reality. Even with a functional prototype, test runs and loads of data, your idea may never make it to the market. Your idea may never make it out of the design lab. All you'll have to show for your hard work is lost hours in the lab and a depleted checking account."

"Then we have to make sure we have the one idea that hits." Determination firmed Grant's chin and voice.

Wait. Why hadn't Kyle discouraged them? His gloom and doom depressed him.

Ava's quick chin nod and straightening shoulders made her look even more determined than Grant. "We have the same odds as everyone else. We just have to be better."

"What if your best still isn't good enough?" Kyle pressed. "Will you look back and regret the four weeks you spent in this design lab? Will you consider all the endless hours and sleepless nights a waste of your time?"

Kyle didn't regret his time spent in the design lab. He only regretted that he had nothing substantial to show for those hours. Nothing to give Tech Realized, Inc. to fulfill his contract.

Ava and Grant looked at each other and nodded as if their Super Squad had just accepted a mission. More likely this was their military training coming to the front line. They wouldn't back down. They wouldn't give up. Yet the third- and fourth-place finalists could be slotted into the top spots if Ava and Grant pulled out. To be honest, he'd have been disappointed in both Grant and Ava if they'd given up that easily. Still, he wasn't backing off yet, either.

"I specialize in sleepless nights," Ava said. "At least I'll have something to work on the next four weeks."

Kyle wanted to know what kept Ava awake.

He concentrated on Grant and dismissed his interest in Ava. "Didn't I see you exchanging contact information with Brad Harrington last night?" Surely Grant wanted to build his résumé and receive a real paycheck rather than work on a contest that might not payout.

"Brad offered me a position at his investigation firm." Grant rubbed his hands together. Anticipation widened his gaze. "He's willing to wait and hire me after the contest ends."

Could Brad have been any more accommodating? One more reason why Kyle liked Brad Harrington. He frowned. He wasn't building a friend list. He was building a case for Grant to drop out. Neither Grant nor Ava looked ready to walk away. They looked like they'd settled into their chairs, as if fully prepared to defend their positions. "Grant, I thought you overextended your stay on your friend's couch? A job on the rental applications will help with a landlord's decision to lease to you."

"I promised if I won the contest, I'd buy new living room furniture for my friend and pay the back rent I owe," Grant said.

The guy was sincere, honorable and intelligent. Kyle pinched the back of his neck before he offered Grant the sofa bed in his apartment— free of charge. Talk about trespassing outside those business boundaries. Bad enough he liked Ava. Now Grant, too.

"Since Grant sounds as if he might need the prize money for first and last month's rent, as well as his friend's furniture, why don't we move to the lab and get started." Barbra stood and motioned toward the door.

Kyle accepted defeat. He wasn't replacing his pair of finalists. His judging panel had picked the right candidates. "Ava, you'll be working with Sam. Grant, you're with Chad. Barbra and I will float between the two teams."

Kyle would have to come up with a new plan to save his contract. The contest was supposed to be his backup plan. With that safety net, why didn't he have ideas pouring out of him as if someone had opened a floodgate? Even the coffee had failed to induce a caffeine rush of new ideas.

Still, he had time to come up with his own idea. Twenty-five days exactly. Not impossible. Just challenging. Kyle had always liked challenges. He usually won. But the stakes had never been so high before. Nor had the outcome affected so many other people.

Sam tapped Grant's shoulder. "We can talk rentals over lunch."

"I might know someone at the hospital who needs to sublease her place." Ava rolled her chair into the table and smiled. "She's getting married soon and moving into her fiancé's place south of the city."

Kyle only ever hit up his contacts for potential job offers for Iris. Business only. His mouth had other ideas. "I can check with a few people, too, for possible rentals."

"Thanks." Grant shook Kyle's hand; his grip was firm and reliable. Relief eased into Grant's voice. "I wasn't expecting to get much more out of this experience beyond an idea."

Neither had Kyle. He'd expected to work on prototypes, not to want to spend time with the finalists beyond the lab.

Barbra extended both arms like a mother bird wrapping her wings around her babies. "We're going to be working closely together for the next few weeks. It helps if we can get along and support each other."

There was the problem. Kyle hadn't anticipated the ramifications of such a small group. He hadn't considered that it might be impossible to remain distant and disengaged.

He'd hoped for inspiration from the finalists and mentor panel. He'd planned to use the winner's idea. Making friends had never been a consideration.

He had to find a new tactic to stay ahead of his emotions and keep everything in the business-transaction box. Starting now.

CHAPTER TEN

AVA WALKED INTO her apartment, dumped her backpack on the counter and dropped into her usual chair at the small kitchen table. Thanks to Joann, Ava's tea was already steeping in her favorite mug. Ben had given Ava the unicorn mug when she'd returned from her last deployment. She used it every morning. The unicorn's mane changed colors with hot and cold liquids and always made her smile.

Ava liked this part of her mornings. This part, she could count on. A quick moment to unwind from whatever work had delivered during the night. She warmed her fingers around the mug and let the steam dampen her face. It was good to be home.

Joann poured her homemade granola into a bowl and set it on Ava's placemat. "You've made the Sunday newspaper."

"That's impossible." Ava swirled honey into her tea. "I haven't done anything newsworthy."

None of their work cases last night had been extraordinary. They'd been routine and typical. Work had been demanding, but manageable. Nothing emotionally or mentally defeating. Nothing nightmare inducing.

Exhaustion made her bones ache, but it was the good kind. The kind that made her appreciate these little moments more. Watching her idea transform into something real with Sam's guidance yesterday only helped energize her. Ava added another dollop of honey to her tea and relaxed into her chair.

"You're a finalist in Kyle Quinn's Next Best Inventor Contest." Joann sat in the chair across from Ava like she had every morning for the past several years. Her typical breakfast—lemon yogurt and a croissant—in front of her. "That seems to be more than enough to start with."

Everything appeared like one of their normal mornings. Everything was in place as it should be. Even Joann and Ava were in their usual seats. But the conversation wasn't routine. The conversation should center on Ava's night, her mother and Joann's plans for the day. Not Ava in the newspaper. Ava lowered her tea mug, afraid to take a sip and burn her mouth. "What do you mean *start with*?"

"It's titled 'Bathroom Confessions.'" Joann reached for the Sunday newspaper on the counter behind her and ran her finger across the front page. "You never mentioned that you and Kyle Quinn were an item."

Ava squeezed the ceramic mug, imprinting the unicorn's mane into her palm. The smile the mug usually pulled from her refused to come. "Because we aren't an item."

"But you'd like to be." Joann peered at Ava over her glasses, looking more like a guidance counselor leading an errant teen to confess than her mom's longtime nurse and friend.

Only in a parallel universe would Kyle and Ava be an item. Like the one where Ava could have everything. Ava set her mug on the table. "Where did you get that idea?"

"It's in this article." Joann pushed her glasses up with her finger and looked at the newspaper. A slow smile spread up toward her eyes. "The writer certainly has a way with words."

And a way with lies. "Can I see it?"

Ava skimmed the article and stared at the picture of the familiar reporter. The woman had the same wide yet sharp smile she'd worn in the bathroom where Ava had first met her. Now she had a name: Nikki James. Ava had chosen her words so carefully after Ava had learned Nikki was a reporter for a local news channel. Nikki had never mentioned she moonlighted as a columnist for the "City Happenings" section in *The Chronicle*. "She was the one who told me that

I should concentrate on winning Kyle, not the contest, because Kyle is the better deal."

"What did you say after that?" Joann asked.

"Nothing. I kept silent." Like she planned to do from here on out. She tossed the paper across the table.

"There's your problem." Joann slathered jam onto every edge of her croissant, painting it a bright strawberry color.

"Since when is keeping quiet a problem?" Ava wanted to smear jam across Nikki James's picture and rub away her mocking grin. Childish, but warranted. "Mom always told me to bite my tongue until I had something nice to say. That's a rule or something for every kid growing up."

"There are exceptions to every rule." Joann lifted her jam-encased pastry toward Ava as if to emphasize her point. "Reporters are an exception."

"She would've twisted my words all around." Ava crossed her arms over her chest and slumped in her chair.

"Most likely she would have, seeing as she twisted your silence to suit her needs." Joann studied Ava over her pastry. "So then, you aren't trying to win Kyle, too."

No. Absolutely not. True, she was interested in Kyle more than she'd been interested in anyone in a long while. She was drawn to him. But attraction faded like a candle flame. Then she'd have to trust in those deep emotions—the ones that were supposed to be lasting and forever, yet never were. Winning over Kyle was a game her heart couldn't afford to play. "There's no room in my life for a man and all the messiness that comes with a relationship."

"It isn't all messy." Joann took a bite of croissant and chewed slowly, as if savoring the jam, even though it was the same jam she ate every morning at Ava's kitchen table.

From the distant look in the older woman's kind eyes, Ava wondered if it was a memory, not the jam, that Joann savored. Would Ava ever look back on her memories with the same fondness and affection?

Finally, Joann shifted her warm gaze to Ava. "There's a lot of good to be found with the right man. And a lot of fun, too."

The sincerity and earnestness in Joann's voice and face pinned Ava to the back of her seat. She wanted to believe Joann. But the childhood memories of her father walking out stopped her. "I'm afraid you married the only good one out there."

Ava knew well the decadelong struggles Joann had endured with her daughter's addictions. Yet Joann and her husband had only strengthened as a couple, raising their two toddler grandchildren and supporting their daughter as best they could. Joann's husband had stayed like husbands were supposed to, but all too often didn't.

"The right man is out there for you, too." Joann finished her pastry and wiped off her mouth, as if that settled everything. "You just have to be open to the opportunity."

"The only opportunity I'm open to right now is the one that offers a fifty-thousand-dollar pay-out at the end." Ava picked up her tea mug and warmed it in the microwave, ready to return to her normal morning routine and avoid any more talk of love and relationships. "That's all I have time for."

Joann clearly had time for more. "Love comes in its own time and its own schedule. You need to remember that it probably won't match your schedule."

"Well, love will have to call and make an appointment," Ava teased. She checked the clock on the microwave. "Right now, I have time for a power nap before mom wakes up."

"When do you need to be at Kyle's place today?" Joann asked.

"After lunch." Ava sipped her tea and burned her tongue. Setting the tea in the sink, she hoped the day would get back on track soon. "Mom has PT this afternoon. Then she's joining Mia's mom for a crafting demonstration of some kind. I should be home before she finishes."

"You can't survive on power naps alone, Ava." Joann set her breakfast dishes in the sink. The plates and silverware clinked together as if echoing the warning and censure in Joann's voice.

"It's not permanent." At least she hoped not. Ava dried her hands on her pants and avoided meeting Joann's gaze. The older woman treated Ava like her own daughter and Ava adored her for that. But like her own mother, Joann often spotted Ava's lies before Ava. "Right now, it's the best I can do."

Joann held the newspaper out to Ava. "You might want to keep this for your scrapbook."

"Very funny. You're aware that I don't know the first thing about scrapbooking." Ava shook her head but didn't return Joann's laughter. Everyone assumed Ava wasn't sentimental. The truth was she kept a few very special items from over the years. The newspaper article wasn't even close to making the cut.

"Nothing like the present to learn a new skill." Joann's eyes sparkled behind her glasses.

The older woman probably had a collection of scrapbooks at home from the memories she'd preserved. Despite the dark times, Joann always seemed to find something to appreciate. Something to cherish. Ava cherished each day with her mom. "I'll stick with what I know. But I'll keep the article. There will probably be questions this afternoon at Kyle's."

Joann hugged Ava. "Get some rest and dream about your right man."

Finally, Ava laughed and set her alarm on her cell phone. "That I can do. Everything is better in dreams."

"Then dreams become reality." Joann touched Ava's cheek and smiled. "And you don't want to sleep, because you might miss all the good parts of your life."

Ava covered her yawn and apologized. "If I miss something good, I'll have to find it later."

Joann shook her head and pushed Ava down the hall. "Get to bed. I'll clean up before I leave."

Ava walked to her bedroom and face-planted on her bed, the article still clutched in her hand.

The crinkling sound jarred Ava awake twenty minutes too early. She tugged the newspaper out from beneath her hip. The article with Nikki James's mocking grin drove her to Kyle's place early.

Recharged with caffeine and determination, Ava rushed through Kyle's arcade room, not needing to be buzzed in as someone was leaving. She barged into Kyle's personal apartment. He stood at the kitchen sink, looking out the window as if more interested in the cars on the street than the commotion Ava was making behind him.

Ava pulled the article from her purse and skipped over any sort of greeting. "I never said any of this to her."

Kyle turned, a yogurt in one hand, a spoon in the other, and leaned against the counter. His smile offered an unspoken welcome. "Did you talk to Nikki James in the suite bathroom?"

"I came out of the stall and she was sort of there." Ava waved the newspaper between them. "She congratulated me. I washed my hands and left."

"You never said anything?" Kyle pressed.

"Okay, fine. I answered her questions, but that was before she told me she was a reporter for some news channel." Ava crammed the newspaper and her frustration back inside her bag. Kyle hadn't made her talk to Nikki James. She'd managed that all on her own. "But Nikki never mentioned the newspaper part of her job."

"They never do give all the details." Kyle tossed the spoon in the sink. "Although they always seem to come up with more than enough for their articles and news stories."

Ava's shoulders slumped at the anger in his voice. "You're mad."

"Irritated," Kyle admitted. "And sorry you were ambushed in the bathroom."

"I believed the women's room was sort of sacred." Ava followed Kyle into the hall. "I thought there was some sort of unspoken rule about bathrooms."

"There are no rules with plenty of reporters," Kyle said.

He sounded just like Joann had that morning with the same disgust and censure. Was she the last one to get that particular memo? "I know that now. Next time, I'll walk away."

She amended her rule about never walking away. If a reporter was involved, she'd step aside.

Outside the conference room door, Kyle stopped Ava with a hand on her arm. "By the way, I'm flattered."

One side of his mouth tipped up, drawing Ava's gaze. "Flattered?"

"That you're trying to win me, too." His voice was quiet and tempting.

Ava jerked her gaze away from his mouth. "I'm not..."

Kyle touched her chin with his knuckles, closing her mouth and stopping her protest. "But there can't be anything more between us than this."

He kept his hand under her chin. One simple adjustment, and he'd be cradling her face. One simple shift, and she'd be leaning against him.

And the *this* that he spoke about became complicated and not so simple. "For now or ever?"

His gaze locked on hers and his hand… His hand curved to cup her chin. His thumb stroked one time across her bottom lip. "Both."

One word that came out raw and rough. The lie was there in his one caress. Ava never stepped away. Never drew back from his touch. She kept her gaze fixed on his, open and unblinking, as if that would prove her next words true. As if that would prove he wasn't lying, either. "That's good. Because I feel the same. There can be nothing more between us."

"Then we both understand." His thumb twitched against her skin.

Ava understood. Understood she needed to keep her distance from Kyle. Understood the threat he posed to her heart. Understood how hard walking away right now was really going to be. She lingered. "Looks like it."

His hand eased farther behind her neck. His touch stalled the breath in her lungs and time itself. If she tipped her face up. If he leaned down. They'd have that one brush of lips against the other. Would their kiss be the truth or another lie?

Ava bit into her lip and dug deep for her voice. She wasn't willing to risk her heart to find out.

"I think they're waiting for us in the conference room."

Kyle blinked as if her words broke him from a trance like the snap of a hypnotist's fingers. He released her and stepped back, far enough that she wouldn't even accidently brush against him on her way into the conference room. The businessman replaced the charmer. Professional polish displaced the earlier tease in his voice. "After you."

Too quickly the distance between them seemed more than an arm's length. Felt deeper, like the ache of something special lost.

Ava should be happy. Should be pleased that he felt the same as her. That he hadn't been willing to take the risk and kiss her, either. This was all part of that messiness she'd told Joann she didn't want in her life.

She sat in the chair the farthest from the one Kyle chose at the head of the table. But that only emphasized how far out of reach Kyle was. She ordered herself to stop being stupid. He'd only touched her face. Yes, his hand had been gentle and the warmth from his palm had extended into her toes. She couldn't allow that to mean something.

Ava concentrated on the conversation between Grant and Barbra, determined to remain as impartial and detached as Kyle.

CHAPTER ELEVEN

KYLE STARED AT the fingerprints on the glass conference table. A spray of glass cleaner would wipe away those smudge marks within seconds. He wondered how long it'd take to wipe away the imprint Ava left on him—an imprint that only etched deeper inside him with every minute he spent with her.

Imprint or not, it didn't matter. Ava was only a finalist. He hadn't lied earlier. This was all they could ever be. If he still wanted to take her out into the hall and kiss her until they both forgot all the reasons they shouldn't be together, well, he'd have to ignore the urge. He wasn't certain he could ever recover from Ava.

He tugged the rolled newspaper from his back pocket and tossed it on the conference table. "If you haven't read the Sunday morning newspaper already, here it is. It's interesting reading, as our very own Ava is a featured column."

Barbra rocked back in her chair, her attention on Ava, not the newspaper. Her face remained neutral, but her eyes widened behind her oval glasses.

He should've known Barbra had read the paper already. She told her students quite often that well-informed was well-prepared. There wasn't much that went on in the city that Barbra Norris wasn't aware of.

Sam grabbed the newspaper and slipped on his round black reading glasses. "How'd you get featured in the paper, Ava?"

Grant leaned toward Sam and read over his shoulder.

Ava's palms smacked against the glass table, pulling everyone's focus to her. She cleared her throat as if the sudden attention unsettled her. "For the record, I'm not trying to win Kyle."

Everyone around the table nodded, slow and in sync.

Kyle focused on Ava, but she refused to meet his gaze. He'd told her they couldn't be anything more. She'd agreed. That pleased him. Except now, slivers of disappointment, not satisfaction, sliced through him.

Ava rushed on, "I'm also not going to turn my sights on Grant if I fail with Kyle."

Again, the whole group nodded in unison, their gazes fixed on Ava. No one spoke.

Ava touched Grant's arm. "No offense."

Grant lifted his hands and managed to pull his smile under control. "None taken."

Ava exhaled. Her words came out less frantic. "That line about me playing Skee-Ball here every night is totally wrong. I mean, I have played obviously, since I own the high score. But not every chance I can find."

One more group nod, as if Kyle had coached them prior to agree to anything Ava said. He hadn't, of course. That made their joint support of Ava all the more impressive.

"Anything else?" Kyle asked Ava.

"I think that covers it." Ava slid her hands off the table and dropped back in her chair.

Twin spots of pink stained her cheeks. She wore flustered quite well. If he'd doubted her before, he didn't now. She wasn't interested in being another one of Nikki James's headlines. Unfortunately for him because he could've dismissed her from the contest. Easily severed his interest in her if she'd wanted to sell a Kyle Quinn story to the press. Too bad Ava wasn't like a number of the other women he'd met recently—the ones more interested in their own fifteen minutes of fame.

"We didn't really believe anything in there." Grant nudged Ava's shoulder. "But thanks for clarifying."

Ava covered her face with her hands. "You could've stopped me."

"You seemed like you really needed to clear the air." Barbra smiled and waved her hand to include the others. "We didn't want to interrupt."

"Thanks for the support." Ava kept her face covered and spoke around her fingers.

"You'd do the same for us," Sam offered. "We're in this together."

Together. They were supposed to be at each other's throats in an effort to beat the other one. Money was on the line. That motivated people. Perhaps not this particular group. Money would motivate Kyle and every decision he'd make in the next few weeks.

"Now that the air is cleared, we should discuss our strategy going forward," Barbra said.

"We need a strategy?" Confusion shifted across Ava's face and lifted her voice an octave. "It was one article, and everyone here knows the truth."

"There will be more articles," Barbra said.

Kyle winced at Ava's gasp.

The rest of the group murmured their agreement.

"How many more?" Ava's voice came out in a breathless squeak.

Definitely not the voice of a fame-seeking woman who was confident in her ability to capture the spotlight and hold it. Ava looked like she wanted to shoot out the spotlight and slide under the table.

Chad tossed the paper on the table and shook his head.

"You roused the interest of the press." Grant picked up the article and frowned. "That woman must have a thing for restrooms, men's and women's."

"Nikki James cornered you in the men's bathroom?" Ava's grimace matched Grant's.

At least Nikki James couldn't be accused of discriminating. Why was he defending a reporter?

Grant nodded. "Nikki stopped me outside the bathroom at Rustic Grille."

"Was that after she came over to our table?" Chad asked.

"Before," Grant said. "I don't think she liked my answer outside the men's restroom, so she followed me to our table."

"What did she want to know?" Kyle asked. Neither Grant nor Ava looked like they wanted to be a part of a news cycle, especially a gossip column. As yesterday's lecture had clearly failed, perhaps this would deter them from continuing with the contest.

"Nikki wanted to know where you and Ava were spending your Saturday evening," Grant said.

Ava coughed and set a pretzel half on the table. "Spending our evening?"

Grant and Chad both held up their hands.

Chad shook his head. "Not that we told her anything."

"Because there was nothing to tell." Kyle rubbed his forehead and glanced at Ava. "Where were you, by the way?"

"What does it matter?" she challenged back. Her mouth set into a stubborn frown.

It mattered a lot. If she'd been on a date, then Kyle could feed that information to Nikki James somehow and end the sudden fascination of the press with them as a couple. He stared at Ava and waited.

"Working," Ava said and smacked her palms on the table. "Some of us have jobs to do."

Something inside Kyle released like a pressure valve. He'd only wanted to know for the reporters. He hardly cared if Ava dated or not. If he didn't meet his contract obligations, he, too, would be reentering the nine-to-five workforce soon. He should stop networking for Iris and start networking for himself.

"Where were you?" Barbra asked him.

All the attention shifted to Kyle. He said, "Here, at home. Working."

Or more precisely, slamming his head against the wall as his list of already patented ideas leaked onto the second page of his legal note-pad. And his confidence that there was an original idea out there dwindled.

Sam rubbed his chin. "Ava's coworkers can verify her presence."

Kyle pressed his fingertips into the table and leaned forward. "What are you getting at?"

"You were here alone." Sam shrugged. "A resourceful reporter could link you to Ava last night."

"The only way to link me to Ava would be if I called 9-1-1 for a medical emergency." Kyle let both frustration and sarcasm drip through his voice.

"Which he didn't," Ava stressed. She looked as confused as Kyle felt.

"Why are we talking about this?" Kyle asked.

"It's simple, really. The press has taken an interest in you both as a couple. You should see the number of comments on the internet boards. There's a flurry of commenters calling for the TV network to announce Kyle as the next star of their reality TV show *Marriage Material*." Barbra set her phone on the table and looked over her glasses at him. The glint in her gaze weakened the seriousness in her tone. "Kyle, did you know that you're one of the city's most elusive bachelors?"

Kyle rubbed his forehead to massage away

the tension. He'd heard that before. Didn't require the reminder now. After all, he'd chosen to be elusive.

Sam swiped across the screen on his phone and handed it to Chad. "Barbra isn't kidding."

Chad laughed and said, "Theweddingplanner101 says that she's the perfect marriage material for Kyle Quinn. But Exfinder disagrees and claims she can win Kyle herself."

Sam leaned over his shoulder. "The comments just keep going on and on. Ava, you're not very popular."

"I think we get the idea." Kyle wanted to grab their phones and lock them in a drawer. "Ava already established that she isn't interested in catching me. I'm not interested in being caught. That's enough said about that."

"We need a new strategy." Barbra tapped her fingers on the table.

"A strategy for what?" Kyle asked. Papa Quinn had cautioned him to never ignore a bad feeling. He and Ava both looked to Barbra as if she had all the answers.

"A strategy to handle the press," Barbra said. "We need to keep the focus on the contest and not let it become a matchmaking ploy."

Sam set down his phone. "What do you have in mind?"

Barbra smiled. "Simple. We only go out as a

group in public. If we're having lunch out, we all go. If we're attending an event, we all go. It's all or nothing. We're even more of a team now."

There was that word again: *team*. Barbra accused him of building a team. That was the last thing he was building. He played on his own team. Kyle filled a glass with water from the watercooler. His mouth dried out with every word. "You can't be serious?"

"Quite." Barbra stared him down. "We've committed to helping Grant and Ava develop prototypes. We can't afford to be distracted from our mission."

Their mission? Their commitment? Those were buzzwords for a team. This was supposed to be a contest, not a run for some national championship title. This was supposed to save him. Barbra talked as if this project would change the finalists in life-altering ways. As if they'd taken oaths and signed player contracts. "We can't do everything together all the time."

"Contest-related activities only," Barbra clarified.

He'd ensure there weren't too many of those types of outings. The *team* belonged in the design lab anyway, not out in the city, being social.

"Barbra is right," Sam said. "We don't want to look biased toward one finalist over another."

"That would ruin the integrity of our contest," Chad added.

Now Chad and Sam had bought into the mission and the commitment. It'd become their contest, too. But it was only ever supposed to be Kyle's contest. He'd named the contest after himself. He'd be the one to damage the integrity of the whole thing by himself in a few weeks.

Disapproval turned down the corners of Barbra's mouth. "We don't want to do anything that could damage our contest's reputation."

"What are you saying exactly?" Clearly, he needed things spelled out. He wasn't usually quite this slow. But teams weren't his specialty and he'd never read a playbook.

"As mentors, we don't want to be seen with one of you alone and have someone accuse us of breaking a contest rule," Chad said.

Kyle should imitate his mentor's lead and become a rule-follower, too. He'd already come too close to breaking his own personal rules with Ava.

"They might accuse Grant and I of having an illicit affair." Barbra's eyebrows lifted with her grin.

Grant rubbed his chin. "We could do that to keep the attention off Kyle and Ava."

Kyle needed a distraction to keep his own attention off Ava. His impending financial ruin should be reason enough. Still, his gaze continued to track to her again and again. "We'll keep that as a backup plan if the reporters insist on making up things that don't exist."

Or if a reporter got too close to the truth. Although Kyle wondered what truth he feared the most: that he was a fraud or that he wanted to win Ava for himself.

"Then everyone understands our strategy going forward?" Barbra looked around the table, letting her gaze rest on each contest member for several seconds.

"The team that works together, wins together," Kyle muttered.

"Looks like we'll get to challenge for the high score on basketball shoot after dinner." Chad tapped his fist against Grant's.

Grant grinned. "Care to make it interesting?"

Kyle looked between the two men. "What are you betting on?"

"Do you want in?" Chad asked.

No. He wanted out. Wanted everyone out. He wanted his team of one back. "We're working in the lab all afternoon."

The two men nodded as if he'd called the perfect play to win the game.

"I agree with Kyle," Sam said. "We don't need to go out when we have the ideal work-and-play space right here."

It was impossible to agree with Kyle. He'd never said anything like that. He hadn't issued an extended invitation to anyone at the table. He'd only agreed to the all-in-or-nothing approach. How had they gotten to his suite becoming the de facto safety zone? All to avoid any more awkward encounters with Nikki James at public restrooms.

"Ava has to work tonight, so we can't all go out for dinner," Chad added.

"That means takeout from that pizza place that Kyle introduced us to," Grant said. "Ava, we'll even give you time to challenge for high score on basketball shoot before you leave."

Ava made the motion of shooting a basketball and laughed. "I only need one chance to win."

Tonight should be the nothing part of the all-in-or-nothing clause. Without Ava, their team was down one player. Surely, they were breaking some contest rule staying at his place for dinner and games. Kyle just needed to figure out what rule that was.

"New rule," Ava said. "No one gets to try for Skee-Ball high score unless I'm here to defend my title."

That was not the rule Kyle expected.

"Now that dinner and games are settled, we can get to the real work." Barbra stood and motioned the group toward the door. "Otherwise it'll be a working dinner with no time to relax."

Kyle stood and rolled his shoulders. He'd relax in four weeks, after the contest ended and he fulfilled his contract. For now, he'd stop getting any further involved.

CHAPTER TWELVE

KYLE STUFFED ANOTHER handful of candy into his mouth to shut himself up. He stared at his laptop and chewed to drown out the suggestions and helpful advice being lobbed around the design lab like tennis balls. The group collaboration kept pulling him in. Apparently, he had endless recommendations for Ava's portable vitals device and Grant's cell-phone security case. And still he had nothing for himself and his own as-yet-to-be-thought-of idea.

He wasn't the only one contributing, either. Yesterday, he walked into the conference room to find a full spread of food for the entire contest crew, courtesy of Haley. She'd left a note on the dry-erase board that she was fueling the group with brain food. Then added an extra-large smiley face.

The group had stayed later than expected last night. This afternoon appeared to be heading in the same direction. Kyle had to get them out. This couldn't become a habit.

He closed his laptop and picked up the bowl of

candy. Maybe if he called it a day, they'd follow his lead. No one noticed him. Ava and Sam, their heads together, studied the computer screen. Chad and Barbra talked beside Grant's station.

Finally, Grant stood up and scooped candy out of Kyle's bowl. "Never could resist a sugar rush."

"My grandmother blamed my grandfather for my sweet tooth." Kyle wasn't sure who to blame for that particular confession. He preferred not to talk about himself. Kyle locked on to Grant's army T-shirt and asked, "Why didn't you move home after you retired from the army?"

Grant looked at him, his face blank. "Don't know where that is."

Kyle studied Grant. Kyle had always known where his home was: his grandparents' house across the bay. The one place he always depended on. There were only warm hugs, freshly baked cookies and encouragement inside their house. Pretenders and phony people weren't ever allowed past the wrought-iron fence. Bad manners were never welcome. "Where did you grow up?"

"Everywhere." Grant shrugged. "And nowhere."

Kyle's parents had lived a block away from his grandparents, where everyone gathered for Sunday dinner and on most weekdays. Security and acceptance had only ever been a bike ride away.

"My grandmother got me out of the foster system when I was five. I was shuffled between aunts and uncles over the years. Until, finally, I was old enough to make my own choice and enlisted in the army." Grant leaned against the counter with the printers. "You grew up here?'

"All my life." Kyle nodded. "My parents and grandparents lived a street away from each other across the bay."

"Nice. You had two homes." Grant's voice was thoughtful. "How did you decide where to have family dinners and holiday celebrations?"

"My grandmother loved to cook. My grandfather loved to have everyone in his home," Kyle said. "He always said life was fuller and richer with the people he loved right beside him."

"I always wanted to be a part of a family like yours." Grant grabbed more candy and pointed at Kyle. "I would've spent most of my time with you growing up."

Kyle shoved off the counter, pushing away that pinch of regret inside him. Kyle knew the truth. Grant wouldn't have spent time with him as kids. Kyle wouldn't have risked it. He was risking too much now. He could only blame himself for asking Grant what was supposed to have been a simple question. That settled it. No more simple questions. Suddenly he wanted to retreat into that solitude he'd created for himself.

Could he kick everyone out? His grandmother would scold him for his poor manners. His grandfather would be disappointed.

"I need to get going." Ava rolled her chair away from the computer she worked on with Sam. Standing up, she pressed her hands into her lower back and stretched. "I promised to take my mom to Creative Craft Warehouse this afternoon."

Kyle relaxed his hold on the candy dish. Thanks to Ava, he wouldn't have to summon his bad manners and end the evening early. Thanks to Ava's exit, he'd have his suite all to himself tonight, like he preferred.

"The Copper Table is in the same shopping complex as the craft warehouse," Chad offered. "We could have dinner there tonight."

"Their sweet potato french fries are the best I've found." Barbra rubbed her hands together. "With their homemade honey mustard sauce, they are beyond divine."

Sam rubbed his stomach. "A bison burger sounds pretty good right now. Or even the open-faced steak sandwich."

Grant saved his work and closed the design application they'd been working in. "I haven't been there, but you had me at burger."

"We aren't all going to the craft warehouse, are we?" Kyle straightened, his muscles tightened along his entire spine. He'd wanted the group to disperse and head to their respective homes. Not take a field trip to a craft store.

Sam shrugged. "It's the all-in policy we agreed to on Sunday."

"But this isn't a contest-related activity," Kyle argued. There was no need for everyone to go. This was an errand for Ava and her mother.

"It's sort of contest-related." Ava swung her bag over her shoulder and frowned at him. "Thanks to Kyle, Creative Craft Warehouse is the only store that has the supplies my mom must now have."

"My suggestion?" Kyle scratched the back of his neck as if that would rewind his conversations.

"Mom told me you suggested the stacked glass bubble bowls with chrysanthemums and orchids for the centerpieces at the fund-raiser." Ava tapped on her phone screen and handed it to Barbra.

"Iris and I saw something at an art exhibit last month." Kyle winced. His sister had conned him into joining her after he'd dragged her to several networking events. He'd spent the evening learning the new features on his upgraded cell phone, including the camera. "I remembered them and mentioned the centerpieces to Karen in a text."

"Those will look absolutely lovely." Barbra

shifted the phone screen to show Chad and Sam. The men nodded and murmured their agreement as if their opinion mattered.

Kyle knew the centerpieces would look really special. He'd shared the idea with Karen, knowing that she'd expand on the simple design. But he'd only shared an idea. He hadn't offered to assemble the centerpieces. Or shop for the supplies.

Sam motioned for the phone. "How many are we going to make?"

We? When had *his* contest crew become *Sophie's* decoration committee for her City Causes gala? When had his contest crew become a team like a family that did everything together? He already had a family and they were the only ones he'd ever needed. Once he brought his family back where they belonged, his life would be full again. Replacing his family had never been a consideration. Or an option. How did he stop this?

"Right now, the count is one hundred." Ava grinned at Kyle as if she hadn't noticed his distress.

"Well, we should get going." Sam closed his laptop and shoved the computer in his leather bag. "That's a lot of supplies to find and order."

"You can't seriously want to go to the Creative Craft Warehouse." Kyle heard the panic in his voice and plowed on. "Craft stores are like the Bermuda Triangle. Or worse, kryptonite."

He'd been more times than he could count with Iris. His sister hadn't coerced him into going. On more than one occasion, it'd been his suggestion. But that wasn't the point. The point now was the group going together as if mandated. As if the contest rules required an excursion. This was too much. How was he supposed to keep his distance? Remain uninterested? He already enjoyed everyone's company too much. Soon he'd consider each of them a friend.

This had never been about making friends. Friends relied on each other. Trusted each other. No one should trust him.

Every morning he woke up without a solid idea of his own to submit, his decision dwindled. Both Ava's and Grant's ideas were better than he'd anticipated. Smart. Workable. Marketable. And would save him from financial disaster. Their ideas would fulfill his contract and keep his bank account flush.

Nausea rolled through him. No doubt the unplanned trip to the craft store was upsetting him. Shopping made him ill.

Sam stood and squeezed Kyle's shoulder as if he sensed Kyle had lost his balance. He'd only lost his focus.

"We'll be with you, Kyle." Laughter bounced

through Sam's voice. "If it gets to be too much, the craft warehouse has quite the wine section. You can seek solace among the shelves of international red wines on sale."

Chad stood as if eager to get to the store, too. Too much candy had distorted his perception. Chad looked like he should be driving his hand-built robot in an international competition. Grant looked more suited for the extreme gym in the Bay View district, instructing beginners on how to climb the massive four-story indoor rock wall. Neither one looked like they should be wandering through a craft store and enjoying it. "You two really want to go there?" To make sure there was no misunderstanding, Kyle added, "To the Creative Craft Warehouse?"

"I just texted Sophie and Brad to see if they needed anything for the backdrop they're designing for the gala." Grant waved his phone at Kyle. "I offered to help with the construction."

"I'm helping, too." Chad zipped up his navy windbreaker and tugged a baseball cap out of the pocket.

When exactly had Kyle's entire team been recruited for Sophie's charity event?

Grant looked at Kyle, his eyebrows lifted while his voice lowered. "I might've volunteered your services, too, Kyle."

Kyle stepped back. He wasn't used to being included. He relied on being the first to refuse. His gaze clashed with Ava's. She tipped her head, her mouth pulled together and her eyes narrowed. Kyle waited for her to point at him and yell, "I knew it."

Ava expected him to back out. She expected him to refuse to help. She assumed he'd disappoint her. Even though he'd told Ava that he'd work on the charity event and watch out for her mom. She didn't trust him to keep his word. She shouldn't trust him—that he admitted freely. But she should know he always kept his word.

"I'm more than happy to help." Kyle pumped enthusiasm into his voice and hid his reservations about this particular field trip behind a grin. "Looks like we're heading to Creative Craft Warehouse, everyone."

Ava blinked as if she hadn't quite understood him. Or perhaps that was confusion from her assumptions being proved wrong. Her mention of shopping at the Creative Craft Warehouse hadn't cleared the room and sent everyone running in the opposite direction. Kyle hadn't let her down.

Kyle stepped closer to her and held on to his grin. "Where are we meeting your mom?"

"Mom," Ava repeated.

He smiled wider at the sudden dismay that Ava failed to hide. Was it wrong that her discomfort pleased him? He was more than happy that he wasn't the only one rattled. "Your mom will want to be there to make the final decision on the supplies for the centerpieces."

"I have Dan's truck. I just need to pick up my mom." Ava squeezed her forehead.

Kyle could've told her not to bother. Nothing would bring sense back to this afternoon.

"That's perfect." Barbra slipped on her jacket and pulled a set of car keys from her purse. "I can take Grant and Sam with me. Chad can ride with you, Kyle and your mom."

"Creative Craft is south of the city," Ava said.

Barbra smiled; her voice was patient. "I know where it is. I even know a shortcut. You'll want to follow me."

"You spend time at Creative Craft?" Ava asked.

Kyle caught his laugh before it escaped. Once again, Ava and he shared the same surprise. He wouldn't have pinned crafter to Barbra's many talents.

"I'm there most weekends, and if I'm lucky, on a weekday like today," Barbra confessed. "I inherited my mother's decorating genes and my father's DIY tendencies."

"Maybe you'll have some suggestions for my wife." Sam followed Barbra into the hallway. "She wants to redesign the guest room and en suite bathroom to help our guests feel more comfortable and welcome."

"You should also get help from Iris." Grant hurried after Barbra and Sam. "Kyle's sister did the bathrooms and the elevator in here."

But Kyle's sister wasn't an interior decorator. Iris was, however, avoiding Kyle's phone calls and his attempts to schedule several job interviews for her. Her text messages had been short, curt reminders that she was currently employed as Mia's photography assistant. No job interviews were required. But she couldn't remain Mia's assistant forever. She'd never stayed with any job for the long-term. Her art was the only consistent piece of her life. She'd been carrying a paintbrush since she had learned to walk, or so their parents had always told them. She'd expanded her hobby from painting to sculpting and crafting over the years. Iris would've been the first one in the car for a trip to Creative Craft. But that didn't make her qualified to give decorating tips.

Barbra glanced back at him. "I'm sure Iris will be decorating the house you're designing in wine country."

Kyle trailed behind the group through the arcade room.

"You're a house designer, too?" Ava asked.

Kyle shrugged. "It's a home for my family."

"Or a place to disappear in," Barbra said. "Haven't you seen the plans on the desk in Kyle's office?"

Everyone shifted like a school of fish toward Kyle's office. "It's nothing special. Just a place for my family to come home to."

The group gathered around the house plans spread out across the drafting table.

Sam whistled and shook his head. "I'd need a map after I checked in."

Chad pushed his glasses up with one finger and leaned closer to the floor plans. "I think the pool house might be larger than my entire apartment."

"You'd have an extra couch for me in this place for sure." Grant laughed.

Chad pointed at the upper corner of the architect drawings. "If you stayed in the west wing, no one would find you unless you wanted to be found."

Kyle watched Ava. "What do you think?"

"It's certainly extravagant." Her voice was contained, almost cold.

But was that such a bad thing? He wanted to give his family everything they wanted and anything they didn't know they needed.

"I think I'm used to city homes and tight quarters." Ava glanced at him. "What's wrong with here?"

"It's not..." Home. Kyle turned and looked out the doorway into the suite. Although with Ava and the contest crew there the past few days and nights, his suite felt fuller and more alive than it had since he'd moved in over two years ago. "My family has drifted in different directions. The house will change that."

"Maybe they like where they are," Ava suggested.

How could his family be happier someplace else? They'd always belonged in the city with Papa Quinn. But his grandfather had died. And Kyle wasn't sure where he belonged anymore. The house would end his wandering. "They're going to love the new place."

And if they didn't?

He saw the unspoken question in Ava's searching gaze.

He wasn't worried. He had the money to design whatever his family wanted. Whatever would get his family home.

CHAPTER THIRTEEN

AVA HAD MORPHED into a taskmaster. For the past two hours, she'd tried to guide the group through the craft warehouse and keep everyone on task. The experience had been more like herding moths. Someone was constantly flittering to the next aisle and getting distracted by the cool items on the shelves.

Only Kyle had cooperated. He'd worked with her through the supply list, offered suggestions and kept her entertained. He'd been more fun and helpful than she'd ever expected.

Now she had to get back on schedule. The group trip to the craft warehouse hadn't been part of her afternoon plans. Nor was dinner at the Copper Table. If dinner proceeded without any hiccups, she could be home in time for her evening conference call. A conference call that could end in a part-time job offer for a telemarketer. Not her first choice in work, but her dwindling checking account couldn't be too picky.

"Could you send over the waiter?" Ava asked the hostess on their way to the table. "Everyone has been discussing what they were going to order since we left the city. They don't need extra time to look over the menu."

The group seated, Ava once again kept everyone on task and urged them to place their orders with the waiter.

Kyle leaned toward her and bumped his shoulder against hers. "Have someplace else you need to be?"

Yes, she had a job interview she hadn't told anyone about, including her mom. She hadn't wanted to hear that she was stretching herself too thin or that she couldn't handle so much. Or that telemarketer might not be a good fit for her. Several of her mother's medications were due to be refilled next week. "I'm just really hungry."

"You should be more relaxed," Kyle said. "It's your day off."

"Easy for you to be so cavalier. Your bank account isn't bordering on empty." Ava shoved her straw in her mouth and soaked her voice with a deep sip of soda. It wasn't his fault or maybe it was. A night off meant unproductive time with no money coming in and that always upped her stress. Anxiety wasn't ping-ponging through her like usual. She'd enjoyed her time with Kyle. Too much. That should make her worry.

"How can I help?" He looked at her, sincerity in his gaze and his tone. "What do you need?"

He probably had enough to cover the balance in his wallet right now. He'd give it to her, if she only asked. Then she'd become another handout like Iris. Like his sister, she'd resent it. She'd earn her money with hard work and pay her own bills. "Sorry, that was the hunger pangs talking. Forget I mentioned anything."

He shifted farther into her personal space and searched her face.

She saw the questions in his blue gaze. Knew from the way his eyes narrowed at the edges he wasn't about to forget anything.

She almost forgot herself and confided in him. Ava reached for a distraction. "You didn't order any food."

"I'm not hungry." He eased away and picked up his iced tea. "I had a big brunch this morning."

"That's a lie," she countered. She could recognize the lie; she'd been telling enough of her own.

He smeared the water drops from his glass across the table and eyed her. "Is that so?"

"It's Thursday and Haley won't come until tomorrow with meals for the weekend. That means you ate yogurt this morning," Ava said.

"That's perceptive."

"And accurate." Had she not been aiming her satisfied smile at him, she'd have missed the quick touch of his fingers on his medical ID band. The big brunch was a cover story to deflect attention away from him. Ava never mentioned her interview to avoid a lecture. Kyle never ordered to avoid anaphylaxis. "Why did you agree to come here if you can't eat?"

"I never agreed," he said.

She'd been too distracted by the group's determination to head to the craft store together. She hadn't stopped to check the list of Kyle's approved restaurants. She wanted to yell at him for not saying something and search his jacket for his EpiPen. Not that it was her business. Irritation shifted into her voice. "You could've stayed home."

"And miss all this? Not a chance." He motioned to the group around the table. Barbra and her mother assembled a sample centerpiece. The guys discussed the latest cell phone upgrade. "I'm flattered you're so interested in my eating habits, by the way."

"Don't be." Ava unzipped her purse, pulled out a nut-free protein bar and handed it to him. He was too close again. Worried he'd think she cared, she pushed disinterest into her tone. "I want to win the grand prize. I'm sure your death would ruin the contest."

His quiet laugh streamed through her and tugged a smile free from deep inside her. She should be practicing for her interview, not edging closer to him.

"Or maybe the contest would become more popular, like an artist's work after their untimely demise." His fingers tapped against the protein bar.

Ava liked him like this: relaxed, funny and engaged. She liked herself with him. She added, "The contest would gain momentum eventually, but not before the investigation over your suspicious death concluded and a suspect was charged."

"If the circumstances of my demise are suspicious, then someone took me out." Kyle leaned toward her until his shoulder touched hers. His chin dipped forward, and his voice lowered into the conspiratorial. "Who do you think did me in?"

"I'm going with Chad in the drafting room with the ruler." Ava kept contact with him as if she relied on his support. "Chad's innocent look will keep the police off his tail for weeks."

"Barbra is more of the mastermind type." Kyle picked up his iced tea glass and shifted it toward Barbra and her mother. The pair studied the different centerpiece items and whispered as if they were plotting world domination. "I'm going with Barbra in the kitchen with the herb garden."

"The herb garden is the least lethal thing in

the kitchen," Ava said. Kyle on the other hand could be dangerous to her and her heart.

"Exactly." Kyle spread his hands across the table as if he'd just dropped the winning poker hand for the jackpot. "She's a mastermind."

Ava's laughter spilled between them.

"What are you two discussing over there?" her mom asked.

The table quieted, and everyone shifted their attention to Kyle and Ava.

Ava straightened away from Kyle.

Kyle lifted his glass and grinned at her. "We're debating who here would be the best evil mastermind of the group. My money is on Barbra."

"Thank you for the compliment." Barbra lifted her glass in a toast to Kyle. "I believe most of my students would agree with you."

A debate ensued over the best qualifications for an evil mastermind and who at the table possessed those skills. Ava's mother offered several suggestions, and to her amusement, the others nominated Karen as the best skilled at subterfuge and mind control. Laughter filled the table and rolled through Ava.

Meals arrived one by one courtesy of the efficient waitstaff. Her interview loomed and yet Ava jumped into the conversation, wanting the joy on her mom's face to stay. She should be encouraging the group to eat faster. She shouldn't be extending the conversation as if it was a leisurely meal. If the group skipped dessert, she'd have time to take the scheduled call from the truck.

No one commented on Kyle's lack of food. Certainly, Ava wasn't the only one who didn't buy his big brunch story. She was just the only one who'd called Kyle out. "You should eat the protein bar."

"I'm not hungry," he said.

"You haven't eaten all day," she argued.

"I'm fine."

"It feels wrong eating in front of you." Ava pushed her plate away. She'd get a to-go box. That could prompt the others, too. Then she'd definitely be home before her interview.

"Really, I don't mind." Kyle nudged her plate back toward her. "I like watching you eat."

"That's weird," she said. "No one likes watching someone eat food that they can't have."

"I like watching you," he said. "I've never seen someone approach every meal so analytically and with such precision."

"It's not that big of a deal." Ava shifted her plate a quarter turn on the placemat.

"She's gotten much better, Kyle." Her mother wiped her napkin in the corner of her mouth, but failed to hide her grin. "When Ava was little, we had to serve each part of her dinner on different plates."

Ava nudged the steamed broccoli away from her chicken parmesan. "Certain foods aren't supposed to touch."

"Is that why you use multiple paper plates when we order takeout?" Grant asked.

Ava aimed her fork at him. "I know what you're going to tell me."

Chad grinned. "That it's all going to the same place."

Ava pointed her fork at Chad's mess of a plate. "But my food is going into my stomach in an organized fashion. It's better for the digestion."

"But sometimes, if you experiment—" Grant said. He stabbed his fork into a french fry and speared a beet from his salad and dipped it into his aioli sauce. He held the loaded fork up and eyed her "—you might discover something unexpected like the perfect bite. The perfect combination."

"Or you might discover that certain foods just don't belong together." Like certain people didn't belong together.

Grant shrugged and shoved his fork in his mouth, willing to take the chance.

"Some things are more of an acquired taste," Kyle said.

"Even though I don't combine my food, it

doesn't mean my palette is any less refined," Ava challenged. "Or that I don't take risks."

She'd taken a risk entering the contest. It meant every day she didn't secure a second job. That was more than enough to upset her stomach and leave her queasy. She'd table the culinary risks for someone else. Every minute she lingered in the restaurant, she wanted to remain beside Kyle and skip her job interview. Kyle was the risk she couldn't take.

The waiter cleared the empty plates while thoughtfully and thoroughly reciting the dessert menu.

"Scared to take a risk on dessert?" Kyle asked.

Ava fumbled with her phone in her lap. So much for her discreet time check. "I'm going to have to pass." At this pace, she might have to take the interview call in the truck, out in the parking lot with Kyle, her mom and Chad listening in.

"What? You don't like your salted caramel sauce mixing with your hot chocolate?" Kyle teased. "There's something tempting about the combination."

She'd never liked hot chocolate and preferred her caramel sauce with a spoon. But she liked Kyle and the challenge in his cool gaze. Ava kept her gaze on Kyle and ordered the bread pudding. She took risks and she was in control. "Now, let me show you how the centerpiece should be put together."

Barbra handed Ava the glass bowls. Between bites of bread pudding and suggestions from the table, Ava rearranged the bowls more than once. Finally satisfied, she sat back and spread her hands over the centerpiece.

Barbra nodded. "It's quite nice."

Her mom offered a small smile.

"That's quaint." Kyle reached over her and pulled Ava's centerpiece apart. "And hardly remarkable."

"You think you can do better?" Ava challenged.

"I know I can." Kyle gathered the different glass bowls, emptied the flowers and decorations from each one. "Watch and learn."

"I never took you for a floral and color guy." Ava worked through her dessert while he organized the decorations across the table.

"I'm not." Kyle switched the glass rocks to the bowl with the flowers.

"Could've fooled me," Ava said. "You're coordinating the ribbon colors and the flowers better than an interior designer."

"These look good together." Kyle held up the glass bowl with the tea lights and silver ribbon inside. "Besides, Iris is the one with the eye for design."

"Creativity seems to run in the Quinn family," Ava teased.

"You might be right." Kyle smiled. "Maybe I have learned a few things from my big sister after all."

Ava finished her dessert and Kyle finished the centerpiece. Barbra sighed, and her mother clapped. He hadn't created a masterpiece. He'd stacked several glass bowls. Although the light caught perfectly on the top glass bowl and reflected into the other bowls, giving the illusion of water. "That's quaint."

"It's perfect." Barbra snapped a picture. "Now we can replicate it on the night of the event."

"I win," Kyle whispered.

Sam edged closer. "My wife is going to want to take one of those home from the event."

Karen touched Sam's arm. "That's a wonderful idea, Sam. We could auction off the centerpieces."

"Or give them away as door prizes," Kyle suggested.

"Even better." Karen typed on her phone. "I'm adding it to my list for Sophie."

"I'm declaring the evening a success." Sam tossed his napkin on the table.

"We should end it now," Grant added. "On a high note."

The table abandoned for the next group, they

walked toward the exit. Kyle held the door open. Ava waited, lingering until everyone else had exited. "Not everything is about winning or losing. It isn't always a competition."

Kyle let the door swing closed and stepped beside her. "Sure it is. Winning feels good."

Ava should be feeling bad she'd missed her interview. Yet all she felt beside Kyle was good. And that was bad.

CHAPTER FOURTEEN

KYLE HAD WANTED to hold Ava's hand during the Creative Craft field trip and every day since. One week later and the urge had only intensified. Worse, he watched the clock every afternoon until the group arrived. He worked on their ideas on his downtime, not his own. He placed several calls to contacts about apartments and flats for Grant. He'd even agreed to be a guest for one of Barbra's lectures next semester.

He'd lost control and become a joiner. He'd never been like this. He had to stop. No good ever came from his willing participation. That he'd proven more than once. Was he trying to prove that he could belong if he chose to? Well, today he changed his mind. He was making a different choice. He wanted his old life back. His safe, controllable life back. The one where he wasn't reaching for a woman's hand as if he craved that personal connection.

Today he chose to detach and reclaim his old self.

Step one: recover his personal space.

Kyle walked into the design lab and tossed nine silver-embossed cards onto the center of the worktable. "Thought we'd change things up tonight. There is an invitation to the grand opening celebration of the Glass Violet Restaurant for each of you. Sam, I included one for your wife. Chad and Barbra, there are two extra invites in case you've been keeping your plus ones a secret from us."

Chad laughed. "Give my plus one to your sister."

"I'm sure Iris will be thrilled to join us." Kyle picked up an invite from the table. He'd have to track down Iris first. He hadn't seen his sister since the finalist after-party two weeks ago. She'd been busy on the days he'd texted and vague about her evening plans, as if she didn't want to reveal where she was.

Barbra slid an invitation across the table. "Reservations for the Glass Violet are full through the New Year. How did you come by these?"

Celebrity status offered invitations to most of the city's events. He usually declined. But tonight, the Glass Violet provided the perfect excuse to get the group out of his place. Even better, there was an open bar and open seating. He wouldn't have to jostle for the chair next to Ava. He wouldn't be tempted to hold her hand like he'd wanted to at the Copper Table. "I can't reveal my sources."

"You can keep your sources." Grant slid an invitation into the back pocket of his jeans. "I'm just excited to eat there."

"I have to call Glenda. She's going to need a few hours to get ready." Sam held up his phone and walked out. "Kyle, you're going to be my wife's favorite person."

He wasn't interested in the title of most popular. He was only interested in reclaiming his personal space, where he could concentrate on himself and his own ideas. "It's no big deal."

"That's the celebrity talking." Sam squeezed his shoulder. "Seriously, thanks."

Kyle nodded, accepting Sam's gratitude. His gaze collided with Ava. She chewed on her bottom lips as if uncertain.

"Are we all meeting at the restaurant?" she asked.

"The press will definitely be there tonight." Chad picked up an invitation.

"We should decide on a time to meet," Grant suggested.

"We can meet out front of the Pacific Bank and Trust building at seven. It's one block away from the Glass Violet," Barbra suggested. "Then we can walk together."

"That works." Ava looked at Barbra. "I've

never been to an event like this. Any ideas on what I should wear?"

"Yoga pants are out." Barbra sat in the chair beside Ava's workstation.

Kyle liked Ava in her workout clothes. Barbra mentioned a black cocktail dress. Kyle liked Ava in the dress she'd worn for the contest party. Ava described a pair of silver rhinestone heels she'd splurged on, but had yet to wear. He'd like those, too. Kyle twisted his chair away from the women and faced Grant's computer. He liked being alone more than he liked Ava with her yoga pants, sparkly heels and contagious laugh.

Grant opened his cell phone case design on the computer screen. "I feel like we should discuss our outfits for the evening, too. We should coordinate our color scheme, like the ladies."

"This is a serious conversation." Ava threw a crumpled-up piece of paper across the lab. It bounced against Grant's shoulder before he caught it.

Kyle ripped a page off the legal notepad, wadded it up and shot the ball at Ava. "We're being serious, too. We don't want to clash tonight and look like we don't know what we're doing."

Ava caught the paper ball. "Good point. We don't want any extra attention. Let's keep the color scheme classic and subdued. Agreed?"

Kyle wasn't convinced Ava could ever be

considered subdued with her perceptive green eyes and bold red hair. "Fine. Now can we get to work?"

Barbra twisted her chair to face Ava's computer. "We'll need to end early to have enough time to get ready."

He'd already anticipated an early release. He'd have his suite all to himself for longer. "Then we should make the most of the afternoon."

THREE HOURS AND an extralong shower later, Kyle walked out of his bedroom in his dress pants. His shirt still hung on a hanger in his closet, and his socks and shoes waited beside his bed. He hadn't ventured into his apartment half-dressed in weeks. His kitchen trashcan wasn't overflowing with takeout containers. He wasn't looking over his shoulder, waiting for Chad or Grant to pop in. Silence surrounded him.

Exactly what he wanted to hear. Why, then, did he want to turn on the music or open a window to hear the street noise? Quiet never bothered him before.

He scratched his chest, stretched his arms over his head, flicked water from his damp hair. Nothing made him comfortable. Even the floor tiles under his bare feet seemed too cold, too hard. He'd always walked around his apartment like this: alone and in charge of his surroundings. That was before the invasion of the contest crew.

Kyle headed into the arcade room, circled around the foosball table and rolled the ten ball across the pool table. The crack of the striped blue ball against the others echoed in the empty room. He flopped onto the couch, set his legs onto the ottoman and assumed his favorite position for a power nap. The conditions were perfect. He had more than enough time for a twenty-minute recharge. His gaze tracked to the wall of champions and refused to close.

He punched the sofa cushion and strode back to his bedroom. Five minutes later, he slammed his front door on the silence and headed out into the noisy city. Iris had texted and told him she'd meet him at Glass Violet. Kyle patted his jacket pocket, confirming he had both the invitation, the check for Penny he planned to drop off first and his EpiPen.

Kyle welcomed the conversation with the taxicab driver about the Pioneers' upcoming game on Sunday. Penny greeted him with a hug and fudge samples from her newest batch.

"The women are busy in the new room." Penny motioned toward the back of the house. "I'm sure they'll welcome your help."

He'd never volunteered at the house before.

He'd only ever dropped off a check and left. "I'm not sure what they need me for."

"Your height for one." Penny laughed and opened a frosted-glass door. "Your sister won't have to haul the ladder through the house with you here."

Iris was here? Kyle stepped into an enclosed patio with one wall of windows and gaped. His sister stood on a folding chair, holding a large picture frame, her back to him. That wasn't the back that captured his focus like a fly trap. Instead, it was the bare back of the woman with his sister—her red hair sweeping across a fitted black cocktail dress. Her silver heels added even more length to her already long legs. What was Ava doing at Penny's Place with his sister?

Iris turned around and shouted, "Kyle. Perfect timing. Can you hang this, please?"

Kyle took the large frame from Iris. "What are you doing?"

"It's their new art room." Iris jumped off the chair and swept her arms wide. "Isn't it fabulous? Doesn't it inspire you to create?"

Ava stepped beside him and pointed at the hook already in the wall. "Iris designed the whole space."

"I never imagined this when we first discussed an art room." Penny clasped her hands under her chin and turned in a slow circle.

"I had help," Iris said.

Kyle looked at Ava.

Ava lifted her hands and took a step back. "I only delivered supplies."

"That was more helpful than you know." Iris carried an easel toward the windows. "Ava saved me a trip to Creative Craft."

"I need to start dinner." Penny wrapped one arm around Kyle's waist. "Your sister is a true gem."

A gem in hiding. Kyle squeezed Penny. "As are you."

"If you need me, just holler." Penny swept out of the room.

Kyle waited until the door closed, set his hands on his hips and asked, "Can someone tell me what's going on?"

Iris frowned at Ava. "I told you he'd do this."

"Do what?" Kyle looked between the women. He'd dropped off a check and hung a picture. Nothing that deserved his sister's censure.

Ava motioned around the room. "Don't you think Iris did fantastic work?"

"I don't understand how," Kyle said. Had she used the money he'd given her for rent and bills? Was that why she hadn't told him?

"You never understand." Iris fisted her hands and walked past him. An old oak table took up the side wall. Art supplies covered every inch.

Kyle glanced at Ava, not bothering to hide his confusion.

"Iris spent her free time the last few weeks and turned this space into an art room for the residents." Ava's tone was pleasant and patient.

Kyle waited, as if he was back in school and had been warned repeatedly not to interrupt the guest speaker.

"The residents needed a space to create their work to auction off at Sophie's City Causes gala," Ava added.

Kyle studied his sister. She sorted paint-brushes on a table in the back and avoided looking at him. The last of the sunlight streamed through the windows and reached for Iris. The sunlight highlighted her free fall of curls and his understanding.

"Iris is teaching them, too." Ava smiled as if pleased with his progress. "Every Friday night."

Kyle walked closer to his sister. "That's why you didn't want to go to the Harrington event."

"It's therapy for the women." Iris's fingers stilled in a bowl of crystal beads. "To create without judgment or hostility is freeing."

It was therapy for his sister, too. Why hadn't he realized that until now?

"I've been trying to tell Iris that there is a degree in art therapy." Ava's voice was encouraging. "And jobs at the hospital and rehab centers."

"Then art becomes work." Again, Iris's hand stilled inside the bead bowl.

"Work that you're passionate about." Kyle left it at that. He'd talk to Iris more about a degree later. Ava might've helped Iris find her niche. One more thing for Kyle to appreciate about Ava. "I think I'm caught up, except for Sophie's gala." A charity gala that kept inserting itself into his world.

"That was my mom." Ava shrugged. "She talked to Penny at the finalist party. Penny's Place became an item on her agenda. Sophie loved it."

He wasn't surprised. At the after-party, he'd peeked at Karen's growing agenda. Everyone had suggestions for the charity event, even his sister. By then he'd been too busy trying to beat Ava at Ping-Pong to pay much attention to the conversation. He was paying attention now. "How can I help?"

"Really?" Iris asked.

"We can make it a family affair." Kyle rolled up his shirt sleeves. "We'll finish faster if we all help. And you need time to get ready for the Glass Violet opening."

"You still have my ticket?" Iris asked.

"Right here." Kyle tugged the invite from his shirt pocket. "You'll be there?"

"I wouldn't miss it." Iris tucked the invite into

her apron pocket. "I helped Ava find a dress this afternoon at that vintage reseller I like."

That store just became one of Kyle's favorites. Ava was breath-stealing in her black dress, stunning and classic and hardly subdued.

"She might've found a dress for herself," Ava added.

Iris patted her apron pocket. "I thought I'd be here finishing up tonight, but I had hope that I'd make it."

Iris wasted no time putting Kyle and Ava to work. Finally, she agreed to leave Ava and Kyle alone to finish the last of the art room setup. She'd refused to leave until Kyle could repeat her instructions word for word. Fortunately, Ava remembered the details Kyle forgot.

The paintings hung on the wall, the easels prepped and waiting, Ava pulled the front door to Penny's Place closed. "I'm starving. Do you know the menu on the buffet tonight?"

Kyle shoved his hands into his jacket pocket to keep from taking Ava's hand. "Nothing was posted on their website." Nothing had been posted about food allergies, either. In his rush to escape the quiet of his apartment, he'd forgotten to grab one of the protein bars Ava had left at his place. "I'm sure everything will be well-prepared and delicious."

"Wait." Ava touched his arm. "You haven't eaten at this restaurant before."

"That would've been impossible," he said, trying to keep his voice light. "It's just opening tonight."

Ava typed on her phone. Frustration rushed her words. "There are caprese pesto bites, macadamia-encrusted Mahi-Mahi and chocolate hazelnut truffles on the main menu. It's like a nut house. You can't eat there."

"But everyone else can." And everyone was out of his apartment, including him. Not exactly how he'd envisioned things. He'd maneuvered the evening to ensure he had his apartment all to himself. Then that very emptiness he'd craved had chased him out of his own place early like a rodent infestation.

"You will not be standing around and watching everyone else eat." Ava touched the small purse at her waist and frowned as if she'd never seen it before.

"It'll be fine," Kyle said.

"It's not fine." Ava waved the beaded purse between them. "If Iris let me bring a useful-sized bag and not this play purse, I'd have been more prepared."

"The silver coordinates with your shoes nicely," he said.

Ava twisted in her heels. "I know. It's really

quite great. But I couldn't shove a single cracker in here, let alone a protein bar."

"You don't need to carry around food for me." He took care of himself. He didn't need someone to look after him.

"I carry around food for myself. That you can eat it, too, is a bonus." Ava typed on her phone again. "I know where we're going."

"To the Glass Violet," he said.

"First, we're eating." She grinned at him.

"There's an entire buffet table waiting for you," he said. For anyone with food allergies like him, buffets were to be avoided and never to be trusted.

She walked down the sidewalk and searched the street. "Then we'll call this an appetizer."

"I'll be fine." He slowed his steps. He never wanted anyone to be forced to go out of their way for him and his food allergies. Why wasn't she listening?

"This is better, trust me. I always overeat at a buffet. Always." She ignored his look of disbelief. "If I'm already full when I arrive, I won't stuff myself at the Glass Violet."

"I haven't seen you overeat once." He crossed his arms over his chest and planted his feet on the sidewalk. Now she was making things up to appease him.

"You haven't seen me at a buffet." She glanced

up and down the empty street. "I always feel like I need to keep eating to get my money's worth."

"You aren't paying tonight." He had her there. She had to back down.

"It's still a buffet." She double downed instead of relenting. "Just take one for the team and have an appetizer with me first."

There was that word again. *Team.* Something about the way she stressed the word and the implication that they were a team settled inside him like a plant taking root. "What if Nikki James is there? What about the all-in policy?"

"She won't be." Ava grimaced. "This is definitely not her kind of place."

"What kind of place is it?" he asked.

"The kind with really good food made by really good people." Ava tapped on her phone screen and twisted the phone toward him. "Best part is that it's on your restaurant approval list."

He swayed as if a sinkhole suddenly shifted beneath his feet. "Why do you have a copy of my list?"

"I took a screenshot so I'd know." Ava shrugged. "It's no big deal."

It was a very big deal. No one outside his family ever took that extra step. They relied on him to know his own weaknesses. She wasn't going out of her way or being put out. She genuinely wanted him to eat safely. Suddenly, he no longer cared about any contest rules. He only wanted to go wherever Ava took him. Kyle smiled and rubbed his stomach. "I hope they have more than appetizers where you're taking us. I'm really hungry."

"We need to get a cab." Ava grinned. Her shoulders relaxed as he matched his steps with hers. Then she stopped in the middle of the sidewalk as if an invisible wall blocked her path.

They were never going to get anywhere if they kept stopping every block. He glanced at her and moved back to her side. She chewed the corner of her lip, as was her habit, and stared down the street. He asked, "What?"

"We could take a cable car." She let the hope linger in her voice.

Kyle glanced at the cable car tracks running down the cross street toward the waterfront. "You want to take a cable car on the most tourist-filled line in the city?"

Ava nodded slowly as if unable to fully commit.

"Why?" he asked. He didn't bother to keep the bewilderment from his voice. "They are slow and packed with tourists."

She stiffened and stepped closer to him. "I sit on a street corner almost every night in an ambulance. I can tell you the exact number of stoplights on any route to most emergency rooms in the city. It's sixteen from this spot to the Bay View Medical ER." She paused and ran her hand over her dress. "I wear boots, cargo pants with pockets for supplies and carry a jump bag with oxygen, an IV starter and a cardiac monitor." Her chin tipped up, her gaze latched on to his. "I don't have opportunities to dress like this. Or to sit in a cable car and just watch the city slowly pass by."

She wanted that chance. Now. With him. He held his hand out to her. "Let's take the cable car."

"Really?" She set her hand in his. The pleasure in her voice spiraled through him, lightened his steps and made him smile.

He squeezed her fingers and pulled her closer into his side. "Do you have your city bus pass? It works on the cable cars, too."

"I'm lucky I got my driver's license into this thing." She frowned. "Are you telling me I could've been using the cable car all this time?"

"I'm glad you haven't," he said. "We can make it a night of firsts."

"What's your first?" she asked.

"Not sure yet," he said. "I'll let you know when I experience it."

Three blocks later, they joined a handful of people at the cable car stop and climbed aboard. Kyle paid the conductor and guided Ava to the front of the cable car with the open spot on the bench. Then he stood in front of her on the footboard.

"You aren't going to stand, are you?" Ava asked.

"The best views are on this side." Kyle nudged Ava back onto the end of the bench. He grabbed the outer pole and steadied himself. "We have to do this right. It's your first time."

"Then I should stand," she said.

He glanced at her high heels. "Do you trust those shoes?"

She settled back onto the bench. "I don't trust myself in these shoes."

He wasn't sure he trusted himself with her. More often than he liked, his gaze tracked back to Ava as if she was the perfect attraction and the only one that mattered. Kyle tightened his grip on the pole and forced himself to watch the city glide by.

CHAPTER FIFTEEN

"THAT WAS THE BEST." Ava stepped onto the sidewalk and watched the cable car continue down the road. She grabbed Kyle's arm and slid her fingers down until she linked her hand with his. As if Kyle was her anchor. And if she let go too long, she'd lose the thrill of the moment. "Now we eat."

"Lead the way." His grip firmed as if he intended to remain in the moment, too.

Several blocks later, the Market Food Park, with dozens of the best food trucks in the city, came into view.

Ava pulled Kyle along faster, weaving around the long line at the Haute Fusion Food Truck. "Do you know where we're going now?"

"I already know I'm ordering the Bacon-and-Bourbon Mac and Cheese."

Ava laughed. "Make that two orders."

Ava and Kyle stepped up to Charlotte's Cheddar Chariot.

A woman leaned over the edge and grinned,

her smile stretching from cheek to cheek. "Kyle Quinn, it's been too long."

Nothing about Charlotte reflected a middle-aged mom of four. The shimmer on her eyeshadow blended with the glitter on her polished fingernails. Her white-blond pixie cut was streaked with lavender. Charlotte was a retro-cool mom with serious cooking skills.

"Charlotte, we had a craving for mac and cheese with a side order of cheese puffs," Kyle said.

Charlotte took in their joined hands and dress attire. "Are you coming or going to your event?"

"Going," he said.

"Then we better fill you up. Can't ever trust those big events to keep things clean and uncon-taminated." Charlotte slipped on a new pair of clear plastic gloves and called to Poppy to take orders. She smiled at them. "I'll cook your orders myself."

"Appreciate it, Charlotte," Kyle took the drinks Charlotte's assistant handed him.

"I thought Charlotte didn't have any kind of tree nut on her truck," Ava said.

"She doesn't." He handed one of the drinks to Ava. "Which is why I first came here."

"The food brought you back," Ava guessed.

"That and Charlotte's hospitality," he said.

"No request is ever too much for her. She reminds me of my grandmother."

"You still miss her," Ava said.

"Every day."

"Then you should eat here more," Ava suggested. "It's good to remember the ones we loved."

"It's also painful," Kyle said.

"But your grandmother's love lives on inside you," Ava said. "It's worth remembering and sharing."

His pinched eyebrows made him look unconvinced. Yet he nodded as if considering her advice.

Charlotte leaned over the counter to give them their order. Straightening, she tapped her ear. "Love the new colors, Kyle. Now I can coordinate my Medi-Spy with my outfit and my truck."

"That's terrific," Kyle said. His words were as forced as his smile.

"You don't like the new color palette for the Medi-Spy." Ava nudged her elbow into his side.

"I don't like any of the new options." His voice was deep and disgruntled, his face set into a stubborn frown.

Ava thanked Charlotte and followed Kyle to an empty picnic table. "But you invented the Medi-Spy."

He handed her several napkins. His voice felt

just as scratchy. "I invented an earbud for my grandfather and people like him."

"What do you mean?" Ava had never considered what had inspired him. She'd assumed the opportunity to make money had motivated him.

"My grandfather was an ironworker. He suffered heatstroke on the job and never survived the ambulance ride to the ER." Kyle studied the crowd. "My device was meant to save other people working in extreme environments, like road crews, factory workers and soldiers in the desert."

He never shifted his attention to her and kept his gaze on the crowd. Ava wondered if Kyle was counting the number of people wearing a Medi-Spy. His voice and gaze were too distant, as if he'd stepped into an uncomfortable memory. Ava wanted him back with her in the present. She asked, "What happened?"

"The market wasn't big enough for Tech Realized, Inc." He poked at his mac and cheese with his plastic spoon. "The execs at Tech Realized, Inc. had a different direction in mind."

"Why didn't you stop them?" Ava asked.

"I liked the money too much." The blue in his gaze was bleak. Even his shrug lacked conviction.

She didn't believe him. There was more to this than the money. He bankrolled his sister and supported Penny's Place. Iris had told her how Kyle had saved the women's shelter with his donations. He was an invisible philanthropist and not a man motivated solely by financial greed. But that was exactly what he wanted her to believe. Good thing she prided herself on making up her own mind. "What's next for you?"

"Another idea and more money." The finality in his voice ended the conversation. As if that was all there was to say.

She'd drop the subject for now. But they'd talked about his invention more later.

KYLE STACKED HER empty bowl on his and stood. "Now, we have a group to meet up with and you have a buffet to attack."

"My dinner was perfect." Ava walked next to Kyle out of the food truck park. "I don't want another bite of anything."

"The desserts have their own buffet table at the Glass Violet." His voice dipped back into the easy and lighthearted.

"I might have to try a few samples." Ava ran her hands over the sides of her dress. "I think I might have room in here. You have to promise to stop me if I overindulge."

"How would you like me to do that?" he asked.

"Distract me." *Dance with me. Kiss me.* Ava

should yank back her words. Tell him she was kidding. She was an adult and could control herself. The gleam in his blue gaze made her suddenly want to know exactly how he planned to distract her.

"I can do that." He took her hand, tugged her closer into his side.

Right where she preferred to be. There was something about how her hand fit in his. Ava stepped onto the empty sidewalk beside Kyle and let the night embrace them.

"Can you jog in those shoes?" Kyle asked.

"Why?"

"If we hurry, we can catch the cable car." Kyle pointed down the street.

Ava slipped off her heels and picked them up. She gladly accepted one more chance to extend the evening with Kyle. "Let's go."

Five minutes and no stubbed toes later, Ava dropped onto the bench and tugged Kyle down beside her. She adjusted the straps of her shoes around her ankles and sat back. "That's another first. Running barefoot in a dress to hop on a cable car."

"I need to catch up." Kyle set his arm on the back of the bench behind her.

Ava curled into his side and watched the high-rises and apartment buildings scroll by like a movie backdrop. "I need to do this more often. Thanks."

"I was happy to be here for your first and second cable car rides," he said.

The smile in his voice encouraged her to lean in closer. His hand dropped onto her shoulder. His fingers brushed against her skin; his touch brushed against her heart. For the first time in too long, contentment washed through her. Staying on the cable car with Kyle seemed like the only logical option. Falling asleep in the security of his arm seemed only natural.

Too soon Kyle nudged her awake, stood and checked for traffic on the street. He helped Ava off the cable car and guided her around a group waiting to board. Stepping onto the sidewalk, he turned. Ava walked into his arms.

He wrapped his arms around her waist and pulled her against him. "That's the first time I've had someone fall asleep on me."

Ava stared at the buttons on his dress shirt, thankful the night concealed the blush she knew extended from her chest to her forehead. "Sorry about that."

"Don't apologize." He tipped her chin up with the back of his hand. "It might be the best part of my night."

"Might be?" she whispered. The warmth in his gaze drained her voice. Anticipation roared through her. She was fully awake now. Fully present.

"This might be better." Kyle tipped his head down.

Ava lifted toward him until her mouth settled on his. And she found exactly where she wanted to be. Curving her arms around his neck, Ava lost herself in the kiss and all the emotions Kyle stirred inside her.

Too soon, Kyle pulled away and pressed a soft kiss to her mouth. His gaze roamed her face. "I'd call that a successful night of firsts. Cable cars and cat naps."

And their first kiss on a crowded city sidewalk at a cable car stop.

"We have to go, don't we?" Ava let her hands slowly glide down the front of Kyle's jacket, unable to let go yet. "We could jump on the cable car. One should be coming any minute."

"We agreed to that all-in policy." Kyle took her hands and stepped out of her embrace. "We can't leave them waiting outside the bank."

"Stupid policy." Or not. Ava touched her mouth as if that would lock in the memory of their kiss. They stood out in the open view of anyone. She searched the sidewalk, looking for a reporter or camera. What if someone had witnessed their kiss? What had she been thinking? "I'm usually the sensible one."

"We'll keep it sensible from here on out." Kyle motioned her forward. "After you."

They turned the corner and blended into the contest group already gathered outside the bank. Ava hugged Barbra, complimented Chad on his dapper bow tie and Grant on his sleek business suit. Kyle welcomed Glenda and Sam. They strolled toward the Glass Violet, separated by the group and too much cement sidewalk. Ava concentrated on the conversation around her, laughed on cue and responded appropriately. She avoided looking at Kyle. Worried someone might accuse her of sharing more than a casual kiss with him. Worried that someone might realize she desperately wanted to share another one with him.

Ava so wanted to grab Kyle's hand. To know what else he hadn't done. She wanted to share her own list of "Someday, I'd like to…"

She wanted to discover more firsts with Kyle. Even more, she wanted her hand tucked inside his again.

CHAPTER SIXTEEN

KYLE FELL ASLEEP and woke up that morning thinking about one thing: kissing Ava.

Last night, he'd only wanted to kiss her again. He'd fallen asleep considering the many possibilities of where they might share another kiss.

Now, coffee mug in hand and caffeine pumping him to full alert mode, he only wanted to forget. Another kiss with Ava could not happen. He'd been distracted by Charlotte's food truck euphoria and Ava's endless appeal. That was a mistake he wouldn't repeat.

Except, everything about holding Ava in his arms had felt right. Nothing about that moment on the sidewalk or the entire evening seemed like a mistake. Still, he had to forget. Because recalling their kiss made him want another one. And that only made him consider what more could be between them.

He already knew the answer: *nothing.*

The contest ended in less than two weeks and they'd no longer be required to share the same space. Lives would return to normal or whatever they'd looked like before the contest had interrupted everything. His life before the contest had not included the complication of a relationship. Or risking his heart.

Ava seemed to resent his money. Money was the only thing Kyle could give Ava. His heart had never been part of any prize package. Love was like maneuvering a big rig on a one-lane road over a snow-covered mountain. At some point, ice and poor visibility would force him off the road. He'd skid off the precipice in love and wind up alone.

He'd heed the warning signs now and take precautions. The road to love he'd leave open to the risk-takers and misinformed.

Laughter and voices echoed from the arcade area. The group had arrived for their daily work session. He turned on the water in the kitchen sink to rinse out his coffee mug and block his urge to listen for one voice in particular. Kyle dried his hands and reminded himself that reaching for Ava was not part of the day's agenda. Or any agenda.

Calling a quick greeting from the conference room door, Kyle pointed to the dry-erase board with the upcoming schedule. He'd written the lengthy list on his second cup of coffee. "We have less than two weeks before the winner is chosen. That means it's crunch time."

Grant whistled and stared at the bullet-point list that filled the dry-erase board. "It's going to get busy."

"Time spent in the design lab is only one part of the process. Now we expand beyond these walls." Kyle walked to the board, picked up a pen and added another bullet point to the schedule. "There's a world outside, waiting for your product. Are you ready to present to that world?"

"I'm not sure how a photo session with Mia is going to prepare us for the outside world," Ava said. Her eyebrows pulled together as her lips flattened into a frown.

He wasn't allowing her to throw up any roadblocks to his schedule. The one he'd created out of sheer self-preservation early this morning. She had never been comfortable in front of a camera. She'd have to get over it. The same way he had to get over her. "Iris and Barbra have agreed to act as stylists for the photo session and consult on appropriate corporate boardroom attire."

"Image is everything." Barbra set her glasses on the table. "If you present the image of success, you find success."

"Or you look uncomfortable and they call you out for being a fake," Ava argued.

"Iris and I already have a power suit picked out for you, Ava." Barbra grinned. "You'll be comfortable and confident in any boardroom, with any executive."

Ava shifted her gaze to Kyle. "This is necessary?"

It was more than necessary. She could blame herself. If she hadn't fit so perfectly in his arms, if she hadn't considered his food allergies and taken him to one of his favorite places to eat in the city, if she hadn't been so much herself, then he wouldn't have had to run now. "The contest is about creating an invention that can be marketed to the public. This is all part of that plan."

Ava nodded and rocked in her chair.

"The marketing meetings will happen over several days, with a focus on an invention name and a full-scale marketing plan." Kyle studied the board rather than Ava. Something inside his chest urged him to ease off. He couldn't. This was best for the success of both finalists. "The marketing group will also handle the mock interviews with the press. Barbra has a professor friend who has agreed to assist with presentation skills and public speaking. Her friend has also agreed to advise on corporate boardroom etiquette and best practices."

Chad cleared his throat. "We've also scheduled meetings with different material manufacturers for Grant's phone case for next week."

"Ava and I will be working with several fabric vendors this week to discuss the most durable fabric options for her Virtual Vitals Buddy." Sam took a long sip of his coffee as if he already needed the extra jolt of energy.

"I'm guessing the fun part might've already happened in the design lab." Grant shook his head, his gaze fixed on the dry-erase board, his voice strained.

"The final judging panel will be looking for a complete product," Barbra said. "Don't forget that a hefty grand prize is at stake."

Grant grinned. "The effort will be worth the payout."

"For one of you." Kyle launched that warning like a fire starter in the middle of the conference table.

Barbra frowned at him and rose. "There's nothing to keep the runner-up from taking everything they've created and conquering the world on their own."

Except that Kyle's company owned the rights to the two finalists' inventions once working prototypes were built. That had been a last-minute change from his legal team. A backup plan for his backup plan. He expected working prototypes would be ready late next week.

Chad rose and grabbed a handful of chocolate candy. "We should've scheduled a final game night. One last hooray with the group."

"There are still two weeks left." Kyle turned away. He should be pleased. No more game nights. No more dinner debates. That was exactly what he wanted. His usual routine hovered, but he didn't feel like opening his arms and embracing his old life.

"Not only do we have meetings and contest work, we've committed to helping Sophie with her gala." Satisfaction was evident in Ava's voice, as if she enjoyed the fact that she had a few roadblocks of her own to put up.

He was supposed to be avoiding *her*. She wasn't supposed to be throwing out more reasons to keep them apart. Kyle squeezed his forehead, forcing himself to remember that he wanted this.

"Make sure you have sturdy work gloves, Kyle." Grant refilled his water bottle. "We're constructing one of the backdrops tonight with Brad and Wyatt."

Kyle glanced at Ava.

She lifted her hands. "Not me. I'm working with my mom and Iris on color schemes and the best arrangement for the auction tables."

"Good thing you didn't start your job with Brad Harrington yet." Chad tapped his knuckles against Grant's shoulder. "You'd need to request an advance on your vacation time to handle all of this."

But Ava was working. Kyle stepped toward the table. Barbra intercepted him before he could back down.

She touched Ava's shoulder, a warning in her voice. "Despite all this, Ava, you need to sleep sometime. You can't keep pushing yourself too hard. It won't do you any good."

"You sound like Joann and my mother." Ava grimaced.

"Those are very wise women," Barbra said.

"What have they been saying?" Grant asked.

"That I can't keep surviving on power naps alone. I can handle this." Ava stood and pushed her chair into the table. Her voice was firm, her smile fixed. "It's only temporary, right? The contest ends in two weeks and Sophie's gala happens two weeks later."

"The pace is only going to pick up," Kyle cautioned. He knew, as he was the one picking up the pace for everyone—intentionally and deliberately.

"I've got everything handled." Ava looked at each one of them. Her gaze challenged as if she dared someone to disagree with her claim.

"Of course you do." Grant nudged her in the shoulder, breaking the standoff. "We're here if you need us."

Everyone nodded, except Kyle. He needed Ava

too much already. She did not need him, his money and closed-off heart.

"Let's get to work." Barbra led the group out of the conference room.

"What are you doing while we're meeting with marketing experts, speech writers and stylists?" Ava caught up to Kyle in the hallway.

Convincing myself that I don't need you. His fingers brushed against her arm. Kyle shoved his hands in his pants pockets. "Working on a few new things for Tech Realized."

"How's that going?" she asked.

"I'm now the high scorer on both Galaxy Defender and Night Racer, if that tells you anything." He didn't mention his high score on the blackjack and pinball machines, either. Too bad his contract didn't rely on his skill with hand-eye coordination and game controllers.

Ava nodded. "Is there anything I can do to help?"

Kiss me. Convince me what's between us is worth my letting my family down. "Make sure Sophie doesn't decide to expand her gala any more in the next few weeks."

"It's my mom we need to watch out for," Ava said.

He wanted to watch out for Ava. He touched her arm before he could stop himself. "Barbra wasn't wrong. You need to remember to sleep."

"I could tell you the same thing." She stepped closer to him, kept his grip on her arm.

It wasn't sleep he needed to remember. He needed to remember all the reasons their first kiss had to be their last. Standing in the hall, he lost himself and his common sense in her green gaze.

"Hurry up, you two," Grant hollered. "We can't start off the day already behind schedule."

Kyle shifted away from Ava and toward the open door. "After you."

CHAPTER SEVENTEEN

YOU CAN'T HAVE EVERYTHING, Ava. Don't ever forget it. Those had been her dad's parting words. His last words of encouragement and fatherly advice.

Ava stepped off the bus and glared at the cable car tracks. Her dad had been right. She couldn't have everything. The kiss she'd shared with Kyle six nights ago at the cable car stop had been a lie. She'd emptied her emergency bank account that same evening to cover the fee for the physician's assistant application she'd submitted. And why not? That night, she'd ridden home on a cloud of hope.

But her father had warned her. She knew better than to believe in hope and wishes inside her heart.

Even worse, she'd told herself she wasn't like her father. She would never be like her father. Now she was about to follow in his footsteps.

She was about to walk away.

She tried to convince herself this wasn't the same. This was necessary. *You don't make mistakes like these, Ava. We're counting on you to be above this.* Those were the encouraging words from her supervisor. She prided herself on being better. She had to be for her brother's sake. He'd trusted her to care for their mom while he was in Washington, DC. She couldn't fail her mom and brother. Just like her father had.

She'd never wanted to be like her father.

Still, walking away was *walking away.*

She had to do that now to protect everyone she loved.

Ava pulled her phone out and checked the time. She had fifteen to twenty minutes max. More than enough time to tell Kyle and leave to pick up Ben. Every minute she paced outside Kyle's building was less time with him. Not that she required a lot of time to explain. Her mind was made up.

She had to drop out of the contest before she made an even worse mistake on the job—the one job that paid her—and could have cost a patient their life. Lives were at stake and something had to give.

She pressed the call button for Kyle's suite and took the stairs to the second floor.

Kyle's door swung open and a surprised smile lit his face. "You're not my ride."

"Oh, you're going out." Ava fumbled with her sling-back bag in the hallway. The pinstriped navy suit and crisp white dress shirt set off his blue eyes. His unbuttoned collar and the tie hanging around his shoulders set off the urge to fall into his capable arms. "I can come back. Or I'll just call you later. Tomorrow."

She had to stop rambling. Pull herself together. All she really wanted to do was wrap herself in his embrace and tell him to lie to her. Let him tell her that everything would work out.

The only way to ensure things worked out was to do them herself. Like she always had.

"I'm not leaving yet." Kyle motioned her into the suite. Concern shifted along his features as his gaze traveled over her. "Come in, please."

He made her feel underdressed. Underprepared. Breathless for no reason. She should've called or, better yet, texted. Why couldn't she stop looking at his tie? Why couldn't she stop the image of knotting that tie into a neat Windsor and then pulling him to her for... "I should go."

She really had to leave. Before she lost her mind. Her legs never moved. Her body never turned to flee. Her traitorous gaze remained fixed on Kyle as if he was everything right in her world.

"You should come in." Kyle opened the door wider. The quiet appeal in his voice was hard to ignore.

Ava remained in the foyer. If she went any farther, she'd probably curl up on his couch and cry. That would be humiliating. She refused to cry over a contest. *A contest.*

It was about more than the contest. That much she recognized. The contest was simple compared to the goodbye. Saying goodbye to Kyle hit her in the heart. Her heart was the one place she'd sworn to protect and the one place that guarded her tears. "I'm dropping out of the contest."

"Wow. Okay." His hand settled on her lower back, and a gentle nudge urged her inside. He asked, "Can you tell me why?"

"It's too much." Ava edged toward him, not all the way as if she belonged nestled against his side like a couple, but enough that her shoulder and arm brushed against his suit coat. Enough that she could pretend that was all the contact she craved. "Everything is just too much."

"How can I help?" His voice was calm.

No. She didn't want his help. Or his compassion. She didn't know what she wanted. But not that. "You can't help. This is all on me."

"Did something happen?" He guided her through the game room and past the offices, walking with her into his apartment, into his personal space, as if he understood this wasn't a professional call.

His hand remained steady and reassuring on her back. His living space was cozy and comforting and reminded her of Kyle. She stopped and finally drew a deep breath. She was safe here. She believed that. Facing Kyle, she decided for full disclosure. "Bad day at work. I messed up. Made a rookie mistake."

He nodded and walked into the kitchen as if she'd confessed she'd spilled milk at lunch.

That was his response: a simple nod. As if he accepted she made mistakes all the time.

Frustration and weariness surged inside her. "My mistake could've cost a woman her life today. Don't you understand?"

One sane corner of her mind recognized that she wasn't being fair. Lashing out at Kyle wasn't right. But the rest of her didn't care. She wanted to have a tantrum. "This woman is in her late fifties and still has many years left on her life. A grandmother-to-be. The woman's only error was calling 9-1-1 and getting my rig. I could've changed her entire family's world in one moment. With one wrong call." She snapped her fingers. "Just like that."

He kept his arms loose at his sides. From his voice to his stance, everything about him was neutral. "But the woman didn't die."

"That was all Dan's doing." Ava yanked on her ponytail and tugged her voice out of the rant setting. "That had nothing to do with me."

"I'm not going to tell you that mistakes happen." Kyle poured hot water from the instant-hot-water faucet at his sink into a mug. "I fully understand that, in your job, mistakes can't happen."

He offered no false sympathy or empty platitudes. He understood her work was life or death. There were no in-betweens or redoes. Thanks to the quick work of a dependable, solid partner, mistakes could sometimes be reversed or overwritten, yet not forgotten. She had to be better than that for the people she served. "I have to get my focus back. I need to concentrate on my job and what I'm good at."

"The contest is a distraction." He opened a cabinet and pulled out a selection of teas.

Including the same tea she drank every morning. Her favorite tea. That meant nothing. She liked a common, well-known brand. It was only a coincidence.

"Yes. No." *He* was the real distraction. He made her want more. He made her wish for the impossible. He tapped on her heart—the one part of her that she'd always assumed was untouchable. Unmovable. Unreachable. "Without my job, I can't support my mom."

"Would it change things if I told you that the prize money is going to be doubled?" He took a bottle of honey out of the cabinet. "The bonus, too."

"Seriously?" He had honey, too. What else did he know about her? She rubbed a hand over her eyes, focused on his words, not his thoughtfulness. "Did you just decide to double the prize money?"

He shook his head. "I decided to do it the night the finalists were revealed. I wanted to wait until the winner was announced to reveal the change."

"Why?" she asked.

He shrugged and squeezed the perfect amount of honey into the teacup. "Seemed like the right thing to do."

"That's a lot of money." Money couldn't be more important than lives. But what if it wasn't the contest? What if she was losing her edge? Losing the part of her that made her good at her job? What if, buried under the exhaustion and mental fatigue, she discovered her passion for her work had burned out?

He held the mug out to her. "Both your idea and Grant's are worth that kind of money."

"Do you really believe that?" She curved her hands around the mug, brushed her fingers against his.

"Yes." He never hesitated. Nothing broke in his voice or face to hint he might be telling her what she wanted to hear. She saw only resolve and certainty.

She paced into the living room and turned her

back on the glass balcony doors and her reflection. She didn't want to see the temptation in her gaze. Or the truth that the money tempted her to remain in the contest. Kyle's support and solid presence tempted her to believe in impossible things. "Money isn't everything."

"No." He closed the distance between them. "But it can help you now."

She stared into the mug as if wisdom could be discovered in the clear liquid if she only looked long enough. "If I win."

"I can't guarantee that."

More honesty. More straight truths. She hadn't come here to be lied to. Could he guarantee he'd be there for her even in the most difficult situations—the ones that tested faith and the bounds of love? It wasn't fair to ask. It was better not to know. "I'm not asking you to promise I'll win. I need to focus on my job and the paycheck that's guaranteed."

And stop focusing on Kyle and the wishes inside her heart, which would only be broken in the end.

He stepped even closer, stopped a sigh away from her hands, holding the tea mug. The nearness drew her gaze up to his solemn face.

"How can I help you so you can remain in the contest?" he asked.

There was that word again. *Help.* But Ava

never asked for help. Never sought it. She helped those around her. "There's…"

He set his finger across her mouth, halting her words and stirring up those longings inside her heart.

"Don't say there's nothing I can do." His voice was low and sincere. "We both know it isn't true."

She wanted so much more than one small touch. She stepped away and lashed out to break up the need swirling inside her. And the growing hope he might be different. Maybe he'd stick like her father never could. "This is all me. Can't you see that? Let's just break down today for an example."

He crossed his arms over his chest and leaned against the marble counter. He looked as if he had nothing more important to do than let her rail against him and the world.

She charged on, stomping on her incessant need for what she couldn't quite say. Only knew Kyle stood at the core. "I worked all night. Only fifteen calls, so the evening was on the slower side. Made a mistake. Filled out paperwork. Listened to a lecture from my supervisor. Took Mom to two appointments and one lunch date for Sophie's gala. Tried to sleep and failed. Ran to the store. Worked here in the lab. Tried to sleep and failed. Gave Joann the evening off to

watch her sick grandchildren. Forgot I'd promised to take Ben for the weekend so Dan and
Rick can do their volunteer firefighter weekend up north."

She paused and checked the time on her
phone. "I have to be at Dan's to get Ben in ten
minutes. I need to take my mom to a doctor's
appointment and pick up her medicine. I promised Sophie I'd drop off extra blankets for the
new rescues she received this afternoon." Ava
stared into the tea again, wanting to sink into
the liquid and shut the world away. No one could
focus being this stretched thin and worn-out.
Still, she struggled to give herself a break. "I
haven't worked on my write-up for the contest.
The weekend is already piling up to be more of
the same."

"Bring Ben here." Kyle's words were simple.
Direct.

Hadn't he heard a thing she'd said? Hadn't he
heard this was all on her? "Excuse me?"

"Pick up Ben and drop him here. Go to the
doctor with your mom, the pharmacy and then
to Sophie's place," Kyle said.

He was composed and reasonable, logical and
rational. Everything Ava wasn't.

"I'll bring Ben to your place later this evening."

"My place," she repeated. Those were the only

words rattling around clear enough in her head. The only words she could hang on to.

"Ben is staying with you at your place this weekend, isn't he?" Kyle grinned.

Her head bobbed up and down. She waved at his suit and tie, hoping the motion would clear the air between them and redirect their conversation. "You have a thing."

"Now I have a thing with Ben." He tugged his tie off and unbuttoned another notch on his dress shirt.

Ava stared at his open collar, wondering when the conversation had derailed. Wondered why he wanted to help her. "I just came over here to tell you I was dropping out of the contest."

"Why don't you sleep on it." He slipped off his jacket. "If we talk to Barbra and Sam, I'm sure we can figure out a solution that won't make your days even more stressed."

"I didn't come here to beg for help." She came to walk away.

"I'm offering to help." He tipped her chin up to bring her gaze back to his. "Let me help. If it's an epic failure, you don't have to accept my help ever again."

It was dangerous to believe in more. So very dangerous. She couldn't stop herself. Nothing about Kyle Quinn seemed to scream failure. "You're sure about this?"

"I wouldn't have offered." He lifted up his tie and coat. "You're saving me from a fund-raiser tonight for the college."

"You like to support the college," she said. She'd heard him talk to Barbra more than once about his alma mater and how to get the other alumni more involved. Always with enthusiasm, never with dread. "It's the one thing you like to do."

"I like you more." He walked into his bedroom before she could respond.

His words bounced around inside her head and finally landed like an arrow in her heart. She knew he was dangerous. Even worse, she wanted to follow him to hug him. Or do something even more crazy, like kiss him. *He liked her.* She forced herself to back away from his bedroom door and yelled, "I'm going to get Ben and will be back in fifteen minutes."

At his muffled okay, Ava turned and ran. Before he could change his mind. Before she changed hers.

The slam of Kyle's front door made him smile. He'd unsettled Ava when he'd confessed he liked her. Heck, he'd unsettled himself when he'd said that. He wasn't sure what had come over him. Knew only he'd meant it. He liked Ava. A lot.

No good could come from any of this. He

should've let her walk. Should've let her quit the contest and move on with her life. But he didn't want her out of his life. Damn, but he was selfish. He didn't deserve someone like Ava.

He'd make things right for her now. After all, it was his fault she'd messed up at work. If he hadn't created such a hectic schedule for the contest crew the past week, she wouldn't have considered dropping out. He'd help her this one time. There had to be nothing between them. *Nothing beyond their one kiss.* Maybe if he kept shouting that at himself, he'd start to believe it.

Back in jeans and a T-shirt, he grabbed his phone and called his sister.

Iris answered on the second ring and sang hello.

Through his laughter, he asked, "Something came up, can you fill in for me tonight at the college fund-raiser?"

Silence reached him first before she pressed. "What came up?"

Certain Iris would find out from one of Ava's friends, most likely her new boss, Mia, he opted for the truth. "I need to help Ava."

"You can't help Ava on her contest without everyone else there," Iris argued. "It's not fair. Not what was decided. It's everyone together or no one together."

Kyle rubbed his forehead. He'd told Iris about

the meeting and their decision, knowing he'd most likely invite Iris on several of their outings for another person in the group. "We aren't working on her contest."

He was working on relieving his own guilt. He shouldn't have pushed so hard. He could've detached from the group and Ava without involving everyone else.

"You can't go on a date with Ava, either." Iris's voice was alarmed as if dating was much worse than working on the contest. She added, "You'll ruin the contest if the public learns you're dating one of the finalists. You won't ever be trusted again."

"It's not a date." He didn't need her dire warning blasting through his head, either. He'd already warned himself enough not to get any more involved. He just hoped he remembered to take his own advice. "Ben is coming over for a while. Then I'm bringing Ben back to Ava's place." But he wasn't hanging out. He could draw a line somewhere and stick to it.

Iris laughed. "If you're going out with Ava, can I take Grant to the event tonight?"

"I'm not going out with Ava." Because it required repeating. Repetition made something a habit. He had to get in the habit of not wanting more from Ava. Not wanting to be with Ava more. "Why Grant?"

"He's fun and large crowds don't intimidate him." Iris paused and added, "He's like having my own personal bodyguard. He watches out for me."

Kyle agreed. There was a lot to like about Grant O'Neal. "You can't date Grant."

"It's not a date," Iris countered. "He'd be helping me out, so I don't have to attend alone. As I'm not technically part of the contest crew, I won't be breaking any rules, unlike other people."

"This really isn't a date with Ava. We're not breaking any rules. The decision was to appear in public as a group. Ava and I won't be together in public tonight." He wasn't exactly sure who he was trying to convince: his sister or himself. "She needed help. I offered."

"Got it. No rule breaking. No dating," Iris said. "Now I need to hang up and get ready. You've left me very little time."

Before he ended the call, Iris said, "Hey, Kyle, if it was a date with Ava, I wouldn't object. After all, breaking the rules isn't always a bad thing."

With that she clicked off and left Kyle staring at his cell phone. Breaking the rules with Ava had been too much of a good thing already. But he had one rule for his heart: never let it get involved. He wasn't breaking that rule for anyone.

CHAPTER EIGHTEEN

BEN PRESSED THE call button outside Kyle's building. At least Ava had stopped pacing. If only her heart would stop racing. She'd already put a moratorium on sharing more kisses with Kyle the morning after their sidewalk kiss. Not that they'd had many opportunities for a repeat in the past week. This afternoon was the first time she'd been alone with Kyle since their impromptu food truck dinner.

Kyle and she were only friends. She'd spent the entire bus ride to pick up Ben convincing herself of that very fact.

Their kiss had been a lapse in judgment. That she wanted to share another kiss with Kyle was proof of her continuously poor judgment. Falling for Kyle would be a mistake she might not recover from. Better to keep her feelings for him in the friend zone and keep her focus on her goals.

This afternoon, she'd accepted the help of a friend. The entire thing was nothing for her heart to melt over. Friends helped friends.

Ava stepped off the elevator and smiled. The

kind of grateful smile one friend gave to another. If her mouth seemed drier than usual, it only meant she needed to rehydrate. It had nothing to do with Kyle, in his jeans and T-shirt and her internal debate on whether she preferred him in dress or casual clothes. She followed Kyle and Ben into the apartment. She waited for Ben to finish his story about telling the kids at school where he was going and the fist bumps to stop.

"I should be back at home in about three hours," she said.

"Take your time." Kyle looked at her as if he'd forgotten she'd walked inside the apartment, too. "There's no need to rush around the city like your hair is on fire."

Ben grinned beside Kyle.

"Why does it feel like you two might be up to something?" Ava asked. "How is that possible when you've only been together for less than five minutes?"

"We don't need five whole, long minutes to hatch really great plans." Kyle managed to sound both insulted and flabbergasted. "The best plans are hatched in a minute, maybe two."

Ben laughed.

Ava crossed her arms over her chest. "What's your *really* great plan?"

"Don't you need to go?" Kyle grabbed both of Ava's shoulders and steered her backward toward the door. "You don't want your mom to be late, and Sophie's rescues are waiting."

Ava dug in her heels to slow her steps. There was a glint in Kyle's gaze she hadn't noticed earlier. Gone was the supportive, empathetic man. Now he looked a little bit like a kid eager to be left alone in the house for the first time. She wanted to stay, too. Irritation rolled into her voice. "He's only ten, Kyle."

Kyle frowned and glanced over his shoulder. "Well, sorry, Ben, I guess that means we can't put on our super suits and fly around the city. You have to be twelve for super suits."

Ben grabbed his stomach and folded over with laughter.

"Super suits?" Ava failed to bite back her own laughter and find her annoyance.

Kyle smiled and shrugged. "If you must know, we're playing Dragon Reign. Three rounds. We're still working out what the winner gets."

"That's your genius plan?" Ava looked from Kyle over to Ben. She wasn't sure what she'd been expecting, but their idea was much less inventive than she'd imagined.

Kyle stuck his hand over his heart like she'd wounded him. "Any plan that includes Dragon Reign is genius. Right, Ben?"

Ben nodded. "It's only the best video game ever."

"What if I'm running late?" Ava lingered near the door.

"Then we get to play even more rounds." Exasperation forced Ben's eyes to roll.

Ava heard the unspoken "duh" coming from the pair. She bit her lip to hide her grin and keep from encouraging them.

"I know the winner gets to choose where we get dinner from." Ben's mouth dropped open and his eyes widened. "I wasn't supposed to say that, was I?"

Kyle looked at Ben then Ava. "Say what?"

"Kyle and I never discussed dinner plans." They also never discussed their first kiss. She never planned to invite him into her home. Into her private world.

"But we all need to eat, don't we?" Ben looked back and forth between them, his gaze eager.

They all didn't *need* to eat together at her house. As if they always shared Friday night dinners at her place. As if this was part of their thing. Ava bit into her tongue, not wanting to disappoint Ben and not wanting to encourage Kyle.

"I accept those terms for the Dragon Reign challenge." Kyle held up his hand to stop Ben's cheer. "As long as your aunt agrees."

Ava studied Kyle. Like a champion poker player, he revealed none of his inner thoughts.

She pressed a mild disinterest into her voice. "You've already helped enough. You've changed your evening for us." She wasn't changing her lifestyle for him.

"I was going to work," he said.

Ben wrinkled his nose. "That's all adults ever do."

"I suppose I could handle video games and dinner," Kyle added.

Ava could handle her attraction to Kyle, too. After all, it was only a quick dinner with a friend. "Then it's settled. Winner of Dragon Reign picks the restaurant."

Ben kicked the toe of his sneaker into the floor. Disappointment settled quick and hard, slumping his thin shoulders. "I forgot my dad already packed my own dinner. It doesn't matter to me where you guys go to eat."

Kyle shook his head. "Nope. That won't cut it. Tonight, we eat as a team."

"But I can't have too many carbohydrates or sugar in my food." Ben touched his hip where his insulin pump was clipped to his jeans. "All the good restaurants like to use lots of that stuff."

Ava's heart broke for the little boy. He rarely complained about his diabetes, took most things in stride. But there were moments, like now. She wanted to let him grumble. She wanted to hug him, promise him his dad's dinner was hands-down better than any restaurant in the city. She stepped forward, but Kyle got to Ben first.

"Is that all you got?" Kyle flipped over his medical ID bracelet and extended his arm into Ben's view.

Ava moved farther away from the door and closer to the pair. Kyle often evaded any questions about his nut allergies. Still, she'd never seen him without his bracelet on or his backpack within easy reach. He never took unnecessary risks with food. The contest group referred to his approved restaurant list on a daily basis.

"Hey, I have a medical bracelet, too." Ben touched the titanium links on Kyle's ID bracelet. "Yours is cooler."

"I like the paracord style you have." Kyle set his wrist against Ben's to compare the two bracelets.

Everything softened inside Ava. She couldn't stop herself. Watching Kyle and Ben bond melted through her, urging her to hold them both close.

"Does yours change colors or show the time in the links?" Ben asked.

"No, but I like the idea." Surprise lifted Kyle's eyebrows.

He stared at his bracelet. Ava assumed Kyle's inventive mind was considering Ben's idea, debating the feasibility and possibilities.

"What's your bracelet for?" Ben asked.

"Pretty bad nut allergy." Kyle shook his wrist, settled his ID band back in place. "I used to sit alone at a table in the far corner of the school cafeteria every day during lunch."

"But you never had to stick needles in your fingers and test your blood all the time." Ben wrinkled his nose and stuffed his hands in his pockets.

"No, but I have to carry this everywhere." Kyle picked up his backpack from the floor near the couch and rummaged inside. He pulled out a plastic cylindrical tube labeled EpiPen. "One little sliver of a tree nut can kill me without this."

"What happens if someone puts a nut in your dinner and you don't know?" Ben asked.

"I jam this needle in my leg." Kyle set the plastic tube against his leg and eyed Ben. "Then you call 9-1-1. If I'm really lucky, your aunt and dad arrive in their ambulance to take me to the hospital really fast."

"Whoa." Ben's eyes widened, and alarm covered his voice, dipping into a strained whisper. "You get even bigger needles when you get to the hospital."

"I like to avoid those needles as much as possible," Kyle said.

"Me, too," Ben added. "The ones that poke my finger don't hurt too bad anymore."

Kyle tucked his EpiPen into his backpack. "Shall we get our video game challenge on?"

Ben's eyebrows pulled together. His expression uncertain. "You should win, though."

"Why?" Kyle asked. Bewilderment was heavy in his tone.

"I don't want to pick a restaurant that could send you to the hospital." Ben's voice was serious, his gaze grave like someone years older and years wiser.

Kyle rubbed the back of his neck. His gaze collided with Ava's and her insides wilted into her feet. Ben's heartfelt words had shaken Kyle. All Ava wanted to do was draw them both into her arms and promise she'd take care of them. Now and forever. Ava kept her feet rooted to the floor. She could make that promise to Ben. But Kyle was a risk she wasn't ready for. Skipping the group hug, she said, "I have an idea."

They both eyed her, but their mutual distrust shifted across their faces. As if a girl's idea could have merit. Kyle crossed his arms over his chest, and Ben mimicked him. Kyle's lips wobbled from the smile she watched him try to hide.

Ava enjoyed their united front too much to take offense. Later, she'd beat them at Dragon Reign and prove that girls were better than boys. "Make a list of restaurants you can eat at. See which ones are the same and the winner gets to pick from those."

"That could work." Kyle rubbed his chin and nudged his elbow into Ben. "What do you think, Ben?"

"Thanks, Aunty." Ben lunged toward Ava and wrapped her in a hug. "I really like to win, and I'd be bored if I had to *let* Kyle win."

"Well, we don't want you to be bored." Ava hugged the boy and locked her gaze on Kyle over Ben's head. She mouthed the words *thank you*.

He nodded, but there was gratitude in his gaze, too. They'd both sort of rescued each other. Like a team. Like a couple would do. She released Ben and reached for the door, rather than Kyle.

Ben picked up his cooler and held it up toward Kyle. "What do I do with this?"

"Bring it along." Kyle grinned and tipped his head toward the theater room. "We might need snacks before dinner."

"Papa Rick calls it first dinner and second dinner." The cooler bounced against Ben's leg as he hurried to keep pace with Kyle. "Aunty says there's no such thing."

Kyle leaned over and whispered loudly, "Girls don't know about two dinners. It's a guy thing."

Ben turned sideways and studied Ava. "Should we tell her it's real?"

"She won't believe us anyway," Kyle said.

"Stop whispering about me." Ava swung open the door and called back to the pair. "And don't pick Savory Window for dinner."

"That's my favorite." Ben banged his cooler against his leg.

"But we always eat there. Always." Ava shut the door and chewed on the corner of her lip. She knew Ben would pick Savory Window. That was the way his ten-year-old mind worked.

She had no idea what Kyle would choose. Or who he'd pick. At least her sudden craving for avocado fried from Savory Window would be satisfied. Kyle was only a friend. She didn't care who he picked.

CHAPTER NINETEEN

KYLE CARRIED THE takeout from Savory Window and followed Ben inside Ava's building. He appreciated that, despite the modern updates like the security entrance in the lobby, the building managed to retain its history. His grandfather's ode to history was his fully restored Ford Mustang.

"Can we take the elevator, please?" Ben rushed through the lobby. The enthusiasm in his voice matched the bounce in his steps. He stopped at the elevator bay and let his hand hover over the up button. "Aunty Ava always makes us take the stairs for the extra exercise."

"You don't like extra exercise?" Kyle smiled. Ava made the group take the stairs quite often, too.

"I like elevators more." Ben's finger tapped the button, but not hard enough to light it up. "Besides, I can take the stairs at my house whenever I want."

"Elevator it is," Kyle said around a laugh. He'd enjoyed the last few hours with Ben. He'd never spent much time around kids, of any age, really. Ben made him laugh, was interesting and liked to play Dragon Reign as much as Kyle. If he had a kid, Kyle would want him to be as likeable and cool as Ben. Cheering, Ben slapped the button. The noise disrupted Kyle's unexpected thoughts. He'd never considered kids before. Or a family of his own.

He followed Ben onto the elevator. The most disturbing part was the thought of kids hadn't sent him into full crisis mode. Clearly, he needed to stick to his revised plan that he'd come up with waiting on their take-out order: he'd decided to drop off the food and leave like a dine and dash, without the dining part. A quick exit should get his thoughts back on track.

Ben ran his fingers over the floor numbers and grinned at Kyle. "Maybe we can miss Aunty's floor and ride longer."

Kyle adjusted the take-out order. "The food is hot, and I think your aunt might be hungry." More time gave Kyle more chances to change his mind and stay longer.

"Maybe after dinner?" Hope hitched Ben's eyebrows toward his red hair.

The kid was relentless. Kyle even liked that about him. "We could see who's faster—your aunt running the stairs or the elevator."

"That would be awesome." Ben stretched the

last word into its own sentence as only a kid could successfully do.

Then Kyle would stay longer. Still, he had a solid out. "Your aunt won't agree."

Ben swiped an avocado fry from the top of the bag and picked up his empty cooler he'd dropped on the elevator floor. They'd polished off their first dinner—the one Ben's dad had packed— during their second game of Dragon Reign. "She will if we make a bet with her."

"What kind of bet?" Kyle had several ideas. Each one pushed the boundaries of their professional-only relationship. Each one sprinted over the line he'd drawn earlier about not staying. First, he'd agreed to dinner. That was bad enough. He couldn't agree to anything else or he'd lose sight of that line completely.

Ben shrugged. "She likes all kinds of bets."

Without the elevator music to dull his thoughts, his sister's earlier warning drifted through him. Iris was worried other people wouldn't trust him. Well, he couldn't trust himself.

New rule: no betting with Ava. He stepped off the elevator, determined to drop off Ben, the dinner and leave. He wasn't normally so careless with the boundaries he set for himself. Those boundaries had served him well over the years. Then he'd met Ava.

Ben tossed the soft-sided cooler on the floor

and used both hands to pound on the door of apartment number 418. "Aunty, it's us."

"It's about time." Ava stepped into the open doorway. "I'm starving."

Ben jumped forward and hugged her. "You're always hungry."

Ava's hair was damp and twisted into a pile on top of her head. Her cheeks had a soap-polished look. Comfort wrapped her up from her yoga pants and oversize sweatshirt to her faux-fur-lined slippers. Being home suited her. She made him want to come home to her, too. Tension curved around his spine.

Ava squeezed Ben. "That's supposed to be our secret."

"Kyle won't tell." Ben glanced over his shoulder, his gaze solemn. "Besides, he has money, so he can buy you food whenever you need it."

Ava glanced away from Kyle and picked up Ben's cooler. "I can buy my own food."

Most women would want Kyle to pay for their dinner. That wasn't Ava's style. One more thing he shouldn't like about her.

"Yes, but Kyle buys appetizers and desserts, too," Ben argued. "He even let me get two orders of avocado fries."

"I buy desserts, too." Ava's mouth opened, her voice lifted.

"Only sometimes." Ben released her and

frowned at Kyle. "Then she makes us take the stairs."

"Let's eat." Ava ruffled Ben's hair. "We can talk about running the stairs after dinner."

Ben groaned and rushed inside. The boy had enough energy to run the stairs several times and keep on going.

Kyle smiled. He'd take the stairs to the penthouse suite in the city's tallest high-rise if it meant time with Ava. Especially if she was this relaxed and appealing. He shifted the bag of food and remained in the hall. Now he handed her the takeout order and left. Told her goodbye and walked away.

Ava never reached for the bag of takeout. She simply waited in the doorway and watched him as if unsure about him and what he offered.

Kyle blinked. He'd have to walk inside willingly. Dropping and running would be awkward once he stepped inside. It was awkward now.

Karen called from the kitchen. "Come on in, Kyle. Ava already set you a place at the table."

Kyle peered at the round kitchen table, already set with four places. Ava wasn't acting like an eager hostess. She looked more like she wanted to slam the door on him. Kyle eased by Ava and set the takeout on the counter. Karen stepped around the counter to give him a warm hug.

Ava remained in the open doorway. Kyle

glanced at Ava over Karen's head. She gripped the door handle. He wasn't sure if she meant to close the door behind her when she left or stay inside.

Ben tugged on Karen's arm. "We talked Kyle into coming over. Well, I talked Kyle into it. Aunty just agreed."

Finally, Ava shut the door, stepped to the counter and pulled out the take-out containers. She organized the containers by meal type across the counter. "Did you talk Kyle into double desserts and double appetizers?"

Ben grinned and handed a plate to everyone.

Ava shook her head at the boy. "Now we'll have to run double the stairs after dinner."

Ben high-fived Kyle. "I win."

Ava opened the salad tin and frowned at Kyle. "Win what?"

Kyle held his paper plate in front of his chest to block Ava's disapproval. "My dessert."

Ben pointed at his chest and then Kyle. "We made a bet whether or not you'd make us run stairs."

"There will be no stair climbing this evening." Karen filled her plate and Ava carried it to the dinner table. Karen added, "We have company tonight."

"Kyle isn't a guest. Kyle is…" Ben giggled and glanced at Ava.

What was Kyle if he wasn't a guest?

Ava loaded one plate with salad and a second plate with two sliders. Her voice was uncertain, as if she struggled to explain herself. "He's Kyle."

Kyle smiled at Karen, an apology in his tone. "We sort of need Ava to climb the stairs."

"Why?" Ava lengthened the one word.

Again, Kyle deflected her disapproval with his plate.

"We made a second bet about whether or not you could run to the lobby faster than the elevator." Ben added more fries to his plate.

Ava set her palms on the counter and leaned forward. "How many bets did you guys make?"

"We can't reveal that," Ben said.

"Fine." Ava straightened. "But if I get to the lobby before the elevator, I get to pick dessert first."

Kyle fist-bumped with Ben on his way to the table.

Ben crammed a bite of slider into his mouth. He smiled around the large bite and nodded. Ben said, "Told you she can't resist a bet."

"I don't mean to be impolite, but I'm on a serious losing streak here. I could use a little help." Kyle swiped a crouton from her salad plate.

Ava grinned and sat down at the head of the

table. "That is why I only accept a bet that I know I'll win."

"That's not true," Karen chided. "You lost the bet with Dan and had to attend the diabetes calendar shoot," said Karen with a satisfied smile.

If she hadn't lost a bet, Kyle might not have met her. She might not have entered his contest. They might not have kissed.

Papa Quinn would call that fate.

Kyle just called it bad luck.

His unlucky streak extended past dinner. Ava won the elevator race, refused to reveal her secret to success and chose his favorite dessert as her own. Ava excused Ben to join Karen in the family room to pick out a movie to watch. Kyle and Ava cleaned up.

"I thought you didn't like Savory Window." He'd tried to persuade Ben to pick a different restaurant, concerned Ava would've been disappointed. As if her happiness mattered to him.

"If I hadn't suggested Savory Window, Ben would've picked someplace else."

"Sneaky." Had she given him a heads-up, he wouldn't have played more games with Ben to win and change the restaurant pick. Again, he'd done that for Ava. Not because he'd been enjoying himself.

"Yet effective." Ava toasted him with the last of her iced tea glass.

Kyle tossed the paper napkins in the trash. "You also assumed I'd lose."

"I think all of Ben's dreams are inside video games."

Kyle wanted to know what Ava dreamed about. That was a conversation for a different kind of dinner. The kind of dinner couples had. They weren't a couple. Ava's dreams weren't his business.

"How is the contest progressing?" Karen asked from the family room. Ben sat on the couch and clicked through movie titles.

"Fine." Ava jumped in. "Just fine."

Kyle concentrated on covering the few leftovers. Ava hadn't mentioned quitting to her mom.

Karen smiled. "Kyle, what are Ava's odds of winning it all?"

Ava turned on the faucet in the sink to wash the silverware. A warning clattered through her voice. "Mom."

"Ava's odds are the same as Grant's. Very good." Kyle's odds of developing his own idea were less than good, especially if he insisted on lingering with Ava and her family. As if evenings like this were more important than his contract. This wasn't his family. He had a family he couldn't disappoint. Expanding his circle only gave him more people to let down.

Dishes returned to the cabinets and Ben's blood check complete, Kyle leaned against the counter. He watched Karen and Ben whispering in the family room. "They seem close."

"Very." Ava wiped down the counter. The affection in her small smile shifted through her gentle voice. "They look out for each other and always team up against everyone else."

"Makes me miss my grandmother." Kyle straightened away from the counter. Why had he blurted that out? He never shared personal things, even in past relationships. Not that he was involved with Ava.

Ava glanced at him; the affection remained, along with an understanding. "Did you spend a lot of time with her?"

"Every day after school, I rode my bike to my grandparents' house. She always had a snack and hug ready for me." Apparently, Kyle's spill-all moment wasn't quite over. His mouth kept rambling despite the protests in his brain to shut up. "When I was old enough, I worked with my grandfather at the steel mill in the summer."

"Wow." Ava's gaze shifted over him as if she tried to picture him in a hard hat. "That's intense work for a teenager."

And deadly. For any person. "The risk was worth it to spend more time with my grandfather."

He really had to stop oversharing. His past had no relevance to anything, especially not the contest. Something about Ava drew him in. Something about Ava made it easier to open up the memories from his past.

Ava smiled at him. "I used to bird-watch and make homemade ice cream with Grandma and fly-fish with my grandpa. I still wish for another day with them."

He *definitely* didn't need to know that about her. Already he tried to picture the girl with the red ponytail, toting around binoculars and a bird book. He'd like to have been there beside her. Clearly, his brain hadn't learned enough about Ava. "Why did you enlist in the army and leave your family behind?"

Ava looked at Karen; love and pride shone clearly on her face. "To honor my mom."

He'd leave it at that. She'd revealed enough about herself. What more did he need to know? She valued her family and was someone Papa Quinn would have called "good, honorable people." Papa Quinn would tell Kyle those were the type of people he should surround himself with if he wanted to succeed. "What do you mean?"

"I enlisted and served my country because my mom always wanted to but couldn't." Ava dried her hands on a towel. "So I did it for her."

Kyle was humbled and even more drawn to

this brave, kind woman. He'd given his family money. That hardly measured up to her sacrifice. "I'm not sure what to say."

"That's what you do for family." Her tone was matter-of-fact.

He'd bought his parents a retirement condominium in Florida. Paid for his younger sister's graduate education. That was what he did for family. But putting your life on the line during active duty was something more. Something special that highlighted the bond Ava shared with her mother. And reminded him where he fell short. "I should go and let you get on with the evening you'd planned."

"You can't miss our TV show marathon." Ben clutched the remote. "Aunty, you gotta tell Kyle that he has to stay."

Ava opened and closed her mouth. Finally, she blurted, "I'm sure Kyle has something he'd rather do."

"As long as it isn't work," Ben said.

Kyle's mind blanked. He failed to come up with an excuse to leave that wasn't work related.

"See, he has nothing else to do." Ben looked pleased.

The Fates continued to do their worst. Kyle continued to lose.

That was how he found himself in the middle seat on the couch, wedged between Ben and Ava.

No one wanted the middle seat on an airplane. Kyle struggled to find a good reason this particular seating arrangement was bad. He couldn't remember why he didn't belong with this family. He couldn't recall exactly why he should leave.

He shouldn't like being smashed on the worn couch, with his feet propped on the ottoman. Their apartment welcomed and embraced him. He should resent the obvious contrast. For all the state-of-the-art things inside his apartment, his place wasn't warm. Ava's apartment wasn't waiting to be lived in like his.

Ava suggested *Dance-Off*. Ben dropped his forehead against Kyle's shoulder and groaned. Kyle added his own groan. Karen settled into her recliner as if content to let them decide what to watch.

"What's wrong with *Dance-Off*?" Ava said.

"Everything," Kyle said.

Ben nodded. "And then there's the whole part about the people dating and someone always cries."

"That doesn't make it a bad show." Ava leaned forward and aimed the remote at them. "I suppose you two boys want to watch *Junkyard Exterminators*."

Kyle wanted to be with Ava. *Junkyard Exterminators* or *Dance-Off*, he didn't care so long as she was beside him. Clearly, his chocolate mousse cake had already settled into his thighs and that prevented him from moving. He'd entered food coma territory. He wasn't staying for Ava. He could get up and leave whenever he chose. He wanted his food to digest first.

"Can we watch *Junkyard Exterminators*?" Ben asked. "They built a go-kart last week and raced it."

"Not if I can't watch *Dance-Off*." Ava scrolled through the listing of TV shows to stream.

"There's a documentary about royal myths on tonight." Karen ducked her head and adjusted her blanket, but not before Kyle caught her grin.

Ava and Ben both hollered *no* at the same time.

"It's good for the mind to watch educational things every once in a while." Karen sipped her tea. "We could use a little more brain power in our lives."

"Those documentaries are good if you want to fall asleep quickly." Ava earned a high five from Ben.

Ben turned toward Kyle. "What do you like to watch?"

"I don't think Kyle is at home as much as us," Ava said.

He wondered if Ava would be surprised to know how many nights he spent in front of the TV at home. Way more often than he cared to admit. Right then, there was nothing appealing about heading back to his place. Nothing at all. "It depends on my mood. I usually try to find a show I haven't seen, then try it."

"What if you don't like it?" Ben's eyebrows pulled together.

"I turn it off and try another one." Kyle adjusted his feet on the ottoman. The middle seat wasn't all bad. "But if I like it, then I stay up way too late and binge-watch the entire season."

"Can we do that?" Ben shifted around Kyle to look at Ava.

"Watch an entire season of a show tonight?" Ava asked.

Ben nodded quick and fast.

"We have to find a show first. One we all agree on." Ava handed Ben the remote and curled her legs up on the couch. "You can drive, Ben, as long as you find us a show quickly."

"Got it." Ben bounced around on the couch. "Are cartoons in or out?"

"Out," Ava said.

They settled on *Everyday Family*, a comedy both Kyle and Ava remembered watching at Ben's age. Two episodes in, Kyle assumed the quiet was from everyone watching the show and reliving memories. Then he glanced at Ava. She was sound asleep, her head resting against his shoulder. Ben was wide-awake.

Karen dropped a thick blanket over Ava, adjusting the fleece around her daughter's shoulder and legs. She kissed Ava's forehead, touched Kyle's cheek and whispered, "Stay as long as you want. This is the most relaxed Ava has been in a long time."

Ben yawned and stood up. "After I help Ms. Karen to her room, can we watch another episode of *Everyday Family*?"

Kyle looked at Karen. He had no idea what time a ten-year-old should go to bed.

Karen smiled. "One more episode. We won't tell your dad or Aunty Ava."

Ben pumped his fists in what Kyle had deemed the boy's silent version of a happy dance and set his hand on Karen's elbow. Together, the pair disappeared down the hall.

Within minutes, Ben climbed onto the couch and curled into Kyle's other side. He leaned over Kyle and studied Ava. "Do you think she's sick?"

"Why do you say that?" Kyle checked Ava. She looked content and peaceful.

Ben shrugged. "She never sleeps. If she does, she jumps up at the smallest noise and tells everyone she was awake the whole time."

"I think she's just really tired." Kyle dropped his voice lower.

"Or dead." Ben whispered that claim right inside Kyle's ear before leaning closer to Ava.

Kyle struggled not to laugh, but the effort forced him to move slightly. Ava followed and curled farther into his side, as if seeking his warmth.

Ben grinned at her movement. Satisfied his Aunt wasn't dead, he settled against Kyle and pressed Play on another episode of *Everyday Family*.

Three episodes later, Kyle found himself sandwiched between a sleeping woman and a sleeping boy. He had to leave. Instead, he hit Play on one more episode, unable to let the evening end.

SOMETHING STARTLED KYLE AWAKE. He had to leave before he awoke in the morning with Ava in his arms and awkward explanations expected. How was he supposed to maneuver himself free without waking either of them?

Four tries and too many yawns later, Kyle finally wedged a pillow between himself and Ava. Then he managed to get Ben into his arms without first rolling the boy on the floor. To Kyle's relief, Ben stretched out in the guest bed and never woke up. Kyle hesitated over turning all the lights off and finally switched on the bathroom light. He'd always slept with a light on as a kid. Even now preferred the city lights streaming into his bedroom. Back in the living room, he adjusted Ava's blanket.

He kissed her on her forehead like a friend: quick and impersonal. Then convinced himself he didn't want more with Ava. That his heart was closed like it'd always been.

If his heart was involved, he'd stay on the couch with Ava wrapped in his arms. If his heart was involved, he'd kiss Ava on the lips like he'd been wanting to since their last, and only, kiss.

If his heart was involved, he wouldn't be walking out the door and returning to his empty apartment.

CHAPTER TWENTY

AVA WALKED INTO the Jasmine Blue Café. She sent another text in a series of "available-to-work" messages to her contacts, and then scanned the restaurant for Dan and her mom.

The journey from the hospital to the café took ten minutes. She'd used the first five minutes considering her options and the last five minutes reaching out to everyone she knew for possible side jobs. All to prove to herself and her supervisor that she didn't require time off. She'd owned her mistake. Made no excuses. But disagreed with the outcome. Now, she'd hopefully fill her free time and her checking account with temp work.

Her mother waved from a table near the windows with a view of a cable car stop. Ava acknowledged her mom and pressed Send on her last text message.

Dan pulled out a chair, skipped the greeting and asked, "What did he say?"

"I'm off for the rest of the week." Ava set her phone facedown on the table and picked up the menu. Time off without pay. She wouldn't panic with witnesses around.

Dan cringed.

Karen sipped her water. "Now you can re-charge, relax and rest."

"Except, Karen, Ava doesn't know how to do that." Dan drummed his fingers on his laminated menu.

Ava lowered her menu enough to frown at Dan. "I can. I just choose not to."

Dan pushed her menu flat onto the table. A challenge dipped into his voice. "When was the last time you spent an entire day reading or sitting around doing nothing?"

She'd never been able to pick up a book and immerse herself in a fictional world. The real world always intruded in the form of bills due, doctors' appointments and responsibilities. With luck, she'd be reading a lot of textbooks soon. If she won the contest. "I might not read all day, but I can relax."

Her phone vibrated against the table as if to point out her lie.

Her mom set her hand over Ava's phone before Ava could pick it up. "You can't work more, Ava. Your body is telling you to take a break and look after yourself." She squeezed Ava's wrist. "This is why we have the emergency savings account."

Except Ava had been using the money in their

emergency account to cover expenses the last three weeks. And she'd withdrawn a large portion to pay the application fee to graduate school. Worse, she hadn't told her mom about any of it. She didn't want to talk about how careless she'd been.

Thankfully, the waitress returned to take their orders.

Ava guided the conversation away from the emergency savings account. "What do you suggest I do on my week off? I need to do something productive with my time."

"Taking care of yourself is productive," Karen countered.

"All I need is one good night's sleep." Certainly, that counted as taking care of herself. The last time she'd slept really well, she'd been sound asleep on Kyle's shoulder five nights ago. However, a repeat of that night wasn't part of her week-off agenda. After all, she knew the error of relying on someone else's shoulders. Her father had taught her that lesson too well.

"You need more than one night of good sleep," Dan argued.

"I've always functioned on less sleep than other people." The army believed in getting more done before noon than most civilians accomplished in an entire day. She still bought into their motto.

"But not while juggling so much." The concern in her mother's voice wasn't covered by her sip of tea.

"The contest is over in less than a week." Regret flickered through Ava. She'd welcomed the reprieve over the past few weeks. "Then it's back to normal."

"Do you want to go back to your normal?" Dan asked.

"What does that mean?" Ava liked her life. True, Kyle opened a new door for her. But it was temporary. She'd known that all along.

"It's okay to have a life outside of work." Dan leaned back to allow the waitress to set down his lunch plate.

"And me," her mom added.

"I know that." She couldn't afford to. The contest might change her finances. Still, she doubted school or the contest was the life Dan meant. He meant a social life. But a social life with Kyle wasn't possible, was it? Ava stabbed her fork into her salad, wanting to pop that hope bubble inside her chest.

"You have the chance to make a life outside of work," Dan added.

"You aren't talking about Kyle, are you?" She couldn't be thinking about Kyle. He was the distraction. She had to win the contest to make everything right with her mom and finally come clean about their finances.

"What other man is in your life?" Exasperation lowered her mom's voice. "Dan, Ben and Rick don't count."

There were men in her life, not her heart. "Being social would cut into my life too much."

"That sounds like something your dad would say." Her mom glanced at her. "For the record, Kyle isn't like your father."

But he could be. Though Kyle hadn't given her any reason to believe he'd be like her dad. There was the problem. Kyle was too good to be true. Her mother had never thought her father would walk away. And that was exactly what her dad had done.

Her mom had labeled her husband a quitter in every sense of the word. From a simple card game to life-challenging stuff, Ava's father had simply quit and walked away. Ava pushed a wilted piece of lettuce off her plate. If Kyle walked away, the blow would be devastating. And she'd have proof her love wasn't enough.

Dan kept his head down and concentrated on his BLT sandwich.

Silence had never bothered her mom. She crushed crackers into her bowl of soup. "Kyle possesses something your father only pretended to have—loyalty. Your dad isn't as evil as you've made him over the years."

"Don't make excuses," Ava said.

"I understand why he left." Her mom cleaned her glasses with her napkin. "I have to wonder what I would've done if the situation had been reversed."

Ava gaped at her mom. Her mother's word was her bond. In sickness and in health meant something to her mom. "You would've stayed."

"You can't be certain until you have stood in those same shoes." Her mom slipped on her glasses and eyed her. "I have forgiven him."

"I haven't." Ava tore a piece of bread from the small loaf and ignored the tear in her own heart.

"You should, or it will hold you back from your life," her mom said.

"I have a good life," Ava argued.

"Not a complete one." Her mom pointed her fork between Dan and Ava. "Neither of you have a complete life."

Dan finished the sandwich that had consumed his attention and wiped a napkin across his mouth. "I like my life. It's more than full and fun."

"Bake sales and volunteering at Ben's school don't count, Dan," Karen said.

Ava took a bite of her salad, pleased to let Dan be the center of her mom's attention.

"What is a complete life, really?" Dan crunched his homemade potato chips.

"A partner." Her mom pushed her empty soup bowl away. "A family of your own."

"I'm pretty much there already with Ben." Dan tossed his napkin on his plate. "And we're partners."

Dan bumped his knuckles against Ava's.

"You both know what I mean." Her mom shook her head and laughed. "Now Ava has free time on her hands."

"A week to have fun." Dan rubbed his hands together. "Do something you've never done."

That sounded much too close to her list of firsts. She wanted to share those firsts with Kyle. But sharing more firsts would tempt her heart to believe.

This week, she had to be practical and concentrate on side work. She wouldn't regret making extra money. She couldn't say the same about spending time with Kyle.

"You could both use a date night." Her mom's voice was mild, but direct.

Ava dropped her fork on her plate and gave up finishing her salad. Or deterring her mom.

"No dates." Dan dropped cash onto the table. "Dates are sticky, with too many strings attached. Keep it string-free."

"The only date I'm concerned about right now

is the day the contest ends." Ava added cash to the bill and pushed her chair into the table. "To reach that day, I need to get over to the development lab."

"Kyle asked if I'd be part of the mock panel for the practice presentations today." Her mom smiled as if she enjoyed Ava's obvious surprise.

"I'm on carpool duty or I would've been there to be a part of the mock panel, too," Dan said.

Frustration rolled through Ava. She couldn't locate the source. She was an adult, and if she didn't want to participate in her mother's matchmaking schemes, she didn't have to. Now she sounded petty and mean. This was a collision of worlds.

The development lab had been an escape for Ava the last few weeks. She wasn't proud, but she liked her time there. Time when she could be Ava, the inventor, not the paramedic moving from one crisis to the next, not a daughter struggling to care for her mom and keep it all together. With her mom in the suite, she couldn't forget how high the stakes really were.

Dan handed her mom her cane and helped her stand. "Ava, you should know Kyle and your mom have a bet riding on your response to her joining the mock panel."

"Mom?" Ava scooted a chair at an empty table out of their path.

"You aren't the only one in the family allowed to place bets," her mom said.

"When did you talk to Kyle?" Ava asked. Why was she only now hearing about this?

"We talk almost every day," her mom confessed.

"Why?" Her tone was abrupt. Her voice stiff. How long had they been talking and about what?

"There's quite a lot to be done on Sophie's gala and Kyle has been a big help." Karen grinned as she walked past Ava out the door. "It's also his way of checking on me without admitting it."

Kyle could've admitted it to Ava. She hadn't asked him to check on her mom. She handled her mother's care. She couldn't stop the flip inside her heart at Kyle's thoughtfulness. "I think it's great you're helping out, Mom. The final presentation is the day after tomorrow and I need a dry run-through."

Her mom met Ava's gaze. "Kyle is worth taking a chance on."

Sighing over Kyle's loyalty to her mom hardly meant Ava was pursuing something more with Kyle than their platonic relationship. She didn't trust the gleam in her mother's eyes, which seemed more than a trick of the afternoon sunlight. "We can leave after the dry run-throughs of the presentations."

"Don't rush on my account." Karen stepped

into Dan's truck with his help. "If I'm bored at Kyle's, then there's a problem with me."

"It's okay for me to worry about you, Mom." Irritated, Ava shoved open the back-passenger door. She wouldn't apologize for being concerned about her mom.

"Don't for a minute think I don't appreciate you." Her mom's soft voice added force to her heartfelt words. "I refuse to be the reason you miss out on your life."

"I'm not…" Ava let her voice drop away beneath the rumble of Dan's truck engine. Rehashing their disagreement from lunch served no purpose. She had a life. She wasn't missing out on anything.

End of discussion.

She closed her eyes. Dan turned up the volume for their usual radio karaoke session. Maybe it was her sudden indigestion or her back-seat position, but she allowed her mom and Dan to sing their own solos. She refused to believe she was taking the back seat to her own life. If her mom was right, then Ava had been missing out on her life. But she liked the life she'd built for herself. Now wasn't the time to second-guess her choices. Being put on mandatory leave had made her doubt herself.

Ava waited for her mom and Dan to finish their rendition of another top-ten pop song, before she helped her mom onto the sidewalk. Dan drove away, already singing another solo.

A receiving line waited for Ava and her mom inside Kyle's suite. Every member of the contest crew stepped forward to welcome Ava's mom with a hug and the assurance they'd help with whatever she needed. Kyle hugged her mom last. He remained by her side and walked with her into the theater room. They talked about the episode of *Everyday Family* that Ava had slept through. Ava frowned at their shared inside jokes. If she hadn't been asleep, she'd have been aware and prepared now. Had her mom lectured Kyle about needing a date, too?

Kyle said, "The best chairs are in here."

Barbra motioned to the coffee and tea set up on the side table. "I wasn't sure if you preferred coffee or tea, so I brought both."

Grant walked in, his arms loaded with a stack of magazines. "I have reading material that I picked up after lunch. Kyle doesn't seem to have anything other than gaming magazines."

Sam pulled a magazine from the stack. "This is a bridal magazine."

"I never said I knew what women liked to read." Grant shuffled through the pile. "I grabbed one of everything."

"We wanted you to be comfortable." Kyle

rubbed the back of his neck as if unsure whether they'd succeeded.

They'd surpassed comfortable and created a space that welcomed her mother. It also made Ava want to hang out for the rest of the day, too. But she had to finish her presentation. She had to secure a few side-jobs. She had to sleep, but not on Kyle's shoulder in his too-comfortable room.

Her mom leaned on her cane with both hands. "You didn't have to go to so much trouble for me."

"It's no trouble." Kyle picked up several blankets in various weights and sizes. Most still had the ribbon from the store wrapped around them. "It can get cold in here. You might need one of these."

Ava eyed the different blankets Kyle draped over a recliner. The light throw looked soft. But the Sherpa fleece invited her to settle in for the night. The same way she'd curled into Kyle's side and fallen asleep the other night. She popped several chocolate candies from the crystal bowl on the sideboard into her mouth and crunched down. The memory of Kyle's warmth proved harder to crush. "Mom, can I get you some tea?"

"Not right now." Karen thumped her cane. "Grant and Ava, you need to get ready to present."

"Looks like we've been given our orders."

Laughter lightened his tone, but Grant followed orders as if Ava's mom was his commander. He held his arm out to Barbra and left.

Ava followed behind the others and stopped in the doorway. She looked back at her mom. "I'm a shout away, Mom."

Her mother waved, but her attention was on Kyle. Even with her brother and his wife, Ava had never felt so displaced. She lingered in the doorway and tried to swallow her urge to yell. Yell at Kyle to stop being sincere and considerate. Yell at him for buying so many blankets. Yell at him for turning her thoughts inside out.

Kyle turned on the massive TV and handed Ava's mom the remote. "If you want to continue watching *Everyday Family*, I can put that on."

"I'll leave the show for you and Ava," Karen said. "You both seemed to have bonded over your favorite characters."

Ava wanted to yell at her mom. There was *no* bond between Kyle and Ava. Kyle was too good to be true. No one was perfect. Couldn't her mom see that?

Kyle smiled. "Your daughter makes me remember the good."

See? Only someone too good to be true would say something so perfect. And make Ava think about things she had no time to think about. Like what if Kyle was really hers?

"My daughter makes us all better," her mom said. "Every single day."

Would Ava make Kyle better? Would Ava be better with Kyle beside her?

"Thanks for sharing her with us these past few weeks." Kyle sounded genuine.

Ava had gained more than she'd given.

"Well, I appreciate you welcoming her family here." Karen pointed toward the door. "I saw the updated score wall when I arrived."

"It's been entertaining among other things." Kyle took Karen's hand. "I'll be back to check on you."

Ava rushed into the design lab and dropped into the chair beside Sam. She opened her notebook before she demanded Kyle explain those other things. Had it been exciting, memorable, eye-opening for him, too?

Kyle walked to his workstation and booted up his computer. With everyone seated in their usual places, the afternoon work session could proceed like every other day.

Except, this wasn't like the other days. Ava wasn't the only one distracted over the next hour.

"That's it." Barbra came into the media room, looking like a stern headmaster arriving to take her unruly students to task. "This past hour, Grant and Kyle have been to the restroom three times and never drank one sip of water. Sam and Chad have refilled their water bottles four times. Grant has disappeared to look for extra paper three times. Ava hasn't spent more than ten minutes straight at the computer."

Quiet settled over the room. Ava watched the entire group shift their attention to the floor and away from Barbra. They were all guilty as charged.

Barbra walked over to the recliner beside Ava's mom, sat and covered her legs with the new red plaid throw. "I'm going to stay with Karen until it's time to present. The rest of you are going to get to work. No one comes in here until we call for you."

The group shuffled out, adding quick smiles for Karen, but avoiding Barbra. Ava hung back.

"That includes you, too, Ava, most of all." Barbra arched an eyebrow as if daring Ava to challenge her ability to look at her mother.

Ava clamped her teeth together. She hadn't gotten much done. Barbra was right. This was the distraction she'd feared. But her mom came first. Certainly, Barbra wouldn't fault her.

Satisfied, Barbra added, "We'll be quite fine, I assure you."

If Ava had to choose anyone to be with her mom, Barbra would be her first choice. Ava respected and liked the older woman. During their short acquaintance, she'd come to value the older woman's opinion on more than the contest.

Karen handed Barbra a plate of desserts. "Want to bet on who comes back first, Ava or Kyle?"

Barbra picked up a brownie. "They should focus on what's right in front of them. It's more important than any contest."

Her mom's ready agreement followed Ava all the way back to the lab.

If Ava focused on what was right in front of her, she saw a friend in Kyle. That was what she had to see. No matter what her mom or Barbra believed. Love wasn't worth the hassle.

Ava squeezed her forehead to push that word from her mind. She blamed her mom for putting *love* into her vocabulary. She hadn't entered the contest for love. She'd entered for money.

She picked up a pencil and stared at her notes. Her mom was in good hands. Ava shoved everything aside, concentrated on her invention and Sam's voice.

An hour later, she was called into the theater room to give her presentation to Barbra and her mom. Returning to the design lab, Ava settled in again, sorted through their feedback and tweaked her presentation with Sam's guidance.

"That's enough for now." Sam stretched his

arms over his head and sighed. "At least until we've eaten."

Ava checked the time on her phone, surprised she hadn't lost focus the past two hours. "It's good, isn't it?"

Sam enlarged the presentation on the screen. "It's a winner."

But would Virtual Vital Buddy win Kyle's contest? Would it be good enough to earn a fifty-thousand-dollar paycheck? "We need to fix the third and last slides. I'm still not sold on the background color."

Sam tugged her hand off the mouse. "First, we eat."

Grant peered around the large monitor across from their workstation. "Did I hear *food*?"

"It's officially early-bird dinnertime." Chad stood up and rubbed his stomach. "The presentations are done. We should be welcomed back into the theater room."

Ava stopped by Kyle's workstation on her way out. "Making progress?"

"Sure. Absolutely." A quick click minimized the screen, but not the false note in Kyle's voice. "How about you guys?"

"The presentation is ready." Excitement surged through her. "It's a real device."

Kyle rolled his chair away from his desk and smiled. "That was the plan."

"I know. It's just incredible to see it come to life." Ava grabbed his hand and held on. "It's amazing to hold the prototype."

He looked at her as if he thought she was amazing. Or maybe those were her inner thoughts spoken out loud.

Kyle untangled himself and stepped away. His focus never retreated from her. "Shall we get in on the dinner conversation?"

Ava blinked. His intensity urged her to reach for him again. Everything that had to remain unspoken swirled in his blue eyes. "Dinner is probably a good idea."

Because the ideas flowing through her were not good ones.

She had to win the contest, not Kyle.

CHAPTER TWENTY-ONE

AVA SWIPED LIPSTICK across her mouth using the mirror inside the elevator to Kyle's rooftop garden. Tonight was the night. The past four weeks had led to this moment. In less than an hour, she'd walk away a winner with money to attend graduate school and change her future. Or she'd be standing among the crowd, where she'd always stood, her direction the same as it had always been.

She checked her hair in the mirror before the doors slid open. The only change to tonight's event: she'd avoid the bathroom. Every bathroom. She'd coerced Iris into checking the guest list earlier that morning. Nikki James had been invited and RSVP'd yes.

Ava stepped off the elevator, spotted Dan's auburn head towering over the crowd and beelined for her friends and family. She took several deep breaths to keep from chewing off her lipstick. No matter what happened, she had shoulders to lean on tonight. More than she'd ever imagined.

Mia wrapped Ava in a welcoming hug. She

adjusted Ava's hair over her shoulders as if she was preparing Ava for a photo shoot. "You look amazing tonight. There's a wonderful glow about you."

Joann hugged Ava. "She looks happy. Truly happy."

That was only Ava's annoyingly permanent smile. The one that had arrived after her food truck dinner and sidewalk kiss with Kyle. Despite Dan's continuous teasing and constant inquiries as to its source, Ava failed to wipe away her smile.

"It's more than that." Mia tipped her head and studied Ava through her camera lens.

"That's her open heart spilling through her and radiating out of her skin." Karen sounded sage and wise and too much like a relationship expert.

Joann eyed Karen and nodded, her voice equally all-knowing. "It's the look of love."

Her mom captured her own widening smile with a hand on each of her cheeks. Mia clapped and pressed her joined hands under her chin. A new awareness shifted through each of their gazes.

Ava shook her head. She wasn't wearing the look of love—whatever that was. If she'd opened her heart to love, she'd know it. An open heart was just that…open. Open wasn't love. Maybe she smiled more often, which should be a good thing. Her heart wasn't connected to her smile.

Surely, if she was in love, she'd know it already.

She was not *in* love.

Ava grabbed Mia's glass of champagne and downed the liquid. The bubbles tripped over the catch in her throat. Or perhaps that was her open heart. She winced at Mia. "Sorry. Nerves."

"Here, have another one." Mia took the empty flute and pressed a full glass into Ava's hand.

Drunk and in love. Not the combination she intended for tonight. Ava clenched the glass and squeezed her emotions into her heart. She tried to slam that lock on her heart back in place. Yet that was the problem with open hearts. They were impossible to close.

"I'm so proud of you." Sophie stepped beside her and wrapped her arm around Ava's shoulders. "You're the complete package—beauty and brains."

Not true. Her brain should be arguing against falling in love. Her brain should be listing all the endless reasons to avoid love. And all the problems with falling in love with Kyle. Her brain remained on mute. Once again, her irritating urge to smile curved through her. "Has anyone seen Kyle?"

"He's around." Dan took her champagne and

replaced the glass with a bottle of water. "Just doing what I was instructed."

"You'll want to stay clearheaded tonight." Her mom settled onto the couch. "You'll probably have to speak to the press."

Like that, Ava wanted the champagne back. The last time she'd spoken to someone from the press, even her silence had been used against her. Sophie and Mia anchored her on either side.

Mia set her arm around Ava's waist. "Don't worry. You won't be alone this time."

But she was alone in love. She'd always vowed not to fall in love alone. She had no idea how Kyle felt. And she stood alone now with Kyle nowhere in sight.

"If you don't want to speak to the press, they can't make you." Sophie pointed at the guys taking seats on the couches around Ava's mom. "Besides, we have lots of reinforcement from a former FBI agent, assistant DA, an ER doc and paramedic."

"Don't forget, Rick is a former fire captain," Mia added.

"Perfect. Brad can interrogate the press for me. Wyatt and Dan can rescue the reporters if Brad's tactics prove too intimidating. Then Drew can defend me if they decide to press charges." Ava twisted off the cap of her water bottle and downed half. She failed to drown the anxiety that she wanted to blame on the news reporters. But the press hadn't made her fall in love with Kyle. She'd made that error all on her own.

"What about Rick?" Sophie asked, laughter in her voice.

"Actually, he's my first defense." Ava scanned the crowd for a familiar head. Kyle would shield her from the reporters, too. That would only encourage her friends' talk of love. "I figure he can get me down the fire escape in record time and to safety before the first question is launched."

"That's a solid plan." Mia adjusted her camera.

"What are you planning?" Iris floated into the group, a swirl of color and light.

"Ava's escape from the press." Sophie clinked her glass against Iris's.

"That's probably wise." The reserve in Iris's tone contrasted with the bright, bold flowers on her dress. "I overheard Nikki James asking Kyle about Ava earlier."

"There's nothing to tell," Ava blurted. Heat pulsed into her cheeks and down her neck. She wanted to press the water bottle against her warm face. Kyle disliked the press. Would he dislike being in love more?

Iris grabbed Ava's arm. "It's going to be fine."

"But for the record, there is something to tell." Sophie eyed Ava over her champagne flute, speculation and understanding in her wide gaze. "Not to the press, but maybe to your best friends."

"Can I plead the fifth?" Ava asked. She cringed at the uncertainty in her own voice.

"Maybe we should talk to Rick about her fire escape idea." Sophie caught Rick's attention with a wave.

"Look." Ava drew her friends' attention to her. She'd need them once she revealed her open heart to Kyle: to celebrate or lean on. "If there's something to share, I will. Right now, I just…"

"You just want to keep your feelings private," Iris finished for her. "As you should. As your friends, we'll wait."

"But not too long." Mia tapped her elbow in Ava's side playfully.

Ava drew the women around her. Good or bad, she'd need each one of them. She could count on them.

"Sophie, did you call me over here to join in on this group hug?" Rick asked.

"I called you over to discuss fire escapes." Sophie linked her arm with Rick's. "Does there need to be a real fire in order to make use of one?"

"Are you planning to burn the garden down if Ava loses?" The twitch in Rick's frown ruined the seriousness in his tone.

Sophie blinked, her voice bewildered. "I hadn't even considered that Ava would lose."

Ava appreciated her friends' unwavering support. "Grant's idea is really good."

The trio looked at Ava as if it was bad luck to praise the competition.

"Grant's invention might be great." Mia snapped several photographs of Sophie and Rick. "But yours is better, Ava."

Grant waited with several of his friends on the other side of the rooftop. He lifted his glass in a toast to her. He could easily have been standing in her circle. Or she could be with him. She wanted the best for Grant and she wanted to win. They'd joked about a tie, even discussed the chance with Barbra. Barbra had insisted a split decision would not happen. A procedure had been set into place specifically to break a tie in the formal contest rules. Win or lose, Ava had gained a friend in Grant.

Yet she wanted her invention to be better. She wanted to build her future her own way, with Kyle beside her. He'd made her more willing to reach for the impossible. "I wish we could jump ahead and get the announcement out of the way."

Then perhaps those anxious jitters would finally subside.

"Have you considered what you'll do if you don't win?" Dan asked.

Ava's gaze collided with Kyle. He stood with the judges behind the podium. Would she dare build a future with Kyle if her life remained the same? Would it be fair to Kyle? He deserved more than her part-time affection. She'd have to get another job. She'd never accept handouts from Kyle. Actually, she'd never considered losing both the contest and Kyle. She let her gaze track to her friends and away from Kyle.

Sophie elbowed Dan in the stomach. A scold in her voice. "You can't ask that now."

"I just did." Dan rubbed his stomach. "It's smart to have a plan B."

Ava watched Kyle weave through the crowd, a quick pause and handshake for a friend. A smile for another acquaintance. He never fully stepped out of his personal space. But he'd let Ava in. She yanked her gaze away. Kyle was so much more than a fallback plan.

"She won't need one when she wins." Confidence bolstered Mia's voice.

"Dan is probably right." Ava switched the water bottle from one hand to the other. She'd never imagined the impossible being possible. She'd never believed she might fall in love. She'd been too busy immersed in the contest. Plan B hadn't ever been a consideration. "I'll make a new plan after the results are announced."

Dan looked concerned. "No matter what the results, you're a winner, Ava. Don't forget that."

"Do you know something we don't?" Mia confronted Dan.

"How would I know anything?" Dan countered. "I arrived with you guys."

"Dan hasn't ever put all his eggs in one basket," Rick said. "Since he was a kid."

Except for his marriage, Ava added in silence. Dan had regretted his decision ever since. Now Dan had Plans A through D for any given situation. He was only looking out for Ava. Reminding Ava, if she didn't win, she had options. The future she wanted could still be hers. She stepped forward and wrapped Dan in a hug. "You're my plan B."

Dan peeled her arms off him like she'd doused herself in bug spray. "I'm your partner and best friend. I can't be your Plan B, too."

Iris raised her hand. "Dan, can you be mine?"

"What about mine?" Mia asked. Her grin refused to be contained.

"You're engaged, Mia. Wyatt is all your plans A through Z. Iris, you don't want me." Sophie lifted her hand along with Karen. Dan dragged his palms across his face. "For the record, I wasn't offering to be anyone's plan B."

"Never mind." Ava shoved Dan in the chest.

"I didn't want you as my Plan B anyway. I have your dad."

Dan shook his head. "He won't do it. My dad has this thing about people living their own lives."

Ava set her hands on her hips. "You're making me come up with my own plan B?"

"I have to come up with my own. Therefore, you do, too." Dan gave her a one-arm hug more like the hardy shake of a coach with a player. "Seriously, Ava, when you win, can you buy me new seat covers for my truck?"

Ava rested her head on his shoulder for a quick minute. Long enough to remind herself of their friendship and his steady support. "I'll buy seat covers for the front and back seats."

"Hey, Kyle has the microphone." Iris squeezed Ava's arm on her way toward the stage. "I better get up there in case he needs something."

Ava walked over to her mom and took her mom's hand. Her friends gathered around them.

This was the moment. She had no plan B.

Kyle welcomed everyone to the finale party, and his next words shifted to a buzz inside Ava's head. Nerves crisscrossed around her spine.

This was her everything plan.

She inhaled, squeezed her mom's hand, exhaled. Nothing loosened inside her.

Barbra accepted the microphone from Kyle.

Ava's nerves buzzed louder than Barbra's voice inside her head.

She only had to hear one thing: her name.

Barbra congratulated both finalists. Commended them for their diligent work, time and effort. She offered an olive branch to the runner-up with the chance to enter again next year.

A scream built inside Ava. Yelling "get on with it" wouldn't earn her any extra credit. But would offer an ideal relief valve for the pressure mounting beneath her skin.

Ava locked her gaze on Kyle standing beside Barbra. As if Kyle was her plan all along.

Barbra locked in the suspense. "And the winner of the first annual Kyle Quinn's Next Best Inventor Contest is…"

Everything blurred around Ava in that time-stalled pause.

Barbra rushed on. "The winner is Grant O'Neal."

Time fast-forwarded as if intent to make up those lost minutes.

Ava lost the contest.

Lost the money.

Lost the chance for a different future.

Her mom's voice, clear and soft, shifted through her. "I love you, Ava. I'm so proud."

Ava set her head on her mom's shoulder for

one quick moment. Long enough to gather herself and stand.

The voices of her friends hummed around her like a white-noise machine set on blaring. Ava accepted hugs and pats on the back. The image of her future dimmed and faded as if someone turned out the lights. Kyle and Grant stood together on the stage, surrounded by congratulations, confetti and photographers. Kyle shook Grant's hand for a round of photos.

Ava wanted Kyle's arms around her. Wanted to lean against him. Wanted to find her future in his embrace. But they'd never discussed anything beyond this night. Never confessed any deep emotions or made promises. He hadn't asked her to be his future. She couldn't expect that now that she'd lost.

Kyle wasn't her plan B.

She'd always made her own plans. Always relied on herself. Loving Kyle wouldn't change that.

The photographs dwindled, allowing Grant and Kyle to step off the stage.

Ava braced herself and stiffened her spine. Her mother hadn't raised her to be a poor loser. No force was required for her to smile at Grant.

Grant picked her up in a bear hug. "Should've been you, Ava."

"It's your moment, Grant. Accept it and

enjoy." She stepped out of his embrace. "You deserve this and so much more."

"So do you." He looked into her eyes, his voice intense.

Nikki James tapped his shoulder and requested a statement.

Grant hugged Ava and whispered, "I'll keep her away from you."

He led Nikki James toward the bar. Even in his moment of victory, Grant watched out for Ava. She wouldn't have wanted to lose to anyone else.

Kyle stepped beside her. He kept his hands stuck in his pockets, his gaze directed toward the crowd. "You okay?"

"I will be." She forced her smile to remain in place and shoved the doubt out of her voice. "This was fun, a good diversion. But we both know I'm not an inventor and this isn't my life." She pressed her lips together, afraid of the wobble in her voice. Her life never included cash windfalls and falling in love.

"Your life is more than this contest," he said.

So was his. Their lives had intersected for this one moment. She understood that one moment wasn't a future together. "I should get my mom home. I'm back to work tomorrow night." Back to her real life. The one with patients, bills and no Kyle.

"Can I walk you out?" he asked.

Ava watched another reporter weave around the guests toward them. "No. You should remain up here. Enjoy the moment with Grant."

"Ava," Kyle said. A plea circled through his voice.

Ava met his gaze. She saw regret looking back at her. Was it for her second-place finish or something else? She was too scared to ask. Too afraid of the truth. "Thanks for this chance."

"I'll call you tomorrow." His voice dropped to a whisper before he twisted and blocked the reporter from reaching Ava.

Ava turned and bumped into Barbra.

"This isn't the end for you or your idea." The older woman wrapped her in an embrace. "Go home and take the night to process. Then you call me."

"Thank you." Ava held on to Barbra, wanting to absorb the woman's confidence. "I never expected to learn so much." Or to hurt so much.

"You have a product that should be made available to the public." Barbra squeezed Ava's shoulders. "I believed before and I still believe it now."

"I'm not sure I'm cut out for this world," Ava admitted. This was only a contest. How would she have a meeting with a corporate board and stand through a face-to-face rejection? She wanted to crumple onto the couch now. "I'm better in crisis mode with patients who need my help."

"This meant something to you, too." Barbra's voice was sincere. She wasn't giving Ava an empty pep talk. "We don't give up on what we care about."

"I'll call you for lunch," Ava said. That was all she'd promise. She wasn't giving up on Kyle. She was protecting herself. That wasn't the same, was it?

"Fair enough." Barbara released her and moved to talk to Ava's mom.

Ava found Rick near the couches. "I think it's time to use that fire escape."

Dan nodded. "I'll follow with your mom."

Rick wrapped his arm around Ava's waist, lending her his strength and support. "Let's get you out of here. I know a place where we can find double-chocolate gelato and homemade fudge brownies to ease the second-place finish."

Ava leaned into Rick and left the rooftop with her family, leaving her heart on the roof with the plants, flowers and Kyle.

CHAPTER TWENTY-TWO

FORTY-EIGHT HOURS after the announcement, the aftershocks of Ava's second-place finish continued. If she'd won, she wouldn't be gaping at the kind pharmacist. Even the tips of her ears burned as if they were twin lighters. "My credit card can't be declined."

"You'll need to contact your bank." The pharmacist tapped against her keyboard and avoided meeting Ava's gaze. "Do you have another card you'd like to try?"

No. She had this credit card. The only card that connected to her bank account. Her apparently *empty* bank account because she'd calculated wrong or forgotten an automatic debit for a monthly bill. Her worst fear came true. She'd failed her mom. She'd used their money on her application fee—*on herself,* like her father. She really was like her dad. She'd certainly jumped into rock-bottom. "Can you tell me the balance for the medicine? I'll come back with cash."

The pharmacist wrote down the balance on a

slip of paper, handed it to Ava and greeted her next customer.

Ava stuffed the paper into her pocket. She didn't require a written reminder of how much the contest had costed her. She should've been working. Accepting every job, every opportunity for overtime. Anything to boost her bank account. Anything to ensure she could pay for her mom's medicine. But she'd been dawdling in a development lab, riding cable cars and buying into a fantasy. Dreaming of a different future. One that was never really within reach. How could she have been so blind?

Stepping inside her building, Ava circled the lobby and wrestled her pride into place. Pride wouldn't help her mom. Ava couldn't go upstairs without her mother's medicine. She didn't want to lie to her mom again or burden her with her own daughter's failures.

Ava had to ask for help.

She pulled out her phone and dialed the one person she knew wouldn't judge her. Rick told her to meet him at Zig Zag Coffee House in fifteen minutes. Grabbing the mail from their mailbox in the lobby wall, she walked to the coffeehouse, determined to pound every fear into the cement sidewalk.

Rick stood at a table in a corner and opened his arms at her arrival. Ava tossed her mail down and stepped into the comfort of his hug. Her apology rushed out in a tumble of words. "I don't know who else to ask. It's just a loan. For Mom's medicine. I get paid next week. I'll pay you back as soon as the automatic deposit clears. I promise."

Rick pressed a large tea into her hands. "Stop. Sit. Breathe."

Ava slumped in the chair closest to her and cradled the cup, letting the warmth leak into her palms. A chill had burrowed into her bones on the night of the contest finale and hadn't released her from its grip yet. "I really appreciate this."

"I'm happy to help." Rick poured three sugar packets into his coffee. "Don't tell Dan, but this really feels like a three-sugar kind of afternoon."

If only three sugars and a teaspoon of honey would cure Ava. "I don't know how it got so complicated. So out of hand. I had everything figured out."

Rick's burst of laughter drew the gazes of the other coffeehouse guests. "There's your problem. Fate likes to remind us that we don't have it all figured out just to keep us in check."

"I got the message loud and clear." She didn't require any more reminders.

Rick stirred his coffee. "Dan mentioned you're not quite the same since the contest ended."

Ava frowned into her tea. What did Dan

know? Why wasn't he talking to her instead of his dad? "I thought I had everything figured out. Then I lost."

"If everyone gave up after one defeat, no one would succeed at anything," Rick said.

She hadn't given up. She'd stepped into her normal routine.

Rick tossed the coffee stirrer on the table like a dagger in a medieval challenge. "You didn't win, but that doesn't make your invention less worthy."

"What am I supposed to do?" Ava asked.

"What do you want?" Rick countered.

Her gaze stuck on the return address on an envelope in her pile of mail. *The San Francisco College of Medicine.* What did she want? To ensure her mother's care and change her own future. "It all seems so impossible."

"What has really changed since last week?" Rick asked. "You didn't win the money, but you never had that money last week. And last week, you believed."

"I believed in the money," she muttered.

"Then perhaps you need to believe in yourself like we all do." Rick stood and kissed the top of her head. "I'm on carpool duty this afternoon. Just remember you may have lost the prize money, but not the friends or the contacts."

Ava rubbed her hands over her face. The contest had opened her to the possibility of a different future. She hadn't won. But was Rick right? Was that future still within reach? If she believed. If she tried.

She picked up the envelope from The San Francisco College of Medicine and tore it open. Tears clouded her eyes at the first paragraph: *We are pleased to welcome you to the San Francisco College of Medicine.*

She'd been accepted into the graduate program. *Accepted.*

Rick's words bounced around inside her head. She hadn't lost her new friends. Hadn't lost her new contacts. Through hopeful tears, Ava unzipped her backpack and dug around for the business card with Barbra's information.

Suddenly, she wanted to schedule that lunch. And perhaps her future.

BARBRA HUGGED AVA outside the Rustic Grille. "Let's get inside. The night is cooler than I expected."

"Thanks for meeting me on such short notice." Ava slipped off her jacket in the waiting area. She'd called Barbra from the coffeehouse, expecting to schedule lunch next week. Barbra, in her usual way, had other ideas.

"It's wonderful to be able to go out without worrying about the press and the contest crew."

Barbra followed the waiter to their table. "It's also lovely to have a dinner companion."

Ava laughed. "I'm sure you have a long list of dinner companions."

"But not a long list of ones I like." Barbra slipped on her glasses to read the menu. "Your call was a welcome surprise."

"I promised to call for lunch," Ava said.

"You did." Barbra closed her menu and looked at Ava. "But you agreed to dinner. Tonight. That tells me this might be more than a quick catch-up between friends."

"It's both business and social. I need your help and guidance, if you're willing."

"I don't give out my contact information to just anyone." Barbra ordered a bottle of white wine and looked at Ava. "Let's get the business out of the way first, then enjoy a leisurely dinner between friends."

"You told me my Virtual Vital Buddy was good," Ava said.

"I still believe that," Barbra said. "There's a market out there for your product."

"Except I don't know how to get it out into the market." Ava exhaled. She'd taken the first step. Suddenly, she was ready to take more.

Barbra sat back and considered Ava. A slow smile shifted across her face. "But you want to try."

Ava nodded as the tension eased. She was taking control and doing the right thing for her. "I need to."

"Why?" Barbra leaned forward. "Because it won't be easy. There'll be more rejections. More defeats. If it's the get-rich-quick you're chasing, then I'd pick a different race."

"It's not about getting rich quick," Ava said. Her mother always told her all good things were worth the hard work. She was ready to work hard. "Although money is a motivator."

Barbra swirled the wine in her glass and considered Ava.

No more lies. No more holding back and pretending everything was perfect in her life. "I was accepted into the physician's assistant program at the San Francisco College of Medicine."

"Congratulations." Barbra tapped her wineglass against Ava's.

"Except I can't attend unless I can supplement my income. I have to support my mother's care."

Barbra sipped her wine. "Without a regular paycheck, your mom's care will suffer."

Ava nodded. She refused to allow her mom's care to change. But borrowing money from Rick wasn't happening again. One time was sobering enough. "I have to keep working."

"What is your plan?" Barbra asked.

"If I could sell Virtual Vital Buddy, I'd have

the money to pay for Mom's care and attend graduate school." This time she wasn't relying on hope. She was relying on herself and Barbra's guidance.

"When does the graduate program begin?" Barbra asked.

"This coming spring," Ava said. Her voice slipped, slowing her breath and her steps.

"Then we have to schedule appointments as soon as possible." Barbra pulled out her cell phone and opened her calendar. "Can you be ready to pitch your idea as soon as next week?"

"I've never done that before other than the contest." Ava had only done mock presentations with Kyle's marketing team.

"I'll help with the presentation and get you into the conference rooms with the right people." Barbra buttered a roll and handed it to Ava. "Selling it will be up to you."

"I can do this." Ava accepted the bread and wished she could accept her abilities to succeed as readily.

"Yes, you can." Barbra sat back and waited for the waiter to set down their meals. Then she added, "You just have to believe."

That was the very same advice Rick had given her earlier in the coffeehouse. "What else can I do?"

"Call Kyle." Barbra sliced into her steak. "He

can make those presentations in his sleep. He'll help us, too."

Ava dropped her roll onto her plate. She had avoided Kyle's calls the last two days. She owed him a return call. Now she had a reason to phone him. She wanted to ask for his help, not his heart. Although she'd accept his heart, too.

After all, she was in a race to change her future.

CHAPTER TWENTY-THREE

"I'VE FULFILLED MY CONTRACT." Kyle stretched his arms over his head and spoke into his speakerphone. The royalty payments from Tech Realized, Inc. would continue. His family's lives would remain the same as yesterday. The construction crew could break ground on the family estate in Sonoma. Except a tightness stretched across his chest as if a fist slammed against his ribs. Kyle rolled his shoulders. He should be taking a victory lap. Instead, he slumped into his chair.

The sound of fingers tapping on a keyboard came through the speakerphone, followed by Terri's voice. "Got your proposal. I'm forwarding everything to the committee now."

"So, everything is good?" Kyle asked. That fist never pulled back, never relaxed.

"Unless they reject your proposal." The air over the speakerphone stalled. Terri's laughter finally filled the silence. "Kidding. I'm certain that won't happen with one of your ideas."

Except that proposal wasn't one of *his* ideas.

That idea belonged to Grant O'Neal, the winner of his contest and the recipient of a one-hundred-thousand-dollar check. An uppercut combination smacked against his chest. Kyle caught his breath and lied, "If that's all you need from me, I have another meeting to get to."

"I'll be in touch if the committee has questions." Terri clicked off.

Kyle stuffed his phone in his pocket, shoved out of his chair and paced around the empty development lab. The computers were powered off. The printers asleep. The dry-erase board wiped clean. He hadn't been in the lab in four days. That was the last day the entire contest crew had been together. The stillness in the lab stifled, rather than comforted. He used to prefer the quiet to think and design. Now he wanted the laughter, the debates over lunch options and the bottomless candy bowls inside the room. He wanted the creative energy bouncing around the hallways. He wanted his friends.

Was that his problem? He was lonely. But he'd chosen to be alone. He preferred to live his life this way, didn't he?

His gaze landed on the laptop. A copy of the proposal he'd submitted to Tech Realized, Inc. was open on the screen, mocking him. He'd taken the easy way out and passed off Grant's idea as his own. But that had been the plan all along.

He slammed the laptop closed and walked out. What was his problem?

Grant was good with the outcome. *Really* good, in fact. Grant was sunbathing on a white-sand beach in the Caribbean with a margarita in one hand and sunscreen in the other. Grant had already texted a series of pictures from the pristine beach that morning to let Kyle know what he was missing. Yesterday, Grant had sent a series of photographs from his first-class plane seat to his private bungalow sitting over the ocean. The tagline read, Thanks for making all this possible. #bestvacationever #noregrets

Why, then, wasn't Kyle good? Why did nothing inside Kyle's body seem to fit right—as if someone had removed several key bones, letting his spine shift sideways? Kyle had abided by the rules he'd created for his contest. Grant had signed the waivers without hesitation. No questions asked. Grant hadn't even asked Kyle what would happen to his invention. He'd simply cashed the prize-money check, traded in his jeans for swim trunks and his glasses for a snorkel and mask.

Kyle should have no regrets, either. He'd done nothing wrong. He hadn't even lied. At least not to the contestants or his friends. The management of Tech Realized, Inc. wanted an original idea. They hardly cared where the idea originated from as long as it wasn't already patented.

His phone vibrated in his pocket. Kyle latched on to the chance to disrupt his circular thoughts. "Hello, Barbra. I thought we had lunch scheduled next week?"

"We do." The noise of passing cars disrupted the connection. "Ava and I are on our way over to your place."

Ava. His heart slammed around his chest. Ava hadn't returned his calls. He hadn't seen her since the finale party. He hadn't held her hand in over two weeks. He missed that the most. She'd pulled away. He had to follow her lead. "What if I'm not home?"

"Kyle Quinn, it is eight o'clock in the morning." Barbra's voice took on the parental tone that suggested now wasn't the time to mess with her. "You're always home at this time. You've never scheduled a meeting before ten in the morning since I've known you."

Except this morning. But that hadn't been a meeting. More of an email exchange with Terri and a quick phone call to ensure his contract remained in place, along with his future. "I might not be dressed."

"Get dressed," Barbra ordered. "We need your help."

Before he could ask anything more, Barbra hung up.

They wanted his help. Surely assisting Ava and Barbra would right whatever had slipped out of alignment inside him. He'd spend the morning with the women and rediscover his balance. By lunchtime, he expected his world would return to normal. Whatever weighed him down would be nothing more than a minor glitch.

The doorbell for the main entrance downstairs buzzed through the suite. Kyle glanced at his wrinkled T-shirt, jeans and bare feet. Not exactly the put-together look he might've chosen for his get-together with Ava. But it was the best he could do. At least he was dressed.

He pressed the button to unlock the doors at the main entrance, opened his suite door and rushed toward his bedroom for shoes.

"You don't need to change for us." Barbra's voice stopped him in his kitchen.

Ava trailed behind Barbra. A quick smile shifted across her face, but disappeared too soon. She hung back as if hesitant to step fully into his space.

Kyle padded back toward the women. "I was getting shoes."

Barbra waved her hand as if bare feet were his usual attire. "You don't need shoes in your lab. Besides, cold feet are often reserved for your wedding day. Fortunately for you, this is not that day."

Cold feet? Wedding day? Why did Barbra sound disappointed, as if she couldn't imagine Kyle ever getting married? Kyle glanced at Ava.

Ava shrugged and followed Barbra toward the development lab.

Kyle dropped in step beside Ava. "What is she talking about?"

"Sounds like she believes you'll have cold feet on your wedding day." Ava bumped her shoulder into him.

He hadn't translated Barbra's words wrong. He muttered, "I won't have cold feet on my wedding day."

Barbra glanced over her shoulder at him. "Because you don't ever intend to get married."

When had this become about him and his as-yet-to-be-scheduled marriage? Kyle tugged on his T-shirt to smooth out the wrinkles and the confusion in his voice. "Why are we talking about this?"

Barbra eyed his bare feet. "Because you have cold feet."

Kyle closed his eyes and pinched the skin between his eyebrows. "Can we rewind and start over?"

"If your feet are that cold, get some shoes." Barbra pressed the power button on one of the desktop computers. "Ava and I will get started in here."

Started with what? Planning his wedding? He frowned at Barbra, not appreciating the bridal brain worm she'd seeded in his head. "What exactly are we doing?"

"We're putting together a pitch and presentation for Ava's Vital Buddy." Barbra rolled a second chair toward hers and motioned for Ava to sit. "You're going to help us once you get over your cold feet."

Kyle touched Ava's shoulder. His grip was casual and impersonal, but still the tension inside him released. He wanted to take her hand and pull her into his side. Remind himself not to let her go again. "You're pitching your invention? When?"

"Soon. Next week. Barbra is lining up the meetings." Ava's gaze locked on his. Words waited in the swirl of copper in her green gaze.

Would she stay this time if he asked? Kyle squeezed her shoulder, trying to draw in more of her with that one simple touch. "That's fantastic."

"It will be if we get the presentation nailed down." Barbra peered at him over her glasses, her voice stern. "And to do that, we need to focus."

"Got it." Kyle walked to the dry-erase board,

picked up the pen and wrote across the board. "Here are the slides we're going to need for a complete, sellable presentation. We'll create the pitch from this information."

Ava stood up and asked, "Can I really do this?"

"You can. Barbra wouldn't be here if she didn't believe in you." Kyle stepped toward her, linked his hands with hers. Nothing felt more right. "I know you can do this, but you have to believe."

She inhaled and firmed her grip in his hands. "I have to try."

That was a start. He'd get her to believe before the end of the day. He had to. Already he felt more like himself. Helping Ava seemed like what he'd been meant to do. He tightened his grasp on her hands rather than kiss her. That would happen later. Now he tried to press his confidence into her.

"Let's sell your invention, Ava." The enthusiasm in Barbra's voice paired with her wide smile and her bright gaze.

The morning dashed into the afternoon as if someone pressed fast-forward on the clock. The time for lunch to be delivered exceeded their eating time by only about five minutes. Energy and excitement burst against the white walls in the development lab. The loneliness inside Kyle that had absorbed him for the past few days dissolved. He felt alive and useful again.

Ideas were shuffled, handed out and discarded like cards in a Crazy Eight game. Still, the trio never relented, never gave up.

Barbra pushed away from the desk and rolled her shoulders. "I think we have everything."

"Except the pitch." Ava rose and stretched her arms over her head.

"It's in there." Kyle pointed at the slides of the presentation filling the computer screen. "We just need to find the right combination of words."

"You'll have to create the pitch without me." Barbra picked up her purse.

"Wait, you can't leave now." Ava grabbed Barbra's arm, her voice rose.

"I have several calls to return to schedule those meetings." Barbra covered Ava's hand with hers and smiled. "And I have dinner plans with your mom."

"My mom?" Ava glanced at Kyle.

He shrugged at her.

"It might surprise you both to learn Karen and I have a lot in common." Barbra hugged Ava. "Most of which we discovered during our afternoon together here."

"But I need a pitch." Ava released her hold on Barbra and her voice dropped away.

"There's no one better at creating pitches than

Kyle." Barbra stopped in the doorway and turned back. "I'll stay with your mom until Joann arrives, so you can work as late as you need to. Remember, your pitch has to be spectacular to hook them from that one line. Better yet, make them buy it from that one line."

"No pressure there," Ava said.

Barbra laughed and waved her hand at the computer. "This is the easy part. The hard part is standing in that conference room and giving the perfect presentation."

Ava slumped into her chair and dropped her head back.

Kyle stepped behind Ava and set his hands on her shoulders. "Enjoy your dinner, Barbra. We got this."

"Most importantly, have fun." Barbra let her last command hang in the silence and left.

"Fun?" Ava stared at the ceiling, her voice strained. "How are we supposed to have fun with all this pressure?"

Kyle ignored her and listened to the front door shut. "Barbra's right. Let's go."

"Where?" Ava pointed at his bare feet. "You still don't have shoes on."

"Trust me." Kyle held his hand out toward her.

She eyed him for more seconds than he preferred, but finally slipped her hand in his.

He guided her through the suite, into the ele-

vator and up to the rooftop. He released her and
turned on the string of soft white lights over the
outdoor kitchen area. He left the seating area
dark and private. He'd always preferred the rooftop like this. No strangers. No crowds. The roof
looked more like a welcome oasis. A private retreat, guarded by the city's high-rises, standing
like sentinels around the building.

Kyle flopped onto one of the couches, stretching his legs across the entire length and adjusting a pillow under his head. He wanted to pull
Ava down beside him, but she had to want that,
too. She had to decide that for herself.

She sat in the chair beside the couch. "It's
sooooo quiet. I've never been up here when it's
been like this."

Neither had he. At least not in a very long
time. He was glad he'd brought Ava up there
with him. Everything was better with Ava. He
almost groaned at his lack of elegant words.

"I like it." Ava relaxed into the chair, stared at
the sky. "I prefer it a lot more like this."

He liked her. A lot. Her arm rested on the
chair. He had only to reach up and he could link
his fingers with hers. He stuffed his hands underneath the pillow. "I used to come up here all
the time to think."

"Why did you stop?" she asked.

He'd only stopped thinking. Instead, he came

to the rooftop and counted the lights on in the apartment buildings around him to remind himself he wasn't alone. Then he'd invited strangers to the rooftop. Again, to not feel alone. He'd never quite figured out how he could feel more alone in a crowd than by himself. "The parties ruined it."

"Yet you keep having them," she said.

"The ones for the contest were the only two I've hosted this year." He stared at the night sky and ignored the lights in the apartments around him. He liked sharing this space and the night with Ava. It was easy, comfortable, natural. Less lonely, both on the rooftop and inside his heart, with Ava beside him.

"Your weekend gatherings made the newspaper every Sunday. According to the society pages, this was the place to be on a Saturday night," she said. "Why did you stop?"

He tipped his head and looked at her. "The truth—I couldn't breathe with so many strangers around me."

"Funny, I prefer not to breathe." She held his gaze, yet her voice was fragile.

"Then you'd have liked my parties," he said. He'd liked them for a time. Until the evenings became more about business networking and social climbing and less about meaningful interactions.

"Perhaps," she said. "I liked the past few weeks in the lab with the crew. I didn't realize how much I'd miss coming over here. How much I'd miss the break from the real world."

He'd missed her. Too much. "Why don't you like to sit and breathe?"

She shifted and stared up at the sky again. Although, from the distance in her voice, he doubted she focused on anything. "If I stop, the past and the present collide. Wounds from a battlefield and wounds from a domestic fight become interchangeable. Both leave me gutted and fighting for air."

Kyle reached over and linked his fingers with hers. He admired her inner strength and courage and so many other things about her. "Still, you put yourself back out there every night you go to work."

"It's my job," she said. "Anyone would do that."

"Not anyone." He wasn't sure he'd have the guts or the fortitude. He was a little in awe of her. "And you take care of your mom. Not everyone would do that."

"I feel like I'm not doing enough for her." Pain and regret echoed through her soft voice.

"I think your mom would disagree." He knew Karen would argue. The pride Karen had in her daughter was second only to her love for Ava. "She wants you to have more."

"The more is marriage and a family." Distaste coated her words. Her grip on his hand never relaxed.

"You don't want that?" he asked. She had to want that, too. Otherwise he'd have to change her mind and he had no idea how he was supposed to do that. Ava made him consider marriage and children. For the first time ever. He didn't want to be alone in this new, unchartered territory.

"It's impossible right now," Ava said.

But she never said she didn't want all that. Kyle relaxed back against the pillows. "My grandfather used to say, 'Lead with your heart and suddenly the impossible becomes possible.'"

"Perhaps we'll see next week if your grandfather was right," Ava said.

"You've put your heart into the Vital Buddy?" he asked. Before, he'd have claimed her heart was in her family and the people she helped.

"Vital Buddy will give me the chance to follow my heart." Her voice faded into the breeze. "If I'm successful next week."

He squeezed her hand, gentle and quick. "You're forgetting to breathe again."

She inhaled and tightened her grip on his. "There are so many ifs. Too many unknowns."

"But not up here. Not in this moment." He

sat up and swung his legs onto the floor. His knees bumped against hers. "My grandparents had a hammock in their backyard. On the nights I couldn't sleep, I'd lie in it and count the stars. My grandmother told me every star was a possibility."

"If only we weren't in the middle of the city, surrounded by high-rises. I could count those possibilities now."

"We don't need the stars." Kyle leaned forward and brushed his lips across Ava's. Just once. Just the smallest caress. But a kiss that left the deepest of impressions. The strongest of possibilities. He pulled back, enough to see her half-closed eyes. "What do you want...?" He paused, watched her eyes close. Held himself still, despite the urge to take more. "What do you want for dinner?"

Her eyes snapped wide-open, locked on him. "Dinner?"

"Let's start simple—stay in or eat out?"

"In."

His choice, too. "Delivery or takeout?"

Her teeth bit into the edge of her bottom lip. "What's in the refrigerator in the kitchen over there?"

"Wine and an unopened appetizer tray that Haley prepared for the finale party." He tucked a piece of her hair behind her ear, let his fingers graze her cheek.

"Sounds like dinner is already up here."

"Are you sure?" he asked. "It's nothing special."

"It's perfect." She stood up and held out her hand.

Together, they created dinner from an appetizer platter, sipped wine and shared secrets. Their conversation interrupted only by a kiss. Each one longer than the last. Each one less about the possibility and more about the reality. The reality of something deeper and heart tangling between them.

Too soon the night chilled the air and sleep beckoned. Kyle walked Ava out to the waiting taxi and opened the cab door.

Ava turned before getting inside. "We didn't write the pitch."

"But we had fun like Barbra told us to do." Kyle grinned.

"We did have that." Ava kissed him. "Thanks for the breather. I didn't realize how much I needed that."

"Anytime." Kyle leaned on the open cab door. "Besides, we have all weekend to write the pitch."

"I have to work."

"Then I'll get to work, too."

"Thanks for all of this." She waved her hand between them.

"My pleasure." He shut the car door, waited until the cab turned the corner and headed inside. The evening had been more than a pleasure. The evening had been special.

Kyle walked through the suite and stepped into the lab to turn off the lights. His phone vibrated on the desk, where he'd left it. Funny, he hadn't even considered checking his messages or working the entire time he'd been with Ava on the rooftop. He'd only wanted to discover as much as he could about such an incredible woman.

He grinned, grabbed his phone and sent Ava a text.

Got the perfect pitch.

She wanted to hear it. He wanted to tweak it first and promised she'd have it before the end of the weekend.

She answered with an emoji blowing a kiss.

Kyle smiled and sat at the desk with his open laptop. Messages flashed in his in-box in the corner of the screen. Most were marked urgent. He wrote several versions of the pitch on a blank document and then opened his in-box.

And his night nosedived from a perfect evening with a perfect woman into a perfect nightmare.

He picked up his phone, pressed Play on his voice mails. Terri's grim voice filled the silence and confirmed the message in the urgent emails.

The committee had rejected his proposal.

Worse, Kyle had until midnight to submit another idea or he'd owe steep penalties. Terri rattled off how much the penalties and fines would cost him. Kyle's hand shook as he wrote the exact dollar amount on a sticky note. The six-figure number filled the entire square sticky note.

The amount was almost twice what he'd calculated. Nowhere near what he had in his bank accounts. He'd invested in property: his suite, his parents' retirement condo, the family estate.

He shouldn't have had the wine. Shouldn't have kissed Ava. Shouldn't have gotten to know her. Now she was more than a friend and that ruined everything.

He couldn't think straight. Couldn't see past the implications to his family and himself. He had another idea with a proposal already written and a perfect pitch. A pitch he'd just come up with after putting Ava in a cab. He'd worked as hard on the proposal and pitch as Ava. He'd invested as much time as Ava. But the idea wasn't his, except according to the contest rules, it was his.

All he had to do was attach the documents in an email to Terri and hit Send.

Only a couple clicks and he'd save himself and his family.

Ava had signed the contest waivers, too. She'd understood the rules and the conditions for the contest.

He'd understood the danger of crossing boundaries. The danger of making friends and opening his heart. He'd understood the consequences. And he'd jumped anyway.

Images of Ava holding his hand, laughing at shared memories and wiping away a tear after hearing about his grandfather—those images interrupted his concentration. Those images made her no longer a stranger. Much more than a friend.

He'd let Ava into his heart. He'd fallen in love.

Now he was going to be alone. Alone and in love.

He deserved all that and more for being so careless and stupid.

He opened a new email, attached the proposal for the Virtual Vital Buddy and typed a quick note to Terri. His fingers shook from the eruption inside his chest.

He'd told Ava outside the conference room that they couldn't be anything more, now or ever. Why hadn't she listened? Why hadn't she run?

She should've known he'd never be good enough for her.

He clicked on the send button.

God, he hated himself.

CHAPTER TWENTY-FOUR

"THANK YOU FOR agreeing to meet with me on such short notice." Ava shook hands with Terri Stanton, the vice president of Tech Realized, Inc.

"Barbra Norris is a longtime friend." Terri motioned to a seating area near the windows in the glass-walled lobby. The windows granted waiting visitors and vendors a view of the towering four-tiered fountain flowing into a massive reflective pool.

Ava smoothed her mouth into a smile, trying to hide her confusion. She'd assumed she'd be giving her pitch in a conference room or a private office. Not out in the open lobby with employees and vendors and guests streaming through like schools of fish. Nothing about her life since becoming a finalist in Kyle's contest had gone as she'd expected. That included Kyle.

Thoughts of Kyle bolstered her courage. He'd tell her to believe and not worry about the setting. Ava straightened her shoulders and reached into her tote bag "I have a printed copy of my presentation."

The woman stopped Ava from handing the color presentation to her and invited Ava to sit beside her on the couch. "I'm not sure how to approach this, as I've mentioned that Barbra is a dear friend."

Ava lowered herself onto the couch. "But... you're not interested in the Virtual Vital Buddy?" That bubble of hope burst inside her, leaking defeat through her. Barbra had cautioned her about being prepared for rejection. She hadn't thought it'd be so soon.

"On the contrary, the invention has merit." Terri crossed her legs at the ankles and folded her hands on her lap.

Ava studied the woman. Terri Stanton wore practical heels, trendy oval glasses and a navy business suit. Everything from her French twist to her starched and ironed white blouse broadcasted a no-nonsense attitude. "I'm afraid I don't understand."

"Neither do I." The woman indicated the presentation Ava clutched inside her binder. "This idea has already been presented to our committee."

"But it's my idea." Ava let the binder drop back inside her tote bag, along with her fear.

"That seems to be up for debate." Terri pushed her glasses up and stared at Ava, straight and not blinking. "I'm not sure what you're trying to prove, but presenting ideas as your own can have disastrous consequences in this industry. Word travels fast."

She was trying to prove her idea—her invention—was worth the investment. Worth the financial commitment of a corporation dedicated to bringing the device to market. "I'm only here now. How has my own idea been submitted already?"

"I'm afraid I cannot discuss the details." Terri rose and brushed her hands over her skirt as if Ava's deception might've clung to her. "However, I can offer a word of caution. Stealing from Kyle Quinn, then scheduling a meeting with his current employer probably wasn't the wisest move. I'm not sure how you convinced Barbra to believe you, but you can be sure I'll be calling her as soon as I get back to my office."

Kyle? Stealing from Kyle? That was impossible. Ava's stomach twisted into knots. The woman had everything all wrong. Kyle had helped Ava create the presentation. He'd even designed the perfect pitch. Ava had spent all morning memorizing the two lines. Ava cleared her throat, discovered her voice. "Can you at least tell me when the idea was presented to you?"

"Late Friday night." The woman checked her watch. "If you'll excuse me, Ms. Andrews, I have important meetings to attend."

Meetings that didn't include thieves like Ava. Those were the words left unspoken in the quick clip of Terri Stanton's heels on the marble floor. The woman wasn't Ava's concern—she could have her fancy business suits and high-powered meetings. Ava never wanted that.

But Kyle—she'd wanted Kyle.

She'd wanted to make the impossible possible with Kyle. She'd wanted to make a life with Kyle. She'd given him the best of her: *her heart.*

She curled her fingers into the presentation binder. Shredding the paper in the lobby of Tech Realized, Inc. would only make a scene. Another one. She was already being discussed on Terri Stanton's floor, whispered about and scrutinized. Even the receptionist at the lobby desk grimaced in her direction.

Ava forced her hands to uncurl the presentation and everything inside her to uncoil. Meltdowns were best handled in privacy. She'd never liked meltdowns—public or private. But Kyle had betrayed her. He'd stolen from her. Stolen more than her idea.

He'd stolen her trust. Her heart.

And that entitled her to a full-scale meltdown.

Ava rose and walked out of Tech Realized, Inc. with her head high, despite the turmoil surging through her.

INSIDE KYLE'S BUILDING, Ava took the elevator, too afraid her shaky legs wouldn't carry her up the stairs. That meltdown tried to suck her down like a fierce undertow. She wouldn't drown in her emotional turmoil yet.

Kyle opened the door, tousled hair, bare feet and a sleepy grin. He reached for her.

Ava shoved past him and kicked off her heels. She'd have her feet firmly on the ground this time. "How could you?"

Kyle eased the door closed, his grin slipped away. But the way his gaze slid from her face betrayed him. "I'm not following."

"I just left Tech Realized." Ava threw her presentation across the room. Papers scattered like shattered dreams. "Barbra scheduled a last-minute meeting with Terri Stanton for this morning."

Kyle thrust his hands in his hair and yanked as if that would right his world. "Barbra never mentioned where she'd scheduled the meetings."

"It never occurred to us that it mattered," Ava shot back. It never occurred to her that he'd betray her. That he'd pretend to help her and pass off her invention as his own. *His own.* It never occurred to her that she'd need to protect more than her heart from him.

"It's not what you think," he said.

"So, you didn't submit the presentation and

pitch for the Virtual Vital Buddy on Friday night?" she lashed out. *Friday night.* Minutes after she'd left the building. Minutes after she'd poured out her heart and shared her secrets. Minutes after she'd fallen into his kisses. Fallen even more head over heels in love. She curled her toes to keep from buckling.

She'd rode home in a taxicab, sighing and smiling from the inside out.

He'd walked into the development lab, no doubt cackling from what an easy mark she'd been.

His mouth opened, closed and opened. Only the air of guilt escaped.

Ava crossed her arms over her stomach to hold the turmoil inside. "At least have the guts to admit it."

"I sent in the presentation." His words rushed out. "But it's not what you think."

Ava thrust her arms over her head and shouted, "I trusted you." Trusted him with her heart.

"I can explain," he said.

"There's nothing to say," she countered. "What? Were you going to put me on the payroll like Iris? Pay me from the profits of the Virtual Vital Buddy sale?"

He rubbed his hand over his mouth, but not fast enough to cover the truth. He'd considered that an option.

"You were," she accused. She gathered her voice around the fist choking her. How stupid could she be? "You think I'm worth nothing more than a monthly handout. After all, Ava's desperate. Did you convince yourself that I'd take whatever meager amount you gave me and believe I'd hit the jackpot? Did you convince yourself that I'd be grateful and in your debt?"

"That's not what I thought. That's not what I planned."

"But you had a plan," she charged. Where she only had one plan: build a different future for herself. She'd known not to reach for more. Known the dangers and yet took the risk. Now she fell, and the impact would be shattering. "What about Friday night up on the rooftop? Was that part of the plan to betray me? And the talk about falling in love."

"I never said…"

"That's right. You never said you loved me." Ava clutched at her own throat, trying to open her airways. She'd felt love in his kiss. Felt it in his embrace. So many lies, and she'd fallen for every single one. "How stupid I am."

Kyle stood silent and distant.

"And you know what's even more pathetic?" Ava narrowed her eyes, trying to stall the spill of her tears. She wouldn't cry over him. "I'd have given you the invention if you'd asked."

"It was already mine." The crisp bluntness in his voice was like a lethal injection.

Ava recoiled.

He had one more shot to inject. "You signed the consent form for the contest, waiving your rights to your idea."

"Of course I did." She'd handed him her life and her heart and only ended up with a dead-end future. She walked to the door and turned around. "We could've been something special."

"We still can." His voice was earnest, but his gaze guarded.

"Just stop." She stepped toward him, met his gaze, heartbroken but not defeated. "We could never work, because you can't believe."

"I believed in us," he countered.

"That's another lie," she challenged. "How do you sleep at night? You should be suffocating on all your lies by now."

He retreated. She followed.

"You need to believe in yourself first." Ava pointed at him and injected her own hard truths. "You need to believe you deserve to be happy. If you'd sit down long enough to really look at yourself, you'd see that it's you who isn't happy. Stop using your money to fix everyone around you. They're already satisfied with their lives. Fix yourself instead."

Kyle crossed his arms over his chest as if intent on deflecting her words. "You're not happy."

Ava flinched and walked toward the door. "I could've been. With you beside me."

CHAPTER TWENTY-FIVE

"You need to go get Ava." Iris rushed inside Kyle's suite, her voice as urgent as her footsteps. "She's down in the lobby and she's crying." His sister drew out the word *crying* into too many syllables, emphasizing her alarm.

Crying. Ava's tears weren't the hardest blow. Her tears had knocked him sideways. The despair in her watery green gaze had made his knees buckle. But the quiet way she'd shut the door and walked out as if he wasn't even worth her anger. That he wasn't worthy. That she'd given up on him. On them. That had flatlined him.

He deserved every bit of pain and more. She'd called herself stupid. He was the idiot. The fool. And fools deserved to be alone. He knelt and picked up the scattered presentation papers. The truth turned his voice raw. "I made her cry."

And he despised himself even more.

"All the more reason to get down there and fix this." Iris bent and yanked on his arm. Everything about his sister was in emergency mode.

Kyle gathered the papers into a pile. If only the same methodical approach could be used to pick up the pieces of his life. But he knew nothing would fit right without Ava. Nothing would ever feel the same. "There's nothing I can do."

"There's always something you can do." Iris dropped onto her knees and shifted until their eyes met. "You have to try."

How did he fix the heart he broke? Confessing his love for Ava now would be like stomping on those broken pieces. *I stole your idea because I love you.* He wanted to crush his own broken heart. "It's complicated."

"Any relationship that is worthwhile is complicated," Iris argued.

"Let it go, Iris." He crumpled one of the presentation slides in his fist.

She opened her mouth.

He lashed out first. "I did the unforgiveable. I chose my family's well-being over the woman I love."

Oh, by Saturday morning, he'd had it all sorted out. The perfect plan. If Tech Realized, Inc. accepted the Vital Buddy, he'd have given Ava money. He'd have given her whatever she'd needed. He'd have given her financial freedom. Ava had been right: he'd have willingly added her to his payroll. After all, money solved everything, even soothed a guilty conscience.

When the Vital Buddy finally rolled onto the commercial market, Ava would've been so madly in love with him, and he with her, that they would've laughed this off. This would've been part of that small stuff his grandfather had always cautioned him not to hang on to. Kyle crammed the last of the paperwork into the pile he held. Could he have been anymore delusional?

"What do you mean your family's security?" Iris pulled away and studied him, her critical mode shifting into idle.

"Shouldn't you be at work?" he countered. He didn't want to talk about this. He didn't want to give any more power to his despicable actions. He already ached in places he shouldn't feel. And he'd hurt Ava even worse. Wasn't that enough? He snapped at his sister. "Did you quit on Mia, too? I warned Ava you weren't dependable."

Iris jerked back at his words. "Don't you dare turn this on me."

"Look, Iris…" He picked up her hand. Why were his apologies getting lodged in his throat today? "I'm confused. I'm afraid."

"Of course you are." Iris stood, set her hands on her hips and glared at him. "You just ran off the best person in the world for you."

"That's helpful."

"It's not meant to be helpful," she challenged. "It's meant to be the truth."

Kyle stared at the papers, his gaze blurred. "Ava isn't…"

His sister stomped on the floor and cut off his words. "You can't do it, can you?"

"Do what?" His voice came out in a tangled snarl.

"Let yourself be happy. Really, truly happy." Iris tapped her foot in front of him, an angry beat. "Why do you sabotage every chance you have at happiness?"

"I don't." Kyle clenched the paperwork and searched for his spine. Ava lectured him on happiness, and now his sister. What did they know?

"You project your inner unhappiness onto everyone around you. Trying to make them change because you've decided they can't possibly be happy as they are." Iris's foot stilled. "You want Callie to give up on Oxford and move home. You want Mom and Dad to leave Florida. You want me to put on a business suit and work in a real office." Iris waved her hands over her head. "You're building some ridiculous monstrosity of a house that no one asked for."

"I want my family home," he said. "What's wrong with that?"

"They are home. Doing what they love, where they love, with the people they love," Iris said.

"But it's not the same." Couldn't she see that? Nothing was the same since his Papa Quinn's death. The home he'd known all his life was gone. The security he'd relied on had moved across state borders.

"Because you aren't doing what you love with the person you love." Iris dropped to her knees and looked at him.

"The money was supposed to bring our family back together. Like we were when Grandpa was alive." The money was supposed to make everyone happy again. There was the word again. He wanted to curse.

"Papa Quinn's death left a hole in each of us." Iris scooted closer to him, her voice gentle and sincere. "But you honored his memory with the Medi-Spy and gave each of us a gift."

"What was that?" Kyle asked. Disbelief turned his tone sarcastic. "All I have is a commercialized earbud that loses its integrity with every update. That isn't the best gift."

"You gave us the chance to live the lives we needed to heal. The lives that let us find our happy again." Iris set her forehead against his. "You just never found your happy."

Kyle closed his eyes and whispered, "Until Ava."

Iris nodded and repeated, "Until Ava."

"I lost her." The breath-stealing ache snagged his voice.

"Then you should probably figure out a way to find her and keep her this time." Iris wrapped her arms around him.

Kyle held on.

Iris stood up. "I'm off to meet Mia. We're doing the publicity photos for the traveling Broadway production of *Cinderella*."

Kyle stopped his sister before she walked out. "Iris, I only ever wanted you to be happy again after the divorce and everything you went through."

"I know, little brother, and I love you for that." Iris blew him a kiss. "I'm finding myself again. Finding my happy. It's just that there are some things we have to discover on our own. In our own time."

"And if it's too late?" he asked.

She smiled. "It's never too late to lead with your heart."

The door clicked shut, leaving Kyle alone with Ava's forgotten presentation. The paper on the top captured his attention. It wasn't part of the original presentation. The letterhead was from the San Francisco College of Medicine. Kyle read the letter and lost his breath. His fingers shook. Blood rushed like a scream through his skull.

On the bottom of the acceptance letter, in bold blue ink, Ava had written: *My future is within reach. Just believe.*

Ava had been accepted into graduate school. She'd never told him, but she'd hinted. Hinted that the money was for more than cushioning her checking account. He'd stolen her idea and her happy.

He'd officially smacked into rock-bottom, slamming face-first into a new low.

His phone vibrated. The text was from his mom.

Turn on your computer. We want to video chat.

Kyle scrubbed his hands over his face and up into his hair. He'd make it a quick call. If he didn't accept their chat, his mom would think something was wrong. Unless Iris had already called them and spilled the truth. But that wasn't his sister's style. They kept each other's secrets. He turned on his laptop in his kitchen and answered the video call from his parents.

His parents filled the screen: wide smiles against tanned skin. The laughter lines creasing their cheeks up into their eyes were new.

Enthusiasm rushed his mom's words. "Kyle, we wanted to tell you in person."

"Tell me what?" Kyle adjusted the screen,

searching his parents' faces. Was the glow on their faces from the sun or something more?

"We're renewing our wedding vows for our fortieth anniversary here in the Keys. We want our children with us." His mom raised their joined hands into view.

His dad kissed his mom's knuckles. "We'll celebrate Thanksgiving together and have a renewal party."

"Wow." That glow wasn't sun-induced. He couldn't recall the last time he'd seen his parents like this. Kyle ran his palms over his jeans.

"Isn't it fantastic?" his mother gushed. His dad pressed another kiss to his mom's cheek.

Kyle peered closer at the screen. His mother was blushing, twin pink bursts colored her cheeks. His father grinned from ear to ear. His parents looked more like a newly engaged couple who just discovered the power of love. Not two adults in their sixties, who'd weathered life together with all its challenges. Perhaps the glow was the deep love shared between two people for more than forty years. A love that never stalled or weakened, despite the struggles and the tests. "Do you have a place picked out for the ceremony?"

"We're taking care of all that," his mom said. "We just want you here for the week."

"You've done more than enough for us, son," his dad added.

"The Florida condominium was nothing…" *Special*. He'd bought them a small, dated condo that his mother had convinced him was perfect. He added, "There's no yard. No toolshed. No garden." His father had spent every weekend when Kyle lived at home inside his workshop in the garage.

"Between Papa Quinn's house and our home, I've done enough yard work and house maintenance to last more than two lifetimes." His dad grinned. "Now I can reach the golf course or the beach in less than ten minutes. And that's walking."

"Our condo is everything, Kyle." His mom leaned into the camera as if to make certain she had her son's full attention. "You gave us the chance to rediscover what we'd lost in the city."

His parents tapped their heads together. He'd never seen them this in love. Or quite so *happy*. Was Iris right? Had his parents healed in Florida and found a new, fulfilling life there? "The ocean breeze suits you guys."

"More than you can imagine," his dad said.

"You need to come and visit soon, Kyle." His mom edged closer to the screen again, blocking out his dad. "You could use some ocean air and sun. You look a little pale. Have you been eating right?"

"I've been eating. Haley delivers meals every week," he added. He knew his mom would call Haley herself to verify that Kyle had been eating. A broken heart leached the color and life out of a person. But his mother didn't need to know that part. "I've been in the lab quite a lot."

"Fluorescent lighting isn't the same as real sunlight," his mother chided. "Even Callie gets out of her lab on the weekends."

His dad shifted back into view. "It's good to work hard, son. But balance can do wonders for your soul."

His dad had gotten philosophical since his retirement. "You sound like Papa Quinn."

"He was a very wise man." His dad grinned. "I only wish I'd listened to him sooner."

"If it helps, I'm listening to you now," Kyle said.

"You always were a faster learner," his dad said. "Your mom is telling me to hang up. We have a lunch meeting with the wedding planner for our renewal ceremony. Book your flight early for a good deal on airfare."

Kyle promised he'd check flights that afternoon and ended the call.

He'd led with his heart once. When he'd designed and sold the first Medi-Spy. That earbud symbolized his love for his grandfather. But he'd started ignoring his heart with every royalty check he had cashed, listening to everyone but himself. Perhaps it was past time he listened to his heart again.

Kyle picked up his phone and dialed the offices of Luxury Vine Home Builders in Sonoma. Twenty minutes later, with his wine country land for sale, Kyle contacted a car auction house for his grandfather's vintage Mustang. Exactly sixty minutes after the call with his parents, Kyle pulled his proposal from consideration with the committee at Tech Realized, Inc. Kyle assured Terri Stanton he'd have the money to pay the penalties and fines for defaulting on his contract within the thirty days granted to him in his contract.

He glanced around the arcade, calculating how much he could get for the game consoles and pool tables. He was going to need a job and perhaps a payment plan with Tech Realized, Inc. But he'd started to right his world and that mattered.

His last call took several minutes of convincing. Finally, Barbra agreed not to cancel any of the meetings she'd scheduled for Ava. More importantly, his mentor and friend agreed to meet him for dinner. Hopefully by dessert, he'd have garnered both Barbra's support and help. He was going to need all the assistance he could get.

After all, no one ever said listening to your heart was easy.

CHAPTER TWENTY-SIX

AVA STOOD IN the door of her mother's bathroom. "Can I help?"

Her mom sat on a stool in front of the bathroom mirror. "Ava, you look stunning. You'll be the most radiant one at the gala tonight."

Her mood was more melancholy than radiant. Even the silver sparkles on her high heels failed to spark her enthusiasm. She'd have stayed home for a sad movie marathon if Sophie wasn't one of her best friends. And if her mom hadn't worked so hard on the gala. "Mom, I need to tell you something. I should've told you sooner."

"We can talk while you help with my makeup." Her mom grimaced at the array of containers and brushes spread across her counter. "I don't miss having to put on all this before work."

"But you miss working, don't you?" Ava stepped over to the counter. She'd seen the excitement in her mom whenever the gala came up.

"I've missed feeling useful." Her mom swiped two different lipsticks across her hand to check the colors. "Helping with Sophie's gala made me realize that. But my working isn't what you want to discuss."

Ava handed her mom the pale rose-colored lipstick. "It's better with your complexion and dress."

Her mom tossed the other lipsticks into the drawer. "Whatever it is, Ava, we'll deal with it together."

Ava hadn't found a cure for her broken heart. She wasn't sure her mom would have one. But she hoped confessing several truths would dull the edges of her distress. "The good part is that I was accepted to the physician's assistant graduate program at the San Francisco College of Medicine."

Her mom spun around on the stool, her gaze wide with pleasure.

Ava rushed on, trampling over her mother's excitement. "But I drained our emergency savings account to pay for the application fee. Lost my second job and the contest. Borrowed money from Rick. And we can't afford for me to go to graduate school." *Oh, and I fell in love.* She left that confession unspoken, unable to give a voice to her heartbreak, as if talking about her pain would somehow make it worse.

"You've been keeping in a lot." Her mom shook her head. "Too much really."

"I should've told you sooner," Ava said. "I didn't want to let you down."

"We're a family," her mom said. "You were never supposed to handle this alone."

"You handled everything alone when Dad left." Ava skimmed a brush in the blush and swept it across her mom's cheeks.

"You were kids. We're adults now." Her mom's voice chided and soothed. "I've let you down. I was so busy lecturing you and I forgot to look at my own life. I stopped being helpful."

Ava studied her mom. "You aren't thinking about going back to work, are you?"

"Not full-time." Her mom spun the stool back to the mirror. "But I have some ideas that might be part-time and flexible."

"I didn't tell you all this so that you'd feel like you have to get a job." Ava set her hand on her mom's shoulder.

"I know. I want to try this while I still have some energy left inside me." Her mom covered Ava's hand with her own. "You entered the contest and inspired me to step out of my comfort zone. You reminded me to look at things from a different perspective. Working in an office forty hours a week isn't possible. But maybe working from home for ten hours a week is. I want to try."

Ava met her mom's gaze in the mirror. "I

should try, too. You think I need to approach things differently?"

"Sure. We'll start with graduate school." Her mom grinned, but the spark in her gaze gave her away. There was something else she wanted Ava to try. "There has to be options for you to attend graduate school."

"I have to work," Ava said.

"Many people work and attend school." Her mom added a small touch of eyeshadow to her eyes.

"I need both jobs." She'd always had more than one job. She'd always worked.

"Maybe it's time we do a budget. See what we can do without," her mom suggested.

"I never checked to see if there was a part-time program," Ava said. It would take longer to complete the program. But she'd be making progress. Taking small steps.

"That's settled. We need a budget and you need a meeting with the dean to plan your graduate program." Her mom plugged in a curling iron. "Now, tell me about Kyle."

"I'm not cut out for relationships, the same as Dad." Like father, like daughter. Ava picked up the curling iron and tested the temperature with the tip of her finger.

"Ava, listen to me," her mom said. She waited until Ava looked at her. "Your dad quit on our marriage long before my diagnosis. I'd quit, too. It was easier to blame my MS when he left. I'm not proud, but it was for the best for us." She touched Ava's arm. "Is it for the best if you walk away from Kyle without hearing his side?"

"He used my idea as his own for money." Ava curled the back of her mom's hair to avoid meeting her piercing gaze. "What else is there to hear?"

"Do you really believe money was his only motivation?" her mom asked.

Money had been her motivation. Kyle had made his millions and clearly wanted more. "Money was the reason I entered the contest."

"But you wanted to pursue a new career," her mom corrected. "What does Kyle want the money for?"

Ava tossed the curling iron on the bathroom counter before she burned herself. Or maybe that was the truth. She hadn't believed Kyle's claim during their food truck dinner that he was all about the money. Even now, her words about him rang false inside her. "He lied, Mom."

"Were you honest with him?"

"It's not the same," Ava argued. Her personal financial problems and professional issues weren't his business. None of it was anyone's business but her own. Still, she admitted her mistake at work to Kyle and he'd helped. Not with money, but something more valuable: his time. Himself.

"Perhaps you're right." Her mom combed her hair. Her voice took on that of a wise advisor. "It's not the same. Just remember we all lie sometimes, even with the best intentions."

Ava had lied to protect her mom. That had backfired. How could she be completely honest with someone else if she continued to lie to herself? Kyle had lied to her. She didn't know why. But she could guess it might've been for family. Same as her. "He lied to protect his family."

Ava sprayed hairspray on her mom's head, wanting to block out the real truth. Kyle lied to protect the people he loved, and Ava hadn't been included. That wound split her open inside.

Her mom grabbed her hand. "Maybe Kyle never imagined he'd have to make a choice."

"Well, he made one." And like with her dad, Ava got hurt.

"Now you have a choice." Her mom squeezed her fingers. "Do you keep running or do you fight?"

Ava tugged her hand free. "For what?"

"Love, of course," her mom said. "Will you fight for love?"

"You make it sound exciting and romantic." Ava smacked the hairspray on the counter.

"It is. It's also painful, challenging and frustrating." Her mom's voice was too pleasant, as if she cherished the good and the bad.

"You're going to tell me love is worth the risk." Ava blinked, wanting to regain her focus. Fighting to understand her mom. "Even while you never fought for your marriage."

"Your father and I wanted to be in love. We had two beautiful children to prove our love to ourselves and the world." A tremor shifted across her mom's mouth. Her gaze dimmed as if old hurts resurfaced. "We put on a good front for a while."

"And then?" Ava pressed.

"It wasn't enough to pretend anymore." Her mom's voice was muted as if her memories muffled her words.

"So, you just stopped?" Ava said. Was that how it worked? She could tell herself to stop loving Kyle and like a snap of her fingers the love disappeared? She snapped her fingers against her leg. Nothing changed.

Her mom touched her cheek. "We let each other go. Finally."

"And you regretted it?" Ava asked. Her regret warred with her pain, each fighting for control.

"I regretted that I settled because I believed I wasn't worth more." Her mom twisted in her stool and slipped on a pair of jeweled flats. "I never regretted my children, who showed me how deep love really can run. I never regretted taking the risk."

"What if I'm settling?" Her voice jammed in her dry throat.

"You've already been settling for a life alone." Her mom held her hand out for Ava to help her stand. "Maybe it's time to try something new."

"What if I fail?" What if Kyle failed to love her like she loved him?

"What if it's better than you ever imagined?" her mom countered.

"You're telling me to try with Kyle." Ava walked beside her mom into the bedroom.

"I'm telling you to listen to your heart." Her mom picked up a wrap from her bed and adjusted it over her shoulders. She smiled at Ava, "But now, my stomach is telling me we need to leave and get to the gala. I plan to sample everything at the buffet stations, since I helped create the menu."

Ava's stomach flipped inside out. She'd skip trying the food at the buffet. As for trying with Kyle, she tightened the straps on her silver heels and loosened the chains around her broken heart.

AVA KEPT HER silver heels on to stall herself from running away and intercepted Kyle near the edge of the dance floor. She offered an apologetic smile to the woman beside him. "Kyle, I need to say something. I need to say it now."

"Ava…" he said.

She held up her hand and dug her heels into the carpet to brace herself. It was now or never. She wouldn't regret taking the leap. She wouldn't regret trying. "We can add another first to our list."

He tipped his head and studied her. The ballroom lights dimmed over the dance floor, shadowing his blue eyes. For a breath, she was certain she saw hope and need in his gaze.

"Our first fight." Ava smiled at the surprise widening his eyes. "I'm mad you lied. We have to promise to be honest with each other or this is never going to work."

He opened his mouth.

She stepped forward and rushed on, "I wanted to ask if we could press the reset button and start all over like two people that just met. But I can't do that. I love you too much to pretend I don't. I have an incredibly long list of firsts I want to do. And I want to share them all with you. I want to cross off more on the list. Here, tonight. Please tell me you want that, too." *Please don't let me walk away.*

Kyle's chin dipped, and his gaze dropped to the floor.

Ava held her breath, trying to keep her stomach from dropping out as if she free fell. She watched his chest rise and fall. Swayed in her heels. This couldn't be the end. Not like this.

Kyle locked his gaze on her. "I loved you when I walked inside this ballroom. I love you more now."

Air rushed through Ava. He loved her. But his voice was too serious, his expression too intense. Love was supposed to be enough.

Kyle motioned to the woman beside him. "I was going to introduce you to Verna Neal from Simply Med-Tech and leave."

Leave. He couldn't walk away. Not now. That free fall continued.

"I've reconsidered that plan." Kyle took both of her hands and caught her.

Ava held on until her world steadied.

"I don't deserve you, Ava. But I'm going to show you how much I love you every single day." He lifted their joined hands and pressed a kiss to her knuckles. "Starting now, if it's okay with you."

A chill raced over Ava's skin from the promise in his gaze. Her mom had been right. This could be better than she'd ever imagined.

Kyle shifted and tipped his head toward the woman waiting beside them. Her soft smile eased up into her bright eyes. Kyle said, "Ava

Andrews, I would like you to meet Verna Neal from Simply Med-Tech."

"It's nice to meet you." Ava would've reached out to shake Verna's hand, but Kyle kept her hands firmly gripped inside his, as if he worried she might run. The only place she wanted to run was into Kyle's arms.

"It's my pleasure. I came to offer you a contract for your Virtual Vital Buddy invention." Verna smiled. "Instead, we're going to deal with business matters on Monday."

A contract. Simply Med-Tech had been one of Ava's meetings that Barbra had arranged. Ava squeezed Kyle's hands. Understood he held on to steady her. He held on to keep her grounded. He held on until she understood how much he loved her. How sorry he was. Ava cleared her throat. "We can talk now."

"We could, but I'm going to browse the silent auction and catch up with my good friend Barbra." Verna waved toward the silent auction tables and grinned. "I think this might be your chance for that first dance. Unless you two have already crossed that off your list."

Ava's joy burst through her. "It's our first dance."

"Then make a memory." Verna nodded and walked away to join Barbra.

Kyle guided Ava onto the dance floor and

pulled her into his embrace. "Did you want to bid on the silent auction?"

Ava curved her arms around Kyle and she pressed a kiss to his lips. "I'm good right here."

After all, she'd already won the best prize.

EPILOGUE

Thanksgiving Day
Florida Keys

KYLE BURIED HIS feet in the white sand on the beach. His feet were warm, but not from the sand. He was full, but not from the Thanksgiving meal that he'd just shared with his family at the hotel. What filled Kyle was something more valuable than he'd ever known.

He took Ava's hand, pulled her into him and kissed her. "I don't have cold feet."

Ava linked her arms around his neck and laughed. "I'd hope not. We're standing on one of the most beautiful beaches in Florida at sunset."

His kissed her again, softer, but no less significant. "I meant Barbra was wrong. I don't have cold feet."

He took her arms from around his neck, held on to her hands and dropped to one knee.

Ava's grip tightened in his. Her gaze was glossy. He heard his name cross her lips, but the ocean breeze blew away her voice.

"I never intended to get married because I never believed I'd find my soul mate." Kyle released her hands and reached into his pocket. "But Ava Andrews, you changed everything. You made me believe in soul mates and true love. You made me realize I don't want to be alone. I found my home with you."

Kyle opened the ring box. Ava grasped her hands together and pressed them against her mouth. Her smile wobbled. Tears spilled down her cheeks.

"Ava, I love you more than you could ever know. Marry me and together we can invent our own dreams."

The ocean breeze couldn't blow away Ava's enthusiastic cry of yes or her declaration of how much she loved him. She lunged into his arms and together they fell onto the beach.

On the hotel veranda, Iris handed out Kleenex to her little sister and parents. She shifted the laptop screen to face her. "In case it wasn't clear, Ava said yes."

The cheers from their family and friends in San Francisco echoed over the video link and drifted across the beach. Love filled the air from coast to coast.

* * * * *

*For more romances from acclaimed author
Cari Lynn Webb, please visit
www.Harlequin.com today!*

Get 4 FREE REWARDS!

We'll send you 2 FREE Books plus 2 FREE Mystery Gifts.

Love Inspired® books feature contemporary inspirational romances with Christian characters facing the challenges of life and love.

FREE Value Over **$20**

Get 4 FREE REWARDS!

We'll send you 2 FREE Books plus 2 FREE Mystery Gifts.

Love Inspired® Suspense books feature Christian characters facing challenges to their faith... and lives.

FREE Value Over $20

HOME on the RANCH

YES! Please send me the **Home on the Ranch Collection** in Larger Print. This collection begins with 3 FREE books and 2 FREE gifts in the first shipment. Along with my 3 free books, I'll also get the next 4 books from the Home on the Ranch Collection, in LARGER PRINT, which I may either return and owe nothing, or keep for the low price of $5.24 U.S./ $5.89 CDN each plus $2.99 for shipping and handling per shipment*. If I decide to continue, about once a month for 8 months I will get 6 or 7 more books, but will only need to pay for 4. That means 2 or 3 books in every shipment will be FREE! If I decide to keep the entire collection, I'll have paid for only 32 books because 19 books are FREE! I understand that accepting the 3 free books and gifts places me under no obligation to buy anything. I can always return a shipment and cancel at any time. My free books and gifts are mine to keep no matter what I decide.

268 HCN 3760 468 HCN 3760

Name	(PLEASE PRINT)	
Address		Apt. #
City	State/Prov.	Zip/Postal Code

Signature (if under 18, a parent or guardian must sign)

Mail to the **Reader Service:**

IN U.S.A.: P.O. Box 1341, Buffalo, New York 14240-8531
IN CANADA: P.O. Box 603, Fort Erie, Ontario L2A 5X3

* Terms and prices subject to change without notice. Prices do not include applicable taxes. Sales tax applicable in NY. Canadian residents will be charged applicable taxes. This offer is limited to one order per household. All orders subject to approval. Credit or debit balances in a customer's account(s) may be offset by any other outstanding balance owed by or to the customer. Please allow 3 to 4 weeks for delivery. Offer available while quantities last. Offer not available to Quebec residents.

HRCBPA18R